# JAMES PATTERSON
## & MAXINE PAETRO

# PRIVATE VEGAS

arrow books

1 3 5 7 9 10 8 6 4 2

Arrow Books
20 Vauxhall Bridge Road
London SW1V 2SA

Arrow Books is part of the Penguin Random House group of companies
whose addresses can be found at global.penguinrandomhouse.com.

Penguin
Random House
UK

First published in Great Britain by Century in 2015

www.randomhouse.co.uk

A CIP catalogue record for this book is
available from the British Library.

ISBN 9780099574132
ISBN 9780099574149 (export)

Typeset by SX Composing DTP, Rayleigh, Essex
Printed and bound by CPI Group (UK) Ltd, Croydon, CR0 4YY

*For Suzie and John, Brendan,*
*Alex, and Jack*

# PROLOGUE

## START YOUR ENGINES

# One

LORI KIMBALL HAD three rules for the death race home.

One, no brakes.

Two, no horn.

Three, beat her best time by ten seconds, every day.

She turned off her phone, stowed it in the glove box.

*On your mark. Get set.*

She slammed the visor into the upright position, shoved the Electric Flag's cover of Howlin' Wolf's "Killing Floor" into the CD drive, pressed the start button on the timer she wore on a cord around her neck.

*Go.*

Lori stepped on the gas, and her Infiniti EX

crossover shot up the ramp and onto the 110 as if it could read her mind.

It was exactly ten miles from this freeway entrance to her home in Glendale. Her record was twelve minutes and ten seconds, and that record was made to be broken.

The road was dry, the sun was dull, traffic was moving. Conditions were perfect. She was flying along the canyon floor, the roadway banked on both sides, forming a chute through the four consecutive Figueroa tunnels.

Lori rode the taillights of the maroon 2013 Audi in front of her, resisting the urge to mash the horn with the palm of her hand—until the Audi braked to show her he wasn't going to budge.

Her ten-year-old boy, Justin, did this when he didn't want to go to school. He. Just. Slowed. Down.

Lori didn't have to put up with this. She peeled out into the center lane, maneuvered around an old Ford junker in her way. As soon as she passed the Audi, she wrenched the wheel hard to the left and recaptured the fast lane.

This was *it*.

At this point, three lanes headed north on the 110, and the lane on the far left exited and merged into the 5. Lori accelerated to seventy, flew past a champagne-colored '01 Caddy that was lounging at sixty to the right of her, and proceeded to tear up the fast lane.

As she drove, Lori amped up the decibels, and the eleven-speaker Bose pounded out the blend of rock and urban blues. Lori was now in a state that was as close to soaring flight as she could get without actually leaving the ground.

Lori was six minutes into the race and had passed the halfway mark. She was gaining seconds on her best time, feeling the adrenaline burn out to the tips of her fingers, to the ends of her hair.

She was in the hot zone, cruising at a steady seventy-two when a black BMW convertible edged into her lane as if it had a right to be there.

Lori wouldn't accept that.

No brakes. No horn.

She flashed her lights, then saw her opening, a sliver of empty space to her right. She jerked the wheel and careened into the middle lane, her car just missing the Beemer's left rear fender.

Oh, wow, the look on the driver's face.

"It's a *race*, don'tcha get it," she screamed into the 360-degree monitor on the dash. She was lost in the ecstasy of the moment when the light dimmed and the back end of a gray panel van filled her windshield.

Where had that van come from? Where?

Lori stood on the brakes. The tires screeched as the Infiniti skidded violently from side to side, the safety package doing all it could to prevent the inevitable rear-end smashup.

The brakes finally caught at the last moment— as the van pulled ahead.

Lori gripped the wheel with sweating hands, hardly believing that there had been no crash of steel against steel, no lunge against the shoulder straps, no shocking blunt force of an airbag explosion. She heard nothing but the wailing of the Electric Flag and the rasping sound of her own shaky breaths.

Lori snapped off the music, and with car horns blaring around her, she eased off the brakes, applied the gas. Sweat rolled down the sides of her face and dripped from her nose.

Yes, she called it the death race home, but she didn't want to die. She had three kids. She loved her husband. And although her job was boring, at least she had a job.

What in God's name was wrong with her?

"I don't know," she said to herself. "I just don't know."

Lori took a deep, sobering breath and stared straight ahead. The Beemer slowed to her speed, and the driver, his face contorted in fury, yelled silently at her through his closed window.

To her surprise, Lori started to cry.

# Two

THE TWO MEN sat in the satin-lined jewel box of a room warmed by flaming logs in the fireplace and the flickering light of the flat-screen.

The older man had white hair, strong features, catlike amber eyes. That was Gozan.

The younger man had dark hair and eyes so black they seemed to absorb light. He was very muscular, a man who took weight lifting seriously. His name was Khezir.

They were visiting this paradise called Los Angeles. They were on holiday, their first visit to the West Coast, and had rented a bungalow at the Beverly Hills Hotel, palatial by any standard. This opulent three-bedroom cottage was as pretty as a seashell, set at the end of a coral pink path and surrounded by luxuriant foliage: banana trees and palms.

It was unlike anything in their country, the landlocked mountainous triangle of rock called the kingdom of Sumar.

Now, the two men held the experiences of this hedonistic city like exotic fruit in the palms of their hands.

"I am giving you a new name," said Gozan Remari to the rounded blond woman with enormous breasts. "I name you Peaches."

There were no juicy women quite like Peaches in Sumar. There weren't many in Southern California either, where women with boylike shapes were considered desirable and ones like Peaches were called fat.

As if that were bad.

"I don't like you," Peaches said slowly. She was doing her best to speak through the numbing effect of the drugs she had consumed in the very expensive champagne. "But..."

"But what, Peaches? You don't like me, but what? You are having a very good time?"

Gozan laughed. He was an educated man, had gone to school in London and Cambridge. He knew six languages and had founded a boutique merchant bank in the City of London while serving on numerous boards. But as much as he knew, he was still mystified by the way women allowed themselves to be led and tricked.

Peaches was lying at his feet, "spread-eagled," as it was called here, bound by her wrists and ankles to table legs and an ottoman. She was naked except for dots of caviar on her nipples. Well, she had been very eager for champagne and caviar a couple of hours ago. No use complaining now.

"I forget." She sighed.

Khezir got up and went to the bedroom just beyond the living room, but he left the double doors open so that the two rooms merged into one. He lay back and lounged on the great canopied bed beside the younger woman who was the daughter of the first. This woman was even sexier than her mother: beautifully fleshy, soft to the touch, with long blond hair.

Khezir ran his hand up her thigh, amazed at the way she quivered even though she could no longer speak.

He said to the young woman, "And I will call you... Mangoes. Yes. Do you like that name? So much better than what your pigs of parents called you. Adrianna." He said it again in a high, affected voice. "Aaay-dreee-annnna. Sounds like the cry of a baby goat."

Khezir had cleansed many towns of people who

reminded him of animals. Where he came from, life was short and cheap.

The girl moaned, "Pleeease."

Khezir laughed. "You want more, please. Is that it, Mangoes?"

In the living room, the CD changer slipped a new recording into the player. The music was produced by a wind instrument called a kime. It sounded like an icy gale blowing through the clefts in a rock. The vocalist sang of an ocean he had never seen.

Gozan said, "Peaches, I would prefer that you like me, but as your Clark Gable said to that hysterical bitch in *Gone with the Wind,* 'Frankly, I don't give a shit.' "

He leaned over her, slapped her face, then pinched her between her legs. Peaches yelped and tried to get away.

"It's very good, isn't it? Tell me how much you like it," said Gozan.

There was a loud pounding at the door.

*"Get lost,"* Gozan shouted. "You'll have to come back for the cart."

A man's voice boomed, "LAPD. Open the door. Now."

# Three

SPRINKLERS SHOT BROKEN jets of water over the lush gardens in back of the Beverly Hills Hotel. Night was coming on. I was armed, waiting behind a clump of shrubbery a hundred feet from bungalow six when I heard footsteps come up the path. Captain Luke Warren of the LAPD, with a gang of six cops right behind him, came toward me.

For once, I was glad to see the LAPD.

I had information that Gozan Remari and Khezir Mazul, two heinous cruds who were suspected of multiple rapes but hadn't been charged, were behind door number six. But unless there was evidence of a crime in progress, I had no authority to break in.

I called out to the captain, presented my badge,

handed him my card, which read *Jack Morgan, CEO, Private Investigations.*

Warren looked up at me, said, "I know who you are, Morgan. Friend of the chief. The go-to guy for the one percent."

"I get around," I said.

Cops don't like private investigators. PIs don't play by the same rules as city employees, and our clients, in particular, hire Private because of our top-gun expertise and our discretion.

Captain Warren was saying, "Okay, since you called this in. What's the story?"

"A friend of mine in the hotel business called me to say that these two were bounced out of the Constellation for assaulting a chambermaid. They checked in here two hours ago. I've got a couple of spider cams on the windows, but the drapes are closed. I've made out two male voices and one female over the music and the TV, but no calls for help."

"And your interest in this?"

I said, "I'm a concerned citizen."

Warren said, "Okay. Thanks for the tip. Now I've got to ask you to step back and let us do our job."

I told him of course, no problem.

And it *was* no problem.

I wasn't on assignment and I didn't want the credit. I was glad to be there for the takedown.

Captain Warren sent two men around the bungalow to cover the back and garden exits, then he and I went up the steps and across the veranda to the front door along with two detectives from the LAPD. Warren knocked and announced.

We heard a shout through the front door; sounded like "Go away."

I said, "He said, 'Come in,' right?"

The captain smiled to show me that he liked my way of thinking. Then he swiped the lock with a card key, cocked his leg, and kicked in the door.

It blew open, and we all got a good view of what utter depravity looks like.

# Four

THE LIVING ROOM was done up in silk and satin in the colors peach and cream. Logs flickered in the marble fireplace, and atonal music oozed from the CD player. Empty glasses, liquor bottles, and many articles of clothing littered the floor. A room-service cart had been tipped over, spilling food and broken china across the Persian carpet.

I served for three years as a pilot in the U.S. Marine Corps. I've been trained to spot a glint of metal or a puff of smoke on the ground from ten thousand feet up. In the dark.

But I didn't need pilot's training to recognize the filth right in front of me.

The man called Gozan Remari sat in an armchair with the hauteur of a prince. He looked to be about fifty, white-haired, with gold-colored, catlike eyes. Remari wore an expensive handmade jacket, an open pin-striped shirt, a heavy gold watch, and nothing else—not even an expression of surprise or anger that cops were coming through the door.

A nude woman lay at his feet, bound with silk ties. Her arms and legs were spread, and she was anchored hand and foot to an ottoman and a table, as if she were a luna moth pinned to a board. I saw bluish handprints on her skin, and food had been smeared on her body.

There was an arched entrance to my right that led to a bedroom. And there, in plain sight, was Khezir Mazul. He was naked, sitting up in bed, smoking a cigar. A young woman, also naked, was stretched on her back across his lap, her head over the side of the bed. A thin line of blood arced across her throat, and I saw a steak knife on the cream-colored satin blanket.

From where I stood in the doorway, I couldn't tell if the women were unconscious or dead.

Captain Warren yanked Gozan Remari to his feet and cuffed his hands behind his back. He said, "You're under arrest for assault. You have the right to remain silent, you piece of crap."

The younger dirtbag stood up, let the woman on his lap roll away from him, off the bed and onto the floor. Khezir Mazul was powerfully built, tattooed on most of his body with symbols I didn't recognize.

He entered the living room and said to Captain Warren in the most bored tones imaginable, "We've done nothing. Do you know the word *con-shen-sul?* This is not any kind of assault. These women came here willingly with us. Ask them. They came here to party. As you say here, 'We aim to please.' "

Then, he laughed. *Laughed.*

I stepped over the room-service cart and went directly to the woman lying near me on the floor. Her breathing was shallow, and her skin was cool. She was going into shock.

My hands shook as I untied her wrists and ankles.

I said, "Everything is going to be okay. What's your name? Can you tell me your name?"

Cops came through the back door, and one of them called for medical backup. Next, hotel management and two guests came in the front. Bungalow six was becoming a circus.

I ripped a cashmere throw from the sofa and

covered the woman's body. I helped her into a chair, put my jacket around her shoulders.

She opened her eyes and tears spilled down her cheeks. "My daughter," the woman said to me. "Where is she? Is she—"

I heard the cop behind me say into the phone, "Two females; one in her forties, the other is late teens, maybe early twenties. She's bleeding from a knife wound to her neck. Both of them are breathing."

I said to the woman whose name I didn't know, "Your daughter is just over there, in the bedroom. She's going to be all right. Help is coming."

Clasping the blanket to her body, the woman turned to see her daughter being assisted to her feet.

A siren wailed. The woman reached up and pressed her damp cheek to mine. She hugged me tight with her free arm.

"It's my fault. I screwed up," she said. "Thank you for helping us."

# PART ONE

90210

# Chapter 1

I DRAFTED BEHIND the ambulance as it sped the two assault victims through traffic on Santa Monica Boulevard toward Ocean Memorial Hospital. When the bus turned inland, I headed north until I reached Pacific Coast Highway, the stretch of road that follows the curve of the coastline and links Malibu to Santa Monica.

My Lamborghini can go from zero to ninety in ten seconds, but this car draws cops out of nowhere, even when it's just quietly humming at a red light. So I kept to the speed limit, and within twenty minutes, I was within sight of home.

My house is white stucco and glass, shielded from the road by a high wall that is overgrown with vines and inset with a tall wrought-iron gate.

I stopped the car, opened my window, and

palmed the new biometric recognition plate; the gate slid open. I pulled the Lambo into my short, tight parking spot and braked next to the blue Jag.

As the gates rolled closed behind me, I got out, locked up the car, checked behind the wall and within the landscaping for anything that didn't belong. Then I went up the walk to the door.

I'd bought this place with Justine Smith about five years ago. Later, after we'd broken up for the third, impossibly painful time, I bought out Justine's share of the house. It was comfortable, convenient to my office, just right—until a year ago last May.

On that night, I came back home from a business trip abroad to find another former girlfriend, Colleen Molloy, dead in my bed, her skin still warm. She'd been shot multiple times at close range, and the killer was a pro. The way he'd fixed it, all of the evidence pointed to me as the shooter.

I was charged with Colleen's murder and jailed, but after some extraordinary work by Private investigators, I was free—if you could call it that. I still opened my door every night expecting that something horrible had happened while I was out.

I put my eye up to the iris reader beside the front door, and when the lock clacked open, I went inside.

A woman's blue jacket and a sleek leather handbag were on a chair, and her fragrance scented the air as I walked through the main room. I followed the light coming through the house, crossed the tile floors in my gumshoes, then peered through the glass doors that opened out to the pool.

She was doing laps and didn't see me. That was fine.

The door glided open under my hand and I went out again into the warm night. I took a chaise, and as the ocean roared at the beach below, I watched her swim.

Her lovely shape was up-lit by the pool lights. Her strong arms stroked confidently through the water, and her flip turns had both grace and power.

I knew this woman so well.

I trusted her with everything. I cared about her safety and her happiness. I truly loved her.

But I was unable to see my future with her—or anyone. And that was a problem for Justine. It was why we didn't live together. And why we'd made no long-term plans. But we had decided a couple of months ago that we were happy seeing each other casually. And at least for now, it was working.

She reached the end of the pool and pulled herself up to the coping. Her skin glistened as light and shadow played over her taut body. She sat with her legs in the pool, leaned forward, and wrung out her long, dark brown hair.

"Hey," I said.

She started, said, "Jack."

Then she grabbed a towel and wrapped herself in it, came over to the chaise, and sat down beside me. She smiled.

"How long have you been sitting here?"

I put my hand behind her neck and brought her mouth to mine. I kissed her. Kissed her again. Released her and said, "I just got here. I've had a night you won't believe."

"I want to take a shower," Justine said. "Then tell me all about it."

# Chapter 2

THE HOT SPRAY beat on me from six shower-heads. Justine lightly placed her palms on my chest, tipped her hips against mine.

She said, "Someone needs a massage. I think that could be you."

"Okay."

Okay to whatever she wanted to do. It wasn't just my car that could go from zero to ninety in ten seconds. Justine had that effect on me.

As she rubbed shower gel between her hands, sending up the scent of pine and ginseng, she looked me up and down. "I don't know whether to go from top to bottom or the other way around," she said.

"Dealer's choice," I said.

She was laughing, enjoying her power over me,

when my cell phone rang. My fault for bringing it into the bathroom, but I was expecting a call from the head of our Budapest office, who'd said he'd try to call me between flights.

Justine said, "Here's a joke. Don't take the call."

I looked through the shower doors to where my phone sat at the edge of the sink. The caller ID read *Capt. L. Warren*. It could only be about the rapists the cops had just arrested at the Beverly Hills Hotel.

"The joke's on me," I said to Justine. "But I'll make it quick."

I caught the call on the third ring.

"Morgan. We've got problems with those pukes from Sumar," the captain said. "They have diplomatic immunity."

"You've *got* to be kidding."

He gave me the bad news in detail, that Gozan Remari and Khezir Mazul were both senior diplomats in Sumar's mission to the UN.

"They're on holiday in Hollywood," Warren told me. "I think we could ruin their good time, maybe get them recalled to the wasteland they came from, but the ladies won't cooperate. I'm at the hospital with them now. They wouldn't let the docs test for sexual assault."

"That's not good," I said. I put up a finger to let Justine know I would be just a minute.

"Mrs. Grove is very grateful to you, Morgan," the captain was telling me. "I, uh, need a favor. I need you to talk to her."

"Sure. Put her on," I said.

Justine turned off the water. Pulled a towel off the rack. "She's in a room with her daughter," Warren said. "Listen, if you step on the gas, you could be here in fifteen minutes. Talk to them face-to-face."

I told Justine not to wait up for me.

By way of an answer, she screwed in her earbuds and took her iPod to the kitchen. She was intensely chopping onions when I left the house.

It was a twenty-minute drive to Ocean Memorial and it took me another ten to find the captain. He escorted me to a beige room furnished with two beds and a recliner.

Belinda Grove was sitting in the recliner, wearing the expensive clothes I'd last seen strewn around bungalow six: a black knit dress, fitted jacket, black stiletto Jimmy Choos. She'd also brushed her hair and applied red lipstick. And although I'd never met her before today, now that she'd cleaned up, I recognized her from photos in the society pages.

This was Mrs. Alvin Grove, on the board of the Children's Museum, daughter of Palmer Tiptree, of Tiptree Pharmaceuticals, and mother of two.

Now I understood. She would rather die than let anyone know what had happened to her daughter and herself.

# Chapter 3

MRS. GROVE STOOD when I came into the room, took my hands in hers, said, "Mr. Morgan, I want to thank you again."

"My name is Jack. Of course, you're welcome, Mrs. Grove. How are you doing?"

"Call me Belinda. I'm ashamed that I was so easily tricked," she said, sitting down again. "We were having lunch in the Polo Lounge, my daughter and I, and we were talking about the Children's Museum. Those monsters were at the next table and overheard us. Gozan said he had many children and would be interested in making a donation to the museum.

"Jack. They were well dressed. Looked well-heeled. They said they were diplomats. They were staying at the hotel. Gozan said he wanted to talk about making a sizable donation to the museum, but he wanted to discuss it privately.

"I ignored any warning signs. We went to the bungalow. I said that we couldn't stay long, but a short chat would be all right. We are always looking for benefactors, Jack. They used Rohypnol or something damned close to it. It was in the champagne."

"Don't blame yourself. These are dangerous men."

"I hope never to see either one of them again unless they're hanging by their balls over a bonfire. I don't think that Adrianna will be physically scarred, but emotionally ... Emotionally, my daughter is in terrible shape."

*Terrible shape* was an understatement. Adrianna had been drugged, probably raped, maybe by both men, and Khezir Mazul had stroked her throat with a serrated blade. She would have a scar across her neck for as long as she lived.

I hated to think what would have happened to these women had I not been tipped off, if we hadn't shown up when we did.

I started to reason with Mrs. Grove, explain to her that if she made a complaint, Remari and Mazul might be deported.

She shook her head, warning me off.

"My daughter is a senior at Stanford. It would be tragic if she had to leave school. What happened today is something Adrianna and I will learn from and, at the same time, try to forget. That's how one deals with horror, don't you think?"

I said, "I'd suggest some counseling..."

She ignored me and went on. "My responsibility now is only to Adrianna, and I'm going to make sure that she has whatever she needs in order to heal."

She stood up. "You take care, Jack. God bless. I mean that."

Belinda Grove left the beige room with her head down, passing Captain Warren, who was on his way back in.

Luke Warren and I talked together for several minutes. There were no angles to work, no strings to pull. But there are a few cases every year that I want to work pro bono, and I thought this might become one of them.

I told the captain to call me anytime, that I would work with him free of charge. Happy to do it.

I thought if we caught them, I could convince Mazul and Remari to leave the country for good.

# Chapter 4

I MADE THE return trip home under the speed limit and in record time, drove up to my gate, and left my car outside on the grass so that it would be easier for Justine to get out in the morning.

I no longer slept in the master suite, not since Colleen's murder. I'd taken over the guest room that faced the front garden and had sliders out to the back deck.

The full moon was perfectly balanced above the ocean, and moonlight came through the glass, bathing the white bedding in a pearly glow. Justine looked ethereal, as if she were made of dreams.

I put my gun on the nightstand and got into bed beside her. She was sleeping soundly, but she turned at my touch and curled against me. I put my arms around her and kissed the part in her hair. She murmured my name and we kissed good night.

I tried to stop thinking, to let myself drift off. But there was too much inside my mind and it all fought for my attention: the men from Sumar; Colleen, dead, with her eyes open, three bullets in her chest.

And I thought about that night in Afghanistan when I was piloting a transport helicopter to Kandahar from base with fourteen Marines in the cargo bay. A ground-to-air missile fired from the back of a pickup hit the aircraft in the belly and took out the tail rotor section.

There was a horrific sound and the CH-46 began its downward spiral through hell. Even though I landed the Phrog on its struts, the missile had done its work.

No amount of time or therapy could erase the afterimages of the events of that night from my mind: the scramble out of the aircraft to the cargo bay, the *chunka-chunka-chunka* sound of .50-caliber guns going off, the stink of burning aviation fuel, the sight of the dead and dying men.

If Justine had been awake, she would have asked me what I was thinking—and I would have lied.

I had lied to Justine many times, and when I got away with it, I suffered. If she found out that I'd lied, we both suffered.

And that's why psychologist Dr. Justine Smith couldn't imagine a future with *me*.

# Chapter 5

THEY WERE HAVING dinner at Spago, Wolfgang Puck's signature five-star restaurant at Caesars Palace, Vegas. Their table was at the back of the room, giving them a fine view of the dazzling chandeliers and the collection of bright, contemporary works of art on the walls.

But Lester was looking only at Sandra.

Right now, he was feeling an edgy kind of high, thinking how close they were to the jackpot. Sandra was almost ready. She just needed a little extra support.

Lester said, softly, "Hey. Talk to me."

"I'm thinking," she said.

Sandra was an angelic-looking twenty-eight-year-old with blunt-cut dark hair to her shoulders and the long, fluid limbs of a dancer. She was dressed in a black Hervé Léger bandage dress with an understated, million-dollar diamond necklace at her throat.

Sandra was perfect; gorgeous, smart, and very cold. She was also the well-cared-for wife of an extremely wealthy man.

Lester Olsen was not that man.

Lester was in his midthirties, of average height and build. His hair was thick, with a mind of its own, and he had a pleasant face of the boy-next-door variety. His fingers were unforgettable. They were misshapen—crippled by disease or a birth defect or some trauma, his dinner partner didn't know.

Lester never discussed his hands.

Tonight, he and Sandra were having a business dinner, but Olsen cared about her. He was her friend and her coach and sometimes she called him the Big O, which made him laugh out loud. He saw no problem mixing business and pleasure.

But the *point* of their relationship was business.

Lester was teaching Sandra how to kill.

Right now, Sandra seemed thoughtful. She idly twisted the massive pink Tiffany diamond and matching wedding band on her ring finger.

"Sandra? What's on your mind?"

She said, "I'm not concerned about going forward. That's not it. I'm worried about how I'm going to feel afterward."

Lester sipped his wine, and then, after the waiter had cleared the table, he said, "Sandy, it's easy for me to say 'Don't worry.' But don't."

"Tell me why not."

"I have some experience in these things."

She smiled. "Not your first rodeo?"

"Not my second either."

They both laughed.

He reached for her hand, squeezed her fingers.

"It's different for everyone," he said. "You may feel down for a little while, but that feeling won't last. I'll be there for you no matter what. We're partners, right?"

"You bet we are," she said.

"You can back out, you know."

"I know."

"Or—keep your eye on the big fat prize. A year from now, you'll be happier than you've ever been, or ever imagined you could be."

"Promise?"

She was lightening up, coming back around. Attagirl.

"Would you like coffee? Dessert?" he asked.

"No. You go ahead."

"Do you trust me?"

"Yes."

Olsen smiled his approval, then signaled for the waiter.

"Sir?"

"The hot chocolate cake and coffee. For two."

Sandra smiled at Lester.

"Thank you," she said. "Thanks very much."

# Chapter 6

CAPTAIN LUKE WARREN sat in his Hyundai Sonata and watched Gozan Remari leave the Men's Central Jail and walk through the gate to Bauchet Street at 10:15 p.m.

The diplomat from Sumar was wearing a charcoal-gray suit, a striped shirt, and no tie, because he had used it to bind a naked woman to a table against her will and the tie had been taken into evidence.

Remari's phone rang.

Warren saw him take his phone from his jacket pocket and talk for a few minutes, looking around him the whole time. When he was done talking, he returned the phone to his pocket and picked up a newspaper from the sidewalk.

After that, he leaned back against the

chain-link fence and began to read the front page under the not-so-bright light of the streetlamps.

About then, a late-model black Lincoln pulled up, a type of car not commonly seen around this neighborhood. Remari stooped to the window and spoke to the driver, and then the driver jumped out, went around to the back passenger side, and opened the door.

Warren had never seen a car with a liveried driver making a pickup at the jail. This was a first.

Remari folded the newspaper under his arm and got into the Lincoln, and the captain started his engine and watched as the Lincoln continued to idle at the curb.

The captain was trying to understand Remari. He wore good clothing, had excellent grooming, spoke with a trace of an English accent of the upper-class kind. He contrasted all that with the crude, criminal assaults on the Grove ladies and the six other brutal, sexual assaults he and his friend were suspected of committing.

Why pick up rich women and torture them? Why draw attention to himself with this pricey car?

Another ten minutes passed and Warren sat there watching. He slugged down the dregs of his cold coffee, and then the other donkey turd came through the chain-link gate.

Khezir Mazul had put bruises on Adrianna Grove's thighs, had very likely raped her, and had definitely perpetrated an ear-to-ear slash across the front of her neck.

The word *cutthroat* suited this guy to a T.

Now Khezir Mazul looked around, saw the black car. A grin crossed his face. He got into the backseat next to his buddy, and as the door closed, the car shot away from the curb.

Captain Warren turned on his headlights; he let a couple of old cars get behind the Lincoln, then he got into line three cars back. It was sickening that these guys were protected by some international law that kept diplomats from persecution and prosecution while they were on a diplomatic mission. Maybe that covered them back east, but that had nothing to do with LA, and *shouldn't* have anything to do with LA.

He was working on his own time, fairly certain that he would be able to explain this to his chief later. He had a feeling he wouldn't have to tail these goons for long. From the way the Sumaris used their diplomatic privileges, Warren was pretty sure they would commit another outrageous crime.

And maybe their next victim would not only survive but also have the guts to press charges.

"So where are you goons going?" Luke Warren said to the Lincoln's taillights up ahead. "What's the plan for tonight?"

# Chapter 7

GOZAN AND KHEZIR had returned to the Beverly Hills Hotel after their long day as guests of the LA Pig D. They found their bungalow locked, their luggage in the baggage room in the main building, and a few bulked-up security guards loitering near the front desk.

Gozan paid the bill, noting the charges for damages, which made him smile. If they'd had more time, they could have really trashed the place.

The two men had already booked the Presidential Suite at the Beverly Hilton, and as they went outside to their rental car, Khezir peed into a potted palm. The bellhop screamed as Khezir laughed and jumped into the car.

It was funny. Khezir was really funny.

Gozan drove them to their new hotel, and after

they showered and changed, they were ready to party.

At present, Khezir was half drunk, but Gozan was largely sober and he was behind the wheel of their rented Bentley GT convertible, an absolutely astounding car.

The light changed at the intersection of Merv Griffin and Wilshire, and Gozan stepped on the accelerator. The tires squealed, the car jumped forward, and the Sumaris headed toward the heart of Beverly Hills.

What Gozan liked enormously was the splendor and history of this town. He thought about all the silent-movie stars who'd lived here in the 1920s, when his father's father was driving goats through the rocky hills of Sumar.

And he thought with affection about his nephew Khezir.

Khezir played "crude" perfectly, but he was extremely smart. He was demonstrating his theatricality now, shouting out the names of the famous places as they passed them, the bars and shops and roads, and he yelled out insults at the other drivers. "You drive like you are a thumb up my ass."

Gozan laughed.

The streets were bright with beautiful people in their exotic cars. Gozan took a right turn onto Elevado, another right onto North Rodeo Drive, which was, at this point, a residential, tree-lined avenue with two lanes in each direction divided by a low, grassy median.

There were magnificent houses here, but too close together, like fancy ladies at the fence of a racetrack. The money, the opulence, the fair-haired people living on a fault line. These Americans always amused him.

He sped up, letting the car out at eighty, edging up to eighty-five, Khezir screaming his delight. There was a stoplight up ahead and a convertible was in the next lane over, a blue Ferrari with two honey-blond girls in the front seat. Gozan pulled up next to it.

Khezir called across the gap between the cars, "Hello, sweeties. You are so beautiful. Come with us to dinner. We are very rich. We have money to burn."

The girls turned, looked with amusement at the passengers in the Bentley, possibly took in the decal Gozan had slapped on the windshield: *Diplomat. Kingdom of Sumar.*

The blond girls laughed together, and then the girl who was driving said, "Not interested. At all."

The light changed, and the women in the blue sports car took a left turn toward West Hollywood. Khezir said to Gozan, "These sweeties are a good omen of things to come. However, I most liked that girl driver. I could see her under me."

He broke into Sumarin and described to Gozan in explicit terms what he would do to her. These were not completely fantasies, as Khezir was practiced in the art of performing sex while delivering pain. It was what turned him on.

Gozan switched on the music and it drowned out Khezir's words. There was a strategy, of course. And Khezir was ingenious, but he was young and could sometimes be a loose rocket.

Gozan had to make sure he didn't blow up the plan.

# Chapter 8

I AWOKE WITH a start, as if violently jerked out of a bad dream, the remains of a sharp sound in my head—but it was gone. A bright yellow light danced around me and licked at the darkness. Something was *burning*.

Was the CH-46 about to blow? Was I there?

Justine grabbed my arm.

"Jack. What's happening?"

"Get dressed, Justine. We may have to leave."

I turned on the light, grabbed the phone from the nightstand, called 911. I gave my name and address as I walked to the east-facing window of the bedroom.

I saw the pale light of the morning sun—and smoke curling through the bars of the gate. The fire was real, and it was burning outside between my front yard and the highway.

I said to the 911 operator, "There's a fire, big one. I don't know what's on fire."

"Fire department is on the way."

I pulled on my jeans, grabbed my gun, jammed it into my waistband, stepped into a pair of moccasins.

"Jack!"

"I'll be right back."

I smelled smoke in the house, but the front door was cool. I opened it and walked outside into the stench of burning rubber and plastic that set off little explosions like land mines along the neural pathways of my brain.

I had no doubt that I was in Malibu standing in front of my house, and at the same time, I was back *there,* carrying Marine Corporal Danny Young over my shoulder and away from the burning aircraft.

Danny was a spectacular young man, funny and brave and filled with hope. I had talked to Danny as I carried him, told him that he was going to make it.

I thought I was telling him the truth.

But the truth was that we both died that night. I was the lucky one. Del Rio brought me back.

Now Justine shouted to me from the doorway.

"Jack! Be careful."

"I will," I said. "Just, please, go inside."

I walked through the gate toward the fire that was being fanned by the sea breeze, gaining strength and momentum, starting to roam and consume new ground. It was alive, leaping up the trunks of palm trees, catching the husks and fronds as it burned.

I was so transfixed by the blaze, I stopped and stared. The concussive wave of the explosion blew me off my feet and dropped me down hard.

I was back there again.

# Chapter 9

I WAS ON my belly, my cheek flat on the grass.

Justine was patting my face, calling my name. I looked past her to the fireball, what was left of my Lamborghini. It crackled with flames and the roiling smoke obscured everything downwind from the fire.

Justine hugged me. "Oh God, Jack. Get up, get up *now.* "

I groaned, said, "Ah, shit. My damned car."

Justine gripped my arm. She helped me up and now she was crying. "Your eyebrows are gone. Eyelashes too."

"They'll grow back."

"I don't care about your *eyebrows*, Jack. Your car *exploded*. You could have been *killed*."

She was panting as she looked at me, eyes wide with terror. I reached out, enfolded her in my arms. "I'm okay, sweetheart."

"Come on," she said. "Come with me."

We walked back toward the house, Justine saying, "You don't take care of yourself, Jack. Do you want to die? Do you?"

I was wondering what the hell had just happened. Cars don't normally spontaneously combust. So what had caused the fire? Had it been deliberately set?

Sirens screamed in the distance, got louder as they closed in on my stretch of highway. Three fire rigs appeared out of the gloom, pulled up on the roadside. Firefighters bailed out of the trucks and trained lines on the burning car.

Steam sizzled, and as the fire died, police cruisers arrived from north and south. Car doors slammed. Police radios chattered. Cops set out markers and closed the highway down.

An unmarked car pulled alongside Justine and me as we walked toward my front gate. Then the car surged ahead, crossed, and braked in front of us, bringing us to a stop.

Two cops got out of the gray Ford sedan.

They were detectives, Mitchell Tandy and Al

Ziegler, and I welcomed them as warmly as I would the stomach flu.

Tandy and Ziegler were dogged career detectives who had taken a special dislike to me.

Tandy was freshly spray-tanned, his teeth bleached to a blinding white. He had put on ten pounds since last year when he'd tagged me for Colleen's murder. Even though I hadn't killed her, Tandy still believed in his black heart of hearts that I had.

"Morning, Jack. What do you know about this?"

"I'm okay. Thanks for asking."

"Sure. I'm glad you're okay. So, now, Jack. What do you know about this?"

I said, "I parked my car outside my gate last night so that Justine could get out in the morning without dinging her car. It was a dumb decision, Mitch, but that's all I know."

"You have any explosives in the car?"

"No, I did not."

"You were insured?"

"Yes. But come on. I set fire to my car for the insurance money?"

Tandy didn't smile, just said, "Anyone got it in for you, Jack?"

"Hell no." It was one of those lies that was so transparent, it was a joke.

Ziegler had been observing the firefighters. Now he came over to us, his hands jammed in his Windbreaker pockets. He was tall with broad shoulders, muscular. Had sleepy eyes that didn't miss anything. Ziegler and I also had a little history that he would prefer to forget.

"Well, Jack, the arson investigator is on the way. Yours is the sixth car that's been torched around here in the last two months. And no, we have no idea if the fires were set by one person or more, if they're protests against the richy-rich, or even if they're linked."

"In other words, you've got nothing," I said.

"We're going to impound what's left of your vehicle and give the arson investigator a crack at it," Ziegler said. "But this much I know: The other car fires weren't accidental. Maybe the first five were misdirection. Maybe you were the real target all along."

It was a theory.

I'd hate for Ziegler to be right.

# Chapter 10

I SAT ON a stool in the kitchen and watched as Justine unloaded the dishwasher, put away the blue earthenware bowls we had bought together.

She said, "I can name a dozen people who want to see you dead, Jack, and that's not counting your brother."

"Don't count Tommy out," I told her. "I wouldn't count out Ziegler and Tandy either."

Justine said, "What does your gut tell you?"

"From now on, park inside the gates."

She laughed, shook her head, put on a pot of coffee.

The intercom buzzed. I went to the surveillance monitor. Del Rio stuck out his tongue. I'd phoned him as soon as the cops left, told him what had happened to my car.

"I'll be there soon," he'd said.

I pressed the button and a moment later, my friend, former copilot, and current chief investigator came inside. He handed me the keys to a fleet car we kept at the office in case I needed wheels.

I smiled at him. "Coffee?"

"Sure. Okay, no eyebrows. Nice look," he said to me. Then: "How ya doing, Justine?"

"I love waking up to a fiery explosion. Doesn't everyone?" she said, handing him a mug.

"I do! The bigger the better," Del Rio said.

I knew Del Rio better than I knew anyone, and he had full knowledge of a part of my life I didn't know at all.

What I remember about that night was that I had set Danny Young's bleeding body down and then it was as though the ground had erupted. I felt a shocking blow to my chest and that was the end.

*I died.* I went through the tunnel and for all I know, I was coming out the other side.

I just remember swimming up to the light. My eyes flashed open and there was Del Rio in my face, his hands pressing down on my chest. He laughed and at the same time tears ran down his sooty cheeks. He said, "Jack, you son-of-a-bitch, *you're back*."

He told me later that a chunk of shrapnel had

struck my chest. My flak jacket prevented it from penetrating my body, but the concussion stopped my heart. Then the helicopter right behind us blew up and was consumed in flames.

I wasn't dead, but so many of my friends died that day. I swear to God, I would have traded my life for any of them.

I watched Del Rio now, joking with Justine. He was wearing jeans and a T-shirt, a brown canvas jacket, and had a two-day-old beard. Rick was a homely guy, not the type that got cast as a hero in movies. He was a hero anyway.

But the *People v. R. Del Rio* didn't care about that.

He said to me, "Want to know what I think, Jack? Whether that car was firebombed because it was available or because it was personal, the price tag on it *makes* it personal. You live in a glass house, you know? Stay at Justine's until this thing is closed."

I looked at Justine.

She said, "Of course. Stay with me."

But she didn't really want that. I didn't know for sure, but I had a pretty good idea that she'd started seeing someone else. Maybe he was a man who could go the distance, the whole length of the aisle.

"I'll be fine at home," I said. "But thanks."

"Well, then, my work here is done." Del Rio put his mug in the sink, headed to the door.

I called after him, "Rick. Make sure you shave."

"Yes, sir." He gave me a salute and a grin. But his eyes weren't smiling. He was worried.

I was worried too.

I said, "This time next week, this whole thing is going to be behind us."

"I always come out on top, right, Jack? When it counts."

"Yes, you do. See you in court."

# Chapter 11

BY THE TIME Justine dropped me off at the Clara Shortridge Foltz Criminal Justice Center, I was caffeinated to the core and worried about Rick's day in court.

"He'll do okay," Justine assured me. "He's got Eric."

I nodded, kissed her good-bye, and watched as she took off down West Temple Street. Then I lowered my shades to hide my missing eyebrows and headed for the entrance to the blocky nineteen-story high-rise commonly known as the Criminal Courthouse.

There was a swarm of tabloid reporters and trial-junkie bloggers at the foot of the stairs. These "journalists" are what I call raccoons, carnivores who sift through garbage cans, and they'll do grave mischief if you don't lock the door behind you and bolt it shut.

The Criminal Courthouse was like a raccoon feeding station. Some of the most famous defendants in the country had been tried here: O.J. Simpson, Phil Spector, Conrad Murray, and other criminal superstars.

Rick Del Rio even at his worst was never in that league, but because he worked at Private Investigations and was charged with a felony, his trial made for a sexy story that could be sold to celebrity magazines and supermarket tabs for big wads of cash.

I worried about Rick and I worried about Private's reputation. Private wasn't "private" when it was top of the news.

I waved to big and small raccoons I'd known for years, shouted out, "No comment, thanks a lot," smiled like I meant it, and kept going, passing between the thick concrete pillars, through the tall glass doors, and into the granite-tiled lobby.

From there, I took an elevator up to the seventh floor and exited into the wide corridor lit with overhead fluorescents and banked with rust-colored benches. I quickly found courtroom 7B, Judge Pat Johnson presiding.

I didn't know Judge Johnson, but she had a

reputation for making quality decisions based on quirky logic. Rick was a quirky guy, and I wasn't sure if the judge's style would help Rick or hurt him.

The sheriff opened the door for me and I entered the courtroom. It was paneled and appointed in blond wood, with six rows of twelve chairs in the gallery behind the bar. All of the chairs were occupied, and there was standing-room only in the rear.

I squeezed into the crowd at the back and took in the whole room at a glance. Rick was sitting at the defense table, his back to me, his head lowered as if he was looking down at his hands. Rick had been in trouble before and had done four years at Chino, which he considered graduate work in underworld connections.

Rick's lawyer, Eric Caine, was Harvard Law, and a former staffer with the CIA. I was lucky he liked Los Angeles and was playing for our team. He was a good friend, and also head of Private's legal department.

Caine was standing before the judge's bench along with the prosecutor, ADA Dexter Lewis, a kid of thirty to Caine's forty-five. ADA Lewis had been schooled in Detroit, was ambitious, crafty, a member of three state bar associations, and a dynamic speaker. I knew he would go far.

But not soon enough.

Right now, Lewis was determined to put Rick Del Rio away for ten years, the maximum the law would allow. Shooting down a decorated war hero would help Lewis land a mid-six-figure job in a top criminal defense law firm.

That would be good for Dexter Lewis, but Rick would lose everything, including his investigator's license and life as he knew it. It killed me to think about that.

I shifted my attention to the bench.

Judge Johnson wore a big diamond brooch at the neck of her robe, and her hennaed hair was held back with a gold headband. She was shaking her head emphatically.

She wasn't buying whatever Eric Caine was selling.

I heard her say, "Good try, Mr. Caine, but I'm not dismissing the charges. Are you ready to begin? Well, even if you aren't, I am. So let's go."

Attorneys Caine and Lewis turned, moved toward their respective tables.

Caine had dialed his expression down to neutral, but I knew he was pissed. Dexter flashed a beautiful set of teeth. I hoped Del Rio would turn around so I could give him a thumbs-up, but his head stayed lowered. He was trying to control his anger.

I hoped with all my heart that he could do it.

# Chapter 12

RICK DEL RIO sat at the defense table next to his lawyer, hardly aware of the muted activity around him: The bailiff talking to the court reporter. People coming into the row of seats behind him. Chitchatting. Giggling. He looked straight ahead, but inside, his mind was ranging around in the past.

Rick had grown up in Branson Point, New Jersey, an industrial wasteland so hard, even weeds didn't grow in the cracks of the pavement. He had lived in a small, overcrowded brick house on a single residential block between two factories. And down the street from his house was a used-car lot, chain-link fence around it, topped with razor wire and patrolled at night by a pair of Dobermans: Bambino and Lassie.

Rick identified with Bambino.

Both he and the big male dog had hair triggers. The dog, though, was permitted to go bug-fuck. That was his job. But after Rick vented his anger, he usually regretted what he had said or done.

Along with his quick temper, Rick's looks had shaped his personality. He knew he was ugly. His flat black eyes were set close together, his lower jaw was undershot, and he was a stocky kid, not very tall. But being stocky and having a first-class uppercut punch had made all the difference in the world.

Rick punched good.

And he'd been cut out for military service.

After he killed a few carloads of Afghanis, after he survived the helicopter crash and brought Jack back from the dead, after he got a medal and a handshake from the high command and had a government pension in the bag, he didn't care what anyone said to him or thought about him anymore.

They had to watch out for *him*.

If he had a motto, it was Do Not Fuck with Me.

And now he was being fucked with.

Rick thought about how, three months ago, he had been home in his very sweet house on Sherman Canal, drinking a Coors and eating pork chops in front of the TV, his plate on his lap, his feet up on the hatch cover he'd made into a coffee table.

*Godfather II* had been on his fifty-inch flatscreen, and just at the point when Fredo was going for his boat ride, Rick heard the footsteps on the deck followed by a loud shout: "Open up. LAPD." And then the door was kicked in and about eleven guys stormed his place.

They threw him facedown on the floor, and one of those assholes put a knee into his back, almost crippling him. Another stepped on his hand with a boot, acting like the remote control was something dangerous. What? A grenade? A piece?

Or were they just fucking with him?

After the cops roughed him up and dragged him downtown, he got his phone call. Twenty minutes later, Jack was there with Eric Caine, who took pictures of the abrasions on Rick's face and told him don't say anything and don't give the cops any reason to pile on extra charges.

Next day, Eric had appeared with him at his arraignment and put up bail, a half million bucks, which had allowed him to go to work and sleep at home.

After today, he might not sleep in his own bed ever again.

The bailiff called out, "All rise," and Rick stood up.

How had this fucking happened?

He just didn't fucking get it.

He sat down. There was a whoosh of the people in the crowd behind him taking seats, adjusting their clothing, whispering to one another. He felt Caine's arm go around his shoulders.

Rick's ears were burning, but, man, he was doing his best not to let Bambino off the leash. Last thing he needed was to start barking at the ADA and his twelve peers in the box who were going to decide what happened to him.

# Chapter 13

AFTER JUDGE JOHNSON instructed the jury, she asked Dexter Lewis if he was ready to make his opening statement.

Rick thought, *Right, like, is a shark hungry?*

The kid said, "Yes, Your Honor," stood up in his sharp blue suit, and went through the short gate to the middle of the courtroom.

He said "Good morning" to the jurors, looking like he could be the kid or grandkid of some of them: a polished, attractive young man with fire in his belly and blood in his eye.

Lewis said, "Folks, this is a straight-up case of aggravated assault. The People will prove to you that on June fourteenth of this year, Mr. Del Rio went to the house of the victim, Ms. Victoria Carmody, a defenseless woman of forty, and gave her a beating that almost killed her.

"Ms. Carmody isn't in court today. She's in a coma because of that beating—but before she slipped into this state of unconsciousness, she did testify to the police that Mr. Del Rio was the one who assaulted her."

Rick clasped his hands together so hard they hurt. He thought of other things: the boat he was building in his garage, what he would name it, what colors he would paint the hull, that if he got out of here, he was going to take a gun to the range and blow off a little steam.

Lewis was saying, "This tragic story actually started a year ago, when Mr. Del Rio was dating Ms. Carmody. Ms. Carmody is an independent tax consultant and a quiet person who lives by herself. She met Mr. Del Rio in a singles chat room, and after a few months of seeing him, she decided that they were ultimately incompatible and she ended the relationship.

"Then, six months after the split—that is, three months ago—Mr. Del Rio called up Ms. Carmody and said he had something that belonged to her and could he bring it over? And Ms. Carmody, having not seen the defendant in a while, said, 'Sure.'

"At the arranged date and time, five thirty the next evening, Mr. Del Rio went to Ms. Carmody's house—and there is no dispute regarding that fact. A UPS deliveryman, Mr. Brad Sutter, is a witness and he will testify that he saw Mr. Del Rio ring Ms. Carmody's doorbell.

"Mr. Sutter knows Ms. Carmody because he does pickups and deliveries from her in-home business. He knows Mr. Del Rio from times he has seen him with Ms. Carmody. Mr. Sutter knows him by name.

"On this particular evening, Mr. Sutter plainly saw Ms. Carmody answer the door and welcome Mr. Del Rio into her house.

"After the defendant went inside and closed the door, Mr. Del Rio slugged Ms. Carmody in the face. He broke her nose, right here at the bridge."

Lewis indicated the site of the break for the jurors, turning so that they all got a good view of it. But he wasn't finished talking.

"Mr. Del Rio then proceeded to crush her right eye socket and knock out three of her front teeth. He also put bruises on her body and kicked her in the kidney, lacerating it.

"As she raised her arm to protect herself, the defendant seized a table lamp, ripping its cord out of the wall, and used it to break Ms. Carmody's right arm in two places."

Rick jumped to his feet, knocking over his chair, which fell, clattering loudly behind him.

*"This is bullshit,"* he shouted. *"That did not happen."*

# Chapter 14

JUDGE JOHNSON SLAMMED her gavel down a few times, the crack of wood against wood sounding a lot like gunfire, causing Rick to violently hunch his shoulders, a startle reflex left over from the war.

The judge said, "Mr. Caine, this is your one and only warning. If your client *ever* speaks in this courtroom again without having been sworn in, he will be excluded from this trial and *you* will be fined. Heavily. Get me?"

"Yes, Your Honor." Caine leaned over to Del Rio, whispered, "Apologize, Rick. Do it now."

Rick sat, feeling the scalding rush of blood through his veins and the fury pushing against the inside of his skull; hearing Bambino's harsh growl, the jangle of his paws against the fence, his teeth gnashing; seeing the drool flying off his chops.

"Your Honor, I'm sorry for my outburst. I won't do it again."

Rick, feeling Dexter Lewis's eyes on him, turned his head and gave the guy across the aisle a look that could peel paint off the *Last Supper*. It had no visible effect on the little shit.

Caine murmured at his side, "Take it easy."

Rick felt shame wash over him. He'd made a mistake, and now Dexter Lewis was a very happy little shit, because the jurors had seen him lose his temper. It would be easier than before for someone to prove to them that he'd beaten Vicky, that sad little bitch.

Lewis was speaking now.

"Your Honor, if I may show this to the jury."

"Go ahead, Mr. Lewis."

The ADA lifted a poster-size photograph of Victoria Carmody in the Cedars-Sinai ICU, looking like roadkill that had been lying in the sun for about a week. Lewis took the photo enlargement over to the jury box and held it up as he walked from one end of the box to the other, talking the whole time.

"Ms. Carmody has had fifteen surgeries. Her face is disfigured, and one of her kidneys has been removed, as well as one of her eyes. And if she comes out of her coma, she will only have sixty percent use of her right arm. The extent of her brain damage cannot yet be assessed.

"Ms. Carmody never stood a chance against the defendant, this ruthless man whom she had trusted."

Lewis said, "That's what this trial is about, ladies and gentlemen. The People will prove to you beyond a reasonable doubt that Mr. Del Rio, a former first lieutenant in the U.S. Marine Corps, well-versed in the art of hand-to-hand combat, currently an investigator for Private, a lawless private investigation firm, did viciously assault Victoria Carmody without provocation, and without mercy.

"It is by the grace of God that she survived, and with your help, we will put Mr. Del Rio where he can't hurt anyone else for a long time."

# Chapter 15

RICK GLIMPSED THE faces of the jurors as Lewis took his seat. They were horrified. Dexter Lewis, that bastard, had done a good job burying him.

Judge Johnson said, "Mr. Caine? Are you ready to give your opening statement?"

Eric Caine stood up, said, "I am, Your Honor."

He buttoned his jacket and stepped out to the lectern in the well. He had no notes. And he didn't need any.

He greeted the jury, then said, "I'm going to make this short and sweet.

"My client, Mr. Del Rio, is entirely innocent. He did not beat Ms. Carmody. Didn't lift a hand to her, had no reason to, and never would.

"On the thirteenth of June, having not had contact with Ms. Carmody in six months, Mr. Del

Rio called to tell her that he had come across a small camera that she had left in his house way back before they broke off their relationship.

"Ms. Carmody said, 'I thought I'd lost that camera. Well, yes, I'd like to have it back.'

"And Mr. Del Rio said, 'When would be good for you?'

"They agreed on a time for the return of this little camera, so the next evening, Mr. Del Rio went to Ms. Carmody's house, where a witness saw Ms. Carmody open the door for Mr. Del Rio, who then entered the house.

"Once he was inside, Ms. Carmody made tea, and these two people had a polite conversation in the parlor lasting about fifteen minutes and consisting of pleasantries and the return of the Coolpix. Mr. Del Rio never touched Ms. Carmody, unless you count the cheek kisses that were exchanged when Mr. Del Rio left Ms. Carmody.

"After Mr. Del Rio left Ms. Carmody's home, he went to his own place in Venice, took a six-pack out of the fridge, and spent the rest of the evening watching *The Fog of War* on the Sundance channel, alone. At eleven, he went to bed.

"That's the end of the story.

"Or at least, it should be.

"But when Ms. Carmody was questioned by the police after she had suffered a traumatic head injury, she identified Mr. Del Rio as her attacker, a statement that cannot be corroborated.

"In legal circles, this is referred to as he-said-she-said, and that, ladies and gentlemen, is *really* what this case is about.

"To continue with this story, late that night, approximately six hours after Mr. Del Rio left her, Ms. Carmody called an ambulance, and en route to the hospital, in this profoundly traumatized condition, she was interviewed by a detective, Sergeant Michael Degano.

"Sergeant Degano videotaped the interview with his phone camera, and when he asked Ms. Carmody who had beaten her, he showed her a picture of Mr. Del Rio, at which point she said Mr. Del Rio's name.

"After that, she went into surgery, and she survived that surgery but has not spoken again; she has been in a coma ever since.

"It's reasonable to ask, Why would Ms. Carmody name Mr. Del Rio as her attacker if he never touched her?

"I would suggest that she recognized his picture, and that she even remembered that he had come to visit her that evening. I would further suggest to you that Ms. Carmody had suffered so much injury to the brain that she was an unreliable witness for herself.

"So what happened then is that the police had their suspect, and they had no reason to look for another. They had testimony from the victim, and because Mr. Del Rio had been in Ms. Carmody's house, they had evidence placing him at the scene.

"Mr. Del Rio had a cup of tea, and left his fingerprints and DNA. He was witnessed going into the house, but he wasn't seen coming out.

"But in fact, he did leave Ms. Carmody's house, and she was fine when they said good-bye. After that, while Mr. Del Rio was watching TV in his own house, someone went into Ms. Carmody's house and attempted to kill her. Someone else did that. Not Mr. Del Rio.

"In the old days, there were colorful terms for the unfortunate sap who took the blame. He was called the dupe. The fall guy. The patsy."

Rick didn't like being characterized as a fool, but he thought Caine was doing a great job telling what had happened. Over at the prosecutor's table, Dexter Lewis played with his pen like it was a drumstick: *tat-tat-tat* on the tabletop, just enough sound to draw the jury's attention and, maybe, break Caine's rhythm.

But Caine didn't acknowledge the sound, didn't look at Lewis at all. He walked to the jury box, all six foot three of Harvard-educated success story.

Caine said, "So now we have the whole short and not-so-sweet story. Someone beat Ms. Carmody. She had a subdural hematoma and an intracranial hemorrhage. She had brain damage, ladies and gentlemen, and during a semilucid moment as she was being taken by ambulance to the hospital, she named my client.

"But Mr. Del Rio didn't lift a hand to Ms. Carmody.

"He's the scapegoat, the designated fall guy. He didn't beat up his friend Vicky. Someone set Rick up. Or Rick was at the wrong place at the worst possible time. We don't know who attacked Vicky Carmody or why it happened.

"But this we know for sure: Rick Del Rio didn't do it."

# PART TWO

# SEPARATED AT BIRTH

# Chapter 16

BY 11:20 A.M., two of Private's top investigators, Emilio Cruz and Christian Scott, had rung fifteen doorbells on both sides of PCH, had talked to as many housekeepers and homeowners, had collected surveillance footage from security cameras, and were now reviewing the footage on their fleet-car computer.

Scotty was blond, lithe, had been a ballet dancer until he ruined his knees. He became a motorcycle cop with CHiPs and was eventually promoted to deputy sheriff. He was bright and motivated, and a very agile athlete.

Jack had brought him in as an investigator last year and was still floating him, pairing him with other investigators until he found him a partner.

Cruz was senior to Scotty.

First thing most people noticed about Cruz was his good looks: the black hair he wore pulled back in a ponytail, and his muscular build. Cruz was a former light-middleweight professional boxer, born and raised in the 'hood, and had highly developed street smarts. At age twenty-eight, after he retired from the ring with his brains intact, Cruz went to work as an investigator for LA's district attorney, Bobby Petino.

Petino and Cruz were second cousins, and Petino had told Jack about this smart young investigator, saying that he thought Cruz had a dynamite future. Jack thought so too. He hired Cruz and teamed him up with Del Rio.

The partnership had stuck.

Cruz had wanted to be in court for his partner this morning, but he had to get a handle on who had firebombed Jack's car.

Scotty downloaded the video to their hard drive, opened the file, said, "This is from the house across PCH. Camera one. Faces the road."

"Roll it," Cruz said to Scotty.

Scotty pressed Play. The camera was pointed across the highway, right at Jack's house, and the angle took in the wall and the Lamborghini that Jack had parked outside his gate.

As they watched, cars flashed past on the road.

Then, on the screen, a sedan with its high beams on came toward Jack's house. And stopped.

Scotty reversed the clip, then forwarded it in slow motion.

"Whoa," said Cruz. "Freeze that."

It was too dark to see anything about the color or make of the car beyond the fact that it was a dark sedan, probably a Chevy. The time stamp read 4:27 a.m.

"I can't read the plates at all," Cruz said. "Not a single number."

"Going to forward it now," Scotty said.

The car in the center of the frame didn't move, but a few other cars passed in the background, both directions. When the road was clear, a figure got out of the backseat and ran toward Jack's Lambo.

"Here we go," said Cruz.

Scotty tried to refine the image, but no amount of fine-tuning brought up the shadowy figure's face. Still, they could see what he was doing: making chiseling motions on the rear flank of the car.

"He's doing something with the gas tank," said Scotty.

"I see that. And now where is he?" Cruz said.

Scotty reversed the clip, played it forward, saw the guy linger near the tank, then duck behind the car and disappear; he was out of sight for four seconds.

"I think he's putting a charge under the chassis. This was planned," Scotty said. "Well planned."

"So was this a plan to torch *a* car?" Cruz mused. "Or a plan to torch *Jack'*s car?"

"Look here, Emilio. There's your fire," Scotty said as flames flashed from beneath the car.

The dark figure fled from the Lambo and ran to the car waiting for him on the shoulder, which started up before he'd closed the rear door. A moment later, the sedan was gone, and the fire was lapping over the fenders of Jack's quarter-million-dollar car.

"Shit," said Cruz. "There's Jack."

The two men stared, mesmerized, as Jack came out of his house and watched his car burn. He just stood there until, moments later, the car went up and Jack was blown off his feet.

"Some kind of timing device. What do you think?" Scotty said, stabbing the Stop button.

Cruz said, "I think if there's any evidence on the remains of that Lamborghini, it's going to be a miracle."

# Chapter 17

DR. SCI ARRIVED at Private's underground lot at just after two in the afternoon. He nosed his 1967 Spider into his spot, then extracted his silver Halliburton case from the passenger seat and went to the back door to Private's forensic lab that ran underneath half of the building.

Standing at the entrance, Sci reached up, touched the mezuzah in the doorframe, then pressed his hand to the biometric plate. The doors opened, admitting him to the airlock, and closed with a whisper behind him.

The metal and explosives detectors scanned him, and after Sci had spent twenty seconds under the UV light, the second set of doors opened and he stepped into the clean, cool, well-lit lab.

He paused inside the entrance, did a quick

check of the various stations around the perimeter of the large room. Criminologists wearing lab coats worked in their bays, which were equipped with the best forensic tools in the world.

Sci waved to Mo-bot, who was crossing the room with a sound tech, then entered his glass-walled office at the hub. His computer recognized him and flashed on. He set his briefcase on a tabletop, removed the flask he was transporting, and read his e-mail.

About ten years earlier, when Dr. Sci, whose given name was Seymour Kloppenberg, was twenty, he had graduated from MIT with a PhD.

LA County, still recovering from the humiliation of the O.J. Simpson trial, had refurbished its forensic lab to the tune of a hundred million dollars, and Dr. Sci was hired right out of school.

Sci was rotated around the numerous forensic disciplines—DNA, trace analysis, toxicology, ballistics—so he could find his niche. But during this training program, Jack Morgan heard about Sci and offered him a job as chief forensic scientist and head of Private's lab. He told Sci that he wanted the lab to become a profit center.

Sci had been dubious. No independent lab could match the county's facilities.

Jack said, "It's yours to outfit, Sci. I want only the best of everything. And I'll make you an equity partner."

Sci was sold on this rare and terrific opportunity. He equipped and staffed Private's new lab one division at a time. He cut no corners. And soon, law enforcement departments from all over the country hired Private's lab when they required impeccable work done fast.

Of course, Private's clients came first.

Sci had just returned from the LA County lab with a sample from the gas tank of Jack's impounded car. He also had a digital chip loaded with 3-D images from all angles of the remains of the Lambo, as well as a preliminary report from the head of the LA Regional Crime Lab, a man Sci had worked with for years.

Sci put the disk into his computer, then made a slide of the gunk from Jack's car. He loaded the slide into the new Olympia 9000 gas chromatograph/mass spectrometer and watched it start its run.

As the machine worked, Sci called psychologist and senior investigator Dr. Justine Smith on the interoffice line.

Her image came up on the screen. She was

wearing a tailored black-and-white-checked jacket, a silk blouse, and a strand of rough-cut rubies around her throat. Her hair was twisted up and held loosely in a few combs, making her look like a figure in a painting by Botticelli.

Dr. Sci had a crush on Justine, but it was safe to say that he was only one of many men who were crazy about her.

He said, "Justine, you were there. What happened this morning?"

"I wish I had some neat observation, but all I saw was the fire, Sci. That's it."

"Let's go over it anyway."

"Whatever I can do to help," she said.

# Chapter 18

JUSTINE'S OFFICE WAS on the fourth floor, fifteen seconds by elevator above Sci's lab. Sci could have gone upstairs or asked Justine to come down, but generally speaking, Sci found virtual contact as informative and satisfying as meeting IRL. And it was usually faster.

He said to Justine's image, "What's the first thing you remember?"

"Well, I was asleep, when suddenly Jack bolted up in bed. It was an abrupt movement. He gets nightmares, you know."

"Yes. He's told me."

"Anyway, I thought he was dreaming, but then I saw light on the wall. And I smelled smoke. Something was burning."

"Did you hear an explosion?"

"Not then. Jack told me to get dressed and he ran out to where he'd parked the car. I ran after him. It took me a moment to realize that the fireball was Jack's car.

"And then, there was a blast," Justine said, "and that knocked Jack off his feet. He's not hurt, Sci, but I worry about what this means. If it was personal, was blowing up the car the whole point? Or was it a warning? You know, at any given moment, a lot of people are pissed off at him."

The machine at Sci's right blinked to show that the analysis was complete, but it also flashed the words *No match*.

"This is odd," Sci said, turning the screen so that Justine could see the display. "See, the gas tank was BLEVE'd. Blown out, so the explosive was in the tank. However, our spectrometer is calling the explosive 'unknown.' "

"An unknown chemical? That has to be a first."

"I'm going to have to research this compound, but I can tell you what it was packaged in. Latex."

"Like a glove?"

"Or like a condom. Yep. The machine is telling me we've got some spermicidal lubricant here."

"Let me get this right. Someone put explosives in a condom? Then put the condom in the gas tank?"

"Correct. A charge was set under the car to start the fire, and when the fire got hot enough, it melted the latex. That put this chemical in contact with the gas, and boom. That's my theory, anyway. That's why there was delay on the explosion. The latex was a delay device."

"And what does that tell you?"

"This is the kind of thing a teenager would think up. A teenager with access to a car and a total disregard for life."

# Chapter 19

MY OFFICE OVERLOOKS downtown LA, and the late-afternoon sun was high and hot, glancing off the glassy skyscrapers across the street, blazing over the fast-moving traffic below.

Dr. Sci was talking to me on the interoffice network, the picture on my screen so high-def, I could see the individual stitches on the seams of his bowling shirt. He was telling me that there was a new chemical explosive at loose in the world.

"I'm calling it barium trichlormanganate for now," he said. "I can't find any reference to its properties."

"What's special about it?" I asked.

"It requires extreme heat and contact with gasoline to make it ignite," he told me. "Works fine on a burning car."

"Yes, it does."

Sci explained how the explosive had been packaged and ignited, went on to say that this new compound was novel but not versatile. He said that there were numerous easily obtained explosives that would work as well or better, including a Molotov cocktail tossed through the car window.

"So this doesn't make a lot of sense," I said.

"In my humble opinion, this is the kind of thing that a teenager or a gang of teenagers would do, not terrorists or, say, organized-crime types."

"Cops told me that mine is the sixth car in two months to go boom in the night," I said.

"That fits with my theory," Sci said.

I said good-bye to Sci just as I heard a commotion outside my office. My assistant, Valerie Kenney, came through my door in a huff.

Val is five eleven, a striking twenty-five-year-old African American woman who went to BU on scholarship, then got her master's in criminology, also on scholarship, at the University of Miami. Same time she was going for her master's, she was working nights as a clerk in the back rooms of the Miami PD and helping her mother with an out-of-control younger brother.

Last year, she learned that I was looking for an assistant and she applied for the job; she accepted the offer with the understanding that she'd get a promotion to investigator in the future if and when I thought she was ready.

In the short time Val had been working for me, I found her to be smart, disciplined, willing to do any kind of work needed and without being asked. She was also very funny. Val didn't rile easily. But she was riled now.

"It's your *brother,* " she said. "He showed up downstairs and says he's coming up here right now. He has no appointment that I know of and no apologies either. You want to see him, Jack? Or you want me to call security?"

My identical twin, Tommy, was named for my miserable father, Tom Morgan. Tommy is older than me by three minutes, arrogant, a bully, and very likely a killer. I've never been able to prove that last, but I have good reason to believe it.

"Call security," I said. "No, I'll do it." I went for my phone but never reached it.

Tommy brushed past Val, managing to touch her inappropriately on his way through the door.

"Oh nooo," he said with a bright, mocking tone. "Bad Tommy's here."

"What do you want?" I asked him.

"How'd you like twenty million bucks?" he said. "Got time for me now?"

# Chapter 20

"DON'T GET COMFORTABLE," I said to my twin.

Tommy went over to the seating area of my office, threw himself onto the blue couch, put his feet on the coffee table.

He sighed contentedly as he took in the wide view through my windows. Then: "How long does it take you to make twenty million, bro? A few years, at least, right?"

I picked up the phone, called security.

"Charles, I need assistance in my office," I said. "Right now." I hung up, said to my brother, "You have ten seconds."

"What happened to your eyebrows?"

"Maybe you'll tell me."

"Me?"

My subconscious had spoken. Yes, Tommy could have done it. Could have blown up cars, set it up the way Detective Ziegler had said. Five cars in my neighborhood, then mine. Made it look like a serial arsonist, but maybe my car was the target all along.

"Oh, are my ten seconds almost over?" he said. "Let me make this fast. I want to buy you out of Private, Jack. Twenty million, cash, before this case against Del Rio drives all your clients away. I'll combine Private Investigations and Private Security and give you a piece of the whole company.

"I think this could be called equity preservation," he added.

"Let me think about it. No."

"It's win-win for you, Jack. So, okay. How much do you want?"

The security team showed up. I told them that Mr. Morgan needed an escort out. Charles looked at Tom, looked at me, looked back at Tom, both of us with the same sandy-brown hair, the same features—except for my lack of eyebrows.

Tommy laughed, said, "Throw the bum out."

I said, "It's your choice, Tom. You can leave by the door or go out through the window."

"Okay, okay," he said, grinning, putting up his hands, getting to his feet. "You're making a mistake."

In a minute, he was gone, with four security guys behind him to make sure that he didn't loiter in the hallways.

Tommy had stirred me up. As he always does. And as he has done since we were about seven. My brother hates me enough to set me up to take a murder rap.

He's done that, and he's done worse.

I just can't prove it.

I called Val back into my office.

"Val, I apologize for my brother."

"I'm okay," she said. "Thanks, though."

Val said she'd put together a list of all the high schools within five miles of my house with names and contact numbers, the theory being the list might help Cruz and Scotty find car-bombing teens, if they existed.

Then she said, "It's none of my business, but . . ."

"Go ahead."

"You think Rick is going to be convicted?"

"Could happen."

If Rick went away for aggravated assault, the raccoons would have a good time picking Private apart. That would be bad for business. Just as Tommy had said.

My brother was sick, but he wasn't stupid.

# Chapter 21

THE SPIRAL STAIRCASE at the core of our building is beautiful, like a cross section of a nautilus shell. It rises from the center of our reception area and expands outward as it winds to the top floor. The staircase ends just outside my office, where it is capped by a skylight that brightens the stairs all the way down.

Tommy was being escorted out by way of the elevator, so I left my office, paused at the railing, and looked down through the staircase to the ground floor. Once security had hustled Tommy to the street, I walked down one flight, to the fourth floor, where Justine's office is right under mine.

I knocked, stepped through the open doorway.

Justine's office is a lot like her: tailored, witty, easy on the eyes. She was putting on her jacket, getting ready to leave for the day.

I said, "I think that Tommy set fire to my car."

"Ummm. He's capable of it, but what about all those other cars that were torched in your neighborhood?"

"That was Tommy. He was practicing," I said.

Justine laughed, straightened her collar, packed up her laptop. She turned off her art-glass desk lamp depicting two fish doing the samba.

She said, "So why did he do it?"

I said, "He needs a special reason?"

My brother's company, Private Security, provided bodyguards for Hollywood's entertainment elite. He had a client list that looked like it had been ripped from the pages of *Variety*, and that list was like gold.

Private Security got lucrative, repeat business, and Tommy knew the rich and famous intimately: where they lived, where they were going, where they got their drugs—their weaknesses and vulnerabilities—and where they went when they didn't want to be seen.

These A-list connections overflowed with perks for Tommy, including insider deals and young women who Velcroed themselves to him when he was attending to his clients in person.

But although he loved himself and the business he was in, what really turned Tommy on was springing traps and perpetrating dirty-dog schemes on his enemies—of which I was enemy number one.

Last year he framed me for murder. He tried to destroy me—and almost did.

Justine said, "I'm not saying you're paranoid, Jack, but I don't think Tommy, as low as he is, would stoop to torching your car. It's too juvenile for him. Too small."

"Maybe I *am* paranoid. But maybe firebombing my car is Tommy's idea of lighting a fuse. Could be he's just getting started."

"Okay." She shook her head, laughed, said, "I don't see it. I'm going to work on Sci's angle. But if you think it's Tommy, get a lease car, Jack."

I said, "Good idea. Want to have dinner?"

"Since I'm the one with the wheels, I guess I get to choose the venue," she said, shooting me a grin, snapping her briefcase closed.

I talked Justine out of the keys and drove her Jag to one of our favorite places, the Water Grill.

I thought about what she'd said about Tommy.

It was true that Tommy was complex and

devious and that a car fire, even a quarter-of-a-million-dollar-car fire, was small spuds. But he'd made his twenty-million-dollar offer just hours after this morning's explosion.

Maybe I was wrong to connect the two events.

But Tommy and I both love sports cars. The big-bang wake-up call had Tommy's warped sense of humor all over it.

# Chapter 22

THE WATER GRILL is appointed in brass and leather, has marble columns and vaulted aquamarine ceilings that give the restaurant an airy feel. I ordered an amaretto sour for Justine and Ellie's Brown Ale for myself, and by the time the drinks arrived, the aromas from the kitchen had driven me half crazy with hunger.

Our waiter announced the specials and we ran the table, ordering Nantucket bay scallops, line-caught swordfish, and the risotto du jour.

Justine was telling me about one of our clients, a woman who'd been caught stealing from her mother, and she was giving the story a hilarious spin.

"Rita's mom is ninety-four," Justine was saying. "Jack, Rita wrote herself a check for two hundred dollars, and her mom hired Krauss and Maber to sue her for damages. I think Sandy Krauss bills his time at twelve hundred dollars an *hour*—"

Justine's phone buzzed. She glanced at it, said, "Sorry, I need a second, Jack."

Justine typed a text, received one, typed a reply, and by then, my thoughts had gone to Bobby Petino.

Bobby looked like a tough guy from Central Casting; he was handsome, smooth, and had been LA's district attorney for about a decade. A while ago, Petino hired Private to work a particularly gruesome series of killings. A dozen high-school girls had been murdered by assorted methods, baffling the cops, leaving them frustrated and clueless for two years.

Justine had asked to be Private's lead investigator on the case. I called her Princess Do-Good and said, "Don't get emotionally involved." She said, "Shut up, Jack," then did nothing but work the case until she nailed it shut. It was heroic. It was historic.

Justine and I were going through one of our off-seasons at the time, and she was dating Bobby Petino. Bobby used the closed-schoolgirl case as a political springboard to run for governor and tried to mend his broken marriage at the same time.

Petino didn't get what he wanted. He lost the election, his divorce was finalized, and now he was back as our city's DA. I'd heard that Bobby was working on Justine, had told her that things would be different for them this time. That this time, he wouldn't break her heart.

Same kinds of things I told her.

Bastards. Both of us.

Justine said my name. I came back to the moment, said to her, "Sorry. I was thinking about Tommy."

"Well, stop doing that," she said.

We talked, we joked, we savored the chocolate cherry devil's food cake, and I wondered if Justine had made plans with Bobby for later that night.

The check came. I put my card down, looked up at Justine, who was looking at me.

She'd said that as far as our relationship went, we were both free agents. Since I'd been unfaithful to her, it was fair for Justine to set the rules.

No matter how much it killed me.

She pulled the clip out of her hair and tossed her mane. My heart rate ticked up by twenty beats a minute. All these years of knowing her, and I still got a rush when I smelled her hair.

"Where to, Jack?" Justine said. "Beach house or my house?"

# Chapter 23

LESTER OLSEN SAT alone at the exclusive Club Privé in the Bellagio Hotel. The private casino was richly appointed in art deco style: black lacquer, dark wood, veiled with silver screens and textured glass. The air smelled like freshly mown money.

Olsen had been banned from the card tables, but that didn't matter. He was still in the game. From where he sat in the plush armchair, he could see Tule.

Tule was twenty-two, petite, with skin as smooth as Baileys Irish Cream. He'd met her when she was serving drinks in the VIP lounge at the Black Diamond Hotel and Casino. Right now, this adorable woman wore a Reem Acra gold-sequined dress that cost around three thousand dollars, Cartier's wrapped citrine earrings, and strappy

Manolo Blahnik sandals, all of which he'd paid for.

Les heard Tule say to the dealer, "Hit me," then saw her peek at her cards. The guy sitting next to her was an industrialist with a heart of stone. He looked very good for seventy-eight, wore an Armani tux and a big diamond-studded Rolex that matched his silver hair. He whispered to the young Filipino woman.

Tule nodded, then said with confidence, "I'll see you and raise you—this much."

She pushed towers of chips toward the pot with both hands.

A waiter walked into Olsen's view, replaced his empty glass with a new tumbler of Woodford Reserve. When Olsen could see the card table again, Tule was dancing around her date, kissing his face, crying out, "Wowee. Honeyyyy. We did it."

Nice sound of chips stacking on their side of the table. Looked like they were having a good time.

Tule moved away from the table, and his phone buzzed.

He picked up, saw Tule's face on his screen.

"Hey," she said, grinning. Les had paid to have

her teeth straightened and veneered. The guy had done a very good job. Perfect, actually.

"How's it going?" he asked.

"I just made ten grand in two minutes."

He laughed. "I know. Good for you."

She said, "Could you meet me near the little girls' room?"

"Absolutely."

He left his drink on the table, walked past the bar, caught up with her when she stopped in the alcove. She stretched up her arms, put them around his neck, and, getting up on tiptoes, kissed him on the mouth.

"I adore you," she said.

He squeezed her, swayed with her a little bit, kissed her neck like she was a baby, making her giggle. Then he straightened them both up and looked into her eyes.

"Tell me, Tule. I really want to know."

"We're getting married," she said. She was keyed up, trying to keep her excitement in check.

"Seriously? That is awesome," said the brown-eyed man. "When?"

"Tonight," said Tule. "In a chapel up the street."

"No way." Then: "You're phenomenal."

"I owe it all to you," she said.

"Not *all* of it."

She grabbed his hand and laughed. They both did.

"I'll call you from Cannes. France. That's where we're going on our honeymoon."

"Wow. Give me another hug. Stay in touch. I mean it."

They hugged and he patted her bouncy little behind "for luck."

Then Olsen went to the elevator, stabbed the button with one twisted finger. He whistled as the car took him down silently, smoothly to the main floor, and from there, he walked out into the timeless neon life of the Strip.

# Chapter 24

THE NEXT MORNING, my iPhone was clogged with alerts and e-mail from friends and clients letting me know that Private was in the headlines again. Rick's past was being dragged through the muck, and Private was dirtied by association.

It made me sick. All of it. And I was particularly worried for Rick. The man had saved my life. And there was no way I could help him with this.

Justine and I arrived at the Criminal Courthouse before nine, sidestepped all but the most aggressive of the reporters who were clumped around the entrance to the building. One of the swamp suckers ran up to Justine, said, "Dr. Smith, what's your opinion of Rick Del Rio's personality? Borderline or full-blown psychopath?"

I shoved the reporter out of our way, almost knocking him to the ground, saying, "Excuse me," and as he howled for the police, we entered the judicial building.

We found two seats together in courtroom 7B, three rows behind the defense table. Across the aisle and about four seats down, my brother lounged in a chair, one sockless, snakeskin-loafer-shod foot crossed over his thigh. He lifted his hand in an exaggerated, brassy wave. Why the hell was Tommy loitering in this courtroom? Was he here to aggravate me? To gather information? If so, what information, and why?

Del Rio must have sensed the tension arcing across the aisle, because he turned for an instant, saw Justine and me. He smiled sadly. I gave him a thumbs-up, hoping it would give him a lift. He nudged Caine, who also turned, nodded, then turned back to face the bench.

Within the next few minutes, the room filled and court convened. The bailiff asked everyone to rise, and Judge Johnson entered from the door behind the bench and took her seat. The clicking of little-dog toenails on the floor meant that her Chihuahua was under the bench.

There was a sudden, muted flurry of

conversation between the prosecutor and Eric Caine. I couldn't hear them, but both attorneys turned and looked at me. Why?

Lewis said, "Your Honor, we need a word."

The judge asked the lawyers to approach, and Lewis quickly got to the point. He pointed at *me*.

"Jack Morgan is a witness for the defense," Lewis said loudly. "He should be barred from the courtroom until he testifies."

I heard some of what Caine said in response: that I was a character witness, that my testimony was not material to the charges. And after some back-and-forth, the judge went along with Caine.

This was good. I needed to be here for Rick.

The jury filed in. ADA Lewis introduced his first witness.

"The People call Ms. Geralyn Brodeski," he said.

I didn't know the name, and I wondered who Dexter Lewis had put at the top of his witness lineup.

A woman in her early fifties came through the double doors. She had short, streaked hair, wore a calf-length skirt and a ruffled print blouse. If I had to characterize her by her looks, I would say that she was a mild person, maybe a good citizen.

She headed for the witness stand, said "Hello, Your Honor," to the judge, then swore on the Bible to tell the truth.

# Chapter 25

I WATCHED DEXTER Lewis leave the prosecution table, walk over to where Ms. Brodeski was fluffing her ruffles and preparing for her fifteen minutes of fame.

At Lewis's questioning, Ms. Brodeski said that she was a postmistress and established that she lived directly next door to Victoria Carmody.

Lewis asked his witness, "Would you say that you and Ms. Carmody are good friends?"

"Good neighbors, anyway. Both of us are divorced, and sometimes we talk about men."

"All right, Ms. Brodeski. Now. Did you see Ms. Carmody on the thirteenth of June, the day before the assault Mr. Del Rio is charged with committing?"

"Yes. I just got home from work, and Vicky was watering her lawn. We exchanged a few words."

"What was the gist of this conversation?"

"Vicky said that an ex-boyfriend was coming over the next night to return her camera. She was glad to have it back, because she had a photo on it that she took of Sylvester Stallone."

"And did Ms. Carmody mention the name of the man who was going to be coming over the next night?"

"Yes. Rick Del Rio."

"Thank you, Ms. Brodeski. Your witness," Lewis said to Eric Caine.

But Brodeski kept talking, explaining to Dexter Lewis's back and everyone in the room, "I didn't like Rick. I told Vicky from the beginning that he was troubled and angry. And I was right. *That's* why she broke up with him."

Eric Caine stood and spoke angrily from the defense table.

"Objection, Your Honor. Let me count the ways. The witness's uncalled-for remarks are her opinion as well as irrelevant and prejudicial. Then she topped it all off with a little hearsay, and I object to that as well."

The judge said, "Quite right, Mr. Caine. Ms. Brodeski, don't volunteer opinions. Mrs. Gray, please strike the testimony from the record. Jurors, please disregard the witness's remark. It may not be considered during your deliberations. Any questions? Mr. Caine?"

Caine said, "I have no questions for this witness."

Dexter Lewis dismissed Ms. Brodeski, who beamed proudly when she walked past Del Rio. Then Lewis said, "The People call Mr. Bradley Sutter."

# Chapter 26

IT JUST KILLED me to sit helplessly by as Rick was accused of bad character and a sickening felony I was sure he hadn't committed. Lacking a smoking gun, the prosecution was going to play on the jurors' emotions. And I had to admit, Dexter Lewis had the superficial charisma of a pretty good dramatic actor.

I glanced up as Lewis called his next witness.

Bradley Sutter looked to be in his late twenties, had thinning hair, and his scalp was pink from the sun. He wore a new khaki jacket and blue pants, a white shirt, no tie, and a wedding ring.

He looked honest. He looked reliable.

Dexter Lewis asked for his occupation, and Sutter answered that he was a driver for UPS, that he'd been on his current route for two years, that he liked his job a lot, and that Ms. Carmody was one of his regular customers.

"I pick up and deliver to her on average two or three times a week," said Sutter. "We talk about local news. I might tell her a joke. She liked a good joke. Excuse me. She *likes* a good joke."

"Now, do you remember delivering a package for Ms. Carmody about three months ago?"

"I call her Vicky, by the way."

"Okay, Mr. Sutter. Do you remember bringing a package to Vicky on June thirteenth?"

"Yes. It was an overnight letter from San Francisco. I checked my log."

"And did anything about that day stand out in your mind?"

"Actually, yes."

"Please tell the jury what you remember," Lewis said.

"Okay. I went up to Vicky's front door, handed her the letter, and asked her to sign. She did and we were talking, and then she said, 'You remember Rick?' I said, 'Sure, what about him?'

"And she said something like, 'He just called. Said he wanted to come by tomorrow, return something I left in his house.' And I said, 'Are you sure that's a good idea?'"

"Mr. Sutter, why did you ask Ms. Carmody that question?"

Sutter said, "Well, about six months before that, a couple days after Christmas, I had a delivery for Vicky, and I parked my truck in front of her driveway, blocked it, actually. I had a couple of boxes for her, and as I was going up her walk, Mr. Del Rio wanted to get his car out and he leaned on the horn."

Lewis said, "What happened after he blew the horn?"

"I said to him, 'I'll be right back, Mr. Del Rio,' and he said, 'Now. You need to move your truck now.' Something like that. And he got a crazy look on his face. He revved the engine like he was going to drive through my truck."

"Go on," Lewis said. He made a half turn so that he could look at the jury as Sutter spoke.

Sutter seemed to me to be a sincere guy and a credible witness. He had a good job and was friends with the victim, who couldn't speak for herself.

It was pretty clear that Sutter's testimony was going to hurt Rick, and I already had a good idea about what he was going to say.

# Chapter 27

DEXTER LEWIS SAID, "Mr. Sutter, please tell the court what happened after the defendant menaced you."

Sutter said, "I brought the boxes up to the porch as Vicky was coming out of her house. I'm figuring that if he runs into my truck, I'm calling the cops, and anyway, the truck is insured to the hilt."

"Please go on."

Sutter said, "So Vicky goes tearing out, shouts to Mr. Del Rio, 'Rick, Brad will only be a minute. Please don't get upset. I'm asking you, Rick.'"

"And then what happened?"

"He said, 'Stay out of it, Vicky.' Then he got out of his car and shouted at me, 'Do you like your job? Do you?'

"He pulled out his phone and I heard him say,

'I want to report one of your drivers for unprofessional behavior and for blocking a driveway.' He gave my license plate number. Nothing I could do, so I went to where Vicky was standing, got her signature, and asked her if she was going to be all right.

"She said she'd broken up with Mr. Del Rio and that he was angry about it. I told her if she had any trouble to call me on my cell phone. And then, as I was trying to leave, he pulled his car in front of my truck and blocked me in."

"Then what?"

"He said, 'You haven't seen the last of me.' And then he called me an effing moron. He drove off a split second ahead of my own call to the cops."

Sutter shot a pointed look at Rick, who had already taken a few pointed looks from Geralyn Brodeski.

Lewis was saying, "Okay, so, to make sure we're all following you: According to Vicky, she broke up with Mr. Del Rio the day of this incident, which was two days after Christmas."

"That's right."

"And then, about six months later, on June thirteenth, Vicky told you that Mr. Del Rio was coming over the next night. June fourteenth."

"That's right."

"And why do you remember this?"

"Because I was worried about Vicky."

Caine objected, said that the witness was speculating, that there was nothing in evidence or anywhere else to show that Mr. Del Rio was a danger to Ms. Carmody or even to Mr. Sutter. All Rick had done was call Sutter a moron.

Lewis countered the objection, saying that the defendant had tried to intimidate the witness, and, further, he said that Vicky breaking up with Del Rio had made the defendant angry and hostile.

But Judge Johnson sustained Caine's objection, which clearly pissed Dexter Lewis off.

The ADA recovered his glossy composure and said to Sutter, "Okay. Now, the next night, did you have occasion to see Ms. Carmody?"

"I had a pickup from the Reynolds family across the street, and I happened to glance over at Vicky's house, and she was at her front door. And Mr. Del Rio's car was in the driveway. It's a gray Land Rover. I see him get out of his car and go up the steps. Vicky let him in and she closed the door."

"And did you see Vicky after that?"

"No. A few days later, I made a delivery to her neighbor Ms. Brodeski, who told me that Vicky had almost died from a beating and was in the ICU."

I wished I could take Sutter's place on the stand, say that Rick's temper was not a true indication of his character. That he had put his life on the line countless times to save soldiers and civilians. That he had helped put killers away in our city. That he was honest. That he was good.

Lewis said, "Thanks, Mr. Sutter. You've been very helpful. Your witness," he said to the defense.

"Were you intimidated by Mr. Del Rio?" asked Eric Caine.

"I need my job. It's a good company, and I didn't have a plan B."

"Were you intimidated, Mr. Sutter?"

"No. I thought he was a jerk."

"Thanks for your testimony. No further questions," said Caine.

# Chapter 28

JUSTINE LEANED IN, whispered to me that she had to go to work. I moved so she could get past me and out into the aisle, and the prosecution's next witness took the stand.

Merle Widner was about five four and had red hair and an intense unblinking stare through his thick glasses. Widner was the 911 operator who had taken the call from Vicky Carmody.

After the preliminary questions, the 911 tape was played, and it was awful to hear. On it, Widner talked to a muffled voice on the other end of the line, identified as belonging to Victoria Carmody. The only understandable word she uttered was *help,* which she got out in one long sigh.

The operator said, "Stay on the line with

me until help arrives, okay?"

What had seemed almost theoretical, because Vicky Carmody was not present in court, suddenly became very real. Widner testified that he'd dispatched two ambulances and the police to the Carmody address, which served to establish the time line and focus the horrified jury.

"The People call Mr. Dandelion Adar," said the ADA.

Dandelion Adar had a shaved head and a confident walk. He cleared the length of the courtroom in five or six strides, swore to tell the truth, got into the box, clasped his hands at his waist, and leaned forward.

Lewis asked Adar what he did for a living, and Adar said that he was a paramedic, that he and his partner had answered the emergency call to go to Victoria Carmody's address.

Lewis asked, "You were the first responder?"

"That's right. The police and another ambulance were right behind me."

"And did you assist the victim, Victoria Carmody?"

"Yes, I did."

"Will you please tell the court where you found her?"

"She was on the floor in the bedroom. She was holding the phone, a landline."

"And can you tell the court about Ms. Carmody's condition?"

"Her head was a bloody pulp. Right eye socket was smashed. Nose broken, and she was breathing with difficulty. Her pulse was very weak. Along with the obvious severe head trauma, her right arm was fractured, bone coming through the skin in two places. I noticed a table lamp with blood on the base that could have been used as a weapon."

"What other observations did you make in your role as a paramedic?"

"I determined that the lady had been lying on the floor for quite a while, because the blood pool had coagulated and hardened. I thought that she had probably been coming in and out of consciousness between the incident and her phone call to 911."

Dexter Lewis nodded soberly, gave the jurors a chance to think about a woman beaten bloody with a lamp and left for dead. I'd seen Rick fight men far larger than him, break bones, knock out teeth.

But I'd never heard of or seen him hitting a woman.

Lewis said, "What action did you and your partner take, Mr. Adar?"

"We strapped her onto a board with a neck brace, loaded her into the bus, gave her oxygen and fluids, rushed her to Cedars-Sinai. I've seen people with less trauma die en route. I didn't expect her to make it to the ER."

"Thanks, Mr. Adar. That's all I have for this witness," said Dexter Lewis.

"I have no questions," said Del Rio's lawyer.

If Caine thought he could discredit the prosecution's witness, he would have questioned him, which led me to the inevitable conclusion: If Caine's argument for the defense didn't annihilate the prosecution's case, Del Rio was going down.

Judge Johnson dismissed the witness, adding that court was adjourned until two in the afternoon. I left the courthouse by a back door, got out to the curb unnoticed to wait for my cab.

I was looking up the street when a red Ferrari zoomed into my view. As the car came closer, the driver honked the horn.

It was Tommy. Our eyes locked, and in that brief moment, he grinned and blew me a kiss.

Asshole.

My brother is a gambler.

He was betting that he was going to take me down.

How did he think he could pull that off?

# Chapter 29

GOZAN REMARI WHISTLED through his teeth as he drove the rented Bentley north on Rodeo Drive, down the three-block-long strip of extravagant stores. The fantastic shopping area was planted with palm trees on the median, and palms poked through the sidewalks fronting the stores.

Palm trees! In Sumar, there were *no* trees, and here, they were everywhere, waving their flirty branches, hellooo.

There were really no suitable words in Sumarin to describe Rodeo Drive, so Gozan spoke in English, telling his nephew that Rodeo was the jewel in the crown of Beverly Hills.

"Khezzy. Look here. Bulgari, Escada, Harry Winston, Gucci. Isn't this wonderful?"

Khezir was in a black mood since they'd gotten

131

evicted from the Beverly Hills Hotel. He had liked the bungalow. He had liked the garden around it. He was not ready to go back to New York. And he might never be ready to go back to Sumar.

"You need a nice new suit of clothes, nephew. That will cheer you up."

The traffic was clotted with flashy high-ticket autos, and wealthy residents and tourists strolled into the designer stores.

Gozan parked the Bentley in a no-parking zone, waited for Khezir to get out, and then locked up. Khezzy called out to his uncle, "You think shopping is going to cheer me up? I don't think so."

"Think again," said Gozan.

A peachy type of woman and a woman who looked just like a younger version of her were heading into a high-end shop called Mariah Koo. Each woman wore tight jeans, a blousy silk shirt, and high heels. The older one had a deep neckline with her bosoms almost spilling out.

The Sumaris walked through the front doors of the shop, and Gozan was impressed by the scent of flowers, the upbeat techno music, and the elegant decor. The walls were seamless black lacquer, and the clothing was displayed on individual stands that were spotlighted islands of color against the black marble floor.

A young man came over to where Gozan and Khezir stood inside the doorway. He was handsome, with blue eyes and thick black hair. A gold stud winked in the lobe of his left ear.

He said his name was Brian and he asked how he could help them today, and would they like coffee or champagne?

Gozan said, "Coffee, please. With milk and sugar."

Gozan saw that men's clothing was to the left, and the women's area was on the right. The two juicy ladies he'd seen going into the store were grazing among the clothing displays. He could tell at a glance that there would be a sparse selection for curvy women, so he and Khezzy would have to strike quickly, before the pair left the premises.

Brian went off to get coffee, and Gozan and Khezir worked out a plan. It was one of their best yet.

# Chapter 30

WHILE KHEZIR TRIED on sports coats, Gozan took possession of a silver-leather club chair in the ladies' section. He was reading the *Financial Times*, smiling at the peachy women, when he got a call and was forced to get up from his fine catbird seat and have a conversation behind a rack of coats.

The voice on the other end of the line belonged to someone he knew well, a man who was not in charge of him but still made demands.

Gozan spoke into the phone, keeping his voice very low.

"You worry too much. I understand. And you should understand whom you are speaking to."

He signed off, put his phone away, and took a moment to return to his earlier mood. Soon he was back in the fine leather chair, nodding approval when the daughter came out of the dressing room to spin in front of the tall, silvery mirrors.

The women were brown-haired, and he preferred blondes, but their full figures were very choice. The daughter's in particular, with its rounded buttocks and narrow waist. She was complaining about her thighs as she twirled in the skinny-girl dress.

Gozan wondered how hard it would be to close the deal. He eased into a conversation with the mother, telling her that he was in the diplomatic corps and that he and his friend were on holiday.

Gozan's subtle accent and the cut of his clothes made a good impression, and soon this lady was telling him that her name was Susan, she was going through a divorce, and she lived in Ann Arbor, Michigan.

She said that her daughter, Serena, was in law school and would be graduating next year. This trip to LA was a birthday present to her.

During the conversation, Khezir came over a few times to get Gozan's opinion of the various jackets in combination with shirts and ties. But now, Khezzy was flirting with Brian, and the flirtation wasn't lost on the women.

When Khezir returned to the men's section, Gozan said, "Susan, it would give me pleasure to take you and Serena out to dinner tonight. A birthday celebration. Khezzy and I are here on business and he is very homesick for good conversation."

Susan said, "Oh, we shouldn't. We have an early flight tomorrow and should really pack and get to bed."

"I understand," Gozan said, looking very disappointed. "I understand that you don't know us. We could be very boring dinner companions."

"No, no, I'm not saying that," said Susan.

"Good. Let's have an early dinner," Gozan said. "I'll find the best restaurant within ten minutes' drive of your hotel. If we pick you up at seven, you will be back in your room by nine thirty. Khezir is a very funny man. You will be glad you had a chance to meet one of the outstanding young heroes of Sumar."

The daughter said, "Please, Mom. It would be fun."

At that moment, a salesgirl said to Serena, "Let me take these for you." The three women went to the desk, and Gozan joined them.

When the purchases were tucked in tissue and

bagged in black, Gozan called to his nephew, "Khezzy, please help these ladies put the shopping bags in their car."

# Chapter 31

KHEZIR HAD BEEN trying on a jacket, and he said to the salesman, "Brian, wait just a moment, won't you? I'll only be a minute."

Brian said, "Absolutely. I have some shoes I want to show you, Mr. Mazul. You will just *die*."

Gozan held the door open for Susan and Serena, then he and Khezir followed the ladies out to their rented BMW that was parked across the street. Khezir, still wearing the three-thousand-dollar lavender-silk jacket, went to the rear of the car, and when the trunk was opened, he put the bags inside.

Gozan opened the driver's-side door for Susan and said, "You can trust me on the choice of restaurants, Susan. I have researched the best of the best and I have some good ideas already."

Khezir said to Serena, "I am eager to be celebrating your birthday with you, young lady."

The girl tittered nervously, likely thinking what a shame it was that Khezir was gay. He stood on the street with Gozan and waved good-bye to the females as they drove up Rodeo toward Wilshire. Then the two men proceeded to the Bentley at the curb.

Gozan ripped up the parking ticket and said in Sumarin, "This place is starting to stink."

Khezzy grinned and waved toward the black glass of the storefront. He was turning toward the Bentley when he felt a touch on his arm. He jerked around and saw the young salesman called Brian standing on the sidewalk, his mouth quivering and his eyes frightened.

"Mr. Mazul. Would you like me to ring up that jacket for you? Or will you want to see some other things I've put aside for you?"

"I want you to kiss your ass," said Khezir. "No joking, I really want to see you do that."

"You can't do this, Mr. Mazul. Please don't do this."

Brian reached out again for the sleeve of the shimmering jacket, and Khezir knocked Brian's arm away. Brian had just enough time to look surprised as Khezir let fly with a blow to Brian's gut, followed quickly with a kick to the thigh.

Brian expelled air, then sucked it in and screamed before he took a chop to the back of his neck and dropped to the ground, squirming in agony.

"You have the keys, Gozan?" Khezir asked.

Gozan held them up and waggled them.

The two men were inside the Bentley when three more boys ran out of the store; two fell to the ground to attend to Brian, while the third raised his phone and shouted, "I have your license plate. I'm on the phone with the police. Give me that jacket, and maybe we won't press charges."

Khezir got out of the car and went toward the salesman, who backed up, screaming into the phone, "I need the police. Mariah Koo, Rodeo—"

Khezir grabbed the phone from the young man's hand, threw it at the store window. Then, as onlookers screamed, he dropped his fist down on the back of the boy's head.

The salesman's knees buckled and he fell.

Police sirens could be heard coming up Wilshire, but the Sumaris had the advantage of time.

Khezir said, "I left my jacket in the store."

"Leave it. This one is better."

Khezir nodded, then said, "Which do you like more? The mother or the daughter? I want the daughter. She is closer to my age. Maybe she can keep up with me."

"Anything you want, Khezzy. Anything at all."

# Chapter 32

CAPTAIN LUKE WARREN arrived on Rodeo Drive at 3:18 that afternoon and found five squad cars double-parked and uniforms keeping the tourists away from the entrance to the ritzy boutique Mariah Koo.

The first responder was Officer Fox Welky. Welky was from the Wilshire Division, Warren's precinct, and was waiting for him at the curb. Warren opened his car door, and Welky walked him to the sidewalk, talking the whole time.

Welky said, "Why I called you, Captain. There were these two guys, one maybe fifty, the other about thirty, foreign accents, sounds like the guys who mugged those women at the Beverly Hills.

"These foreigners were in the store for about a half hour then left with a couple of women plus a jacket that had a ticket price of two thousand nine hundred ninety-nine dollars plus tax. They didn't pay.

"Brian James Finnerty, he's a salesclerk here." Welky indicated the store with his thumb. "He ran out to get the crooks to come back in and pay up. He put his hand on the younger one's arm and the guy turned on him and used some kind of karate. Really hurt the kid. Broke some of his ribs, for sure.

"Then the same thirtyish guy beat up on this other kid. Ravi Hoffman. Hoffman is on his way to the hospital to be checked for head trauma.

"Hold on, Captain, I got the goon's name here."

Welky took out his notebook, said, "Khezir Mazul. I think I said that right. He's the one did the beatings, and Finnerty can identify him. Said he had a lot of weird tattoos over most of his body. And he also had tattoos circling his arms that looked like writing."

Warren said, "Is the Finnerty kid okay?"

Welky said, "I think so, Captain. He's hurt, but he's talking. Ambulance is on the way for him." Then Welky went on. "Mazul and the other one were last seen driving toward Santa Monica in a midnight-blue Bentley with rental plates. Those are the guys you're looking for, right, Captain?"

"Nice work, Welky. Very good job."

Sirens were singing up Wilshire.

Welky said, "Thanks, Captain. Finnerty is still inside, and we also got other witnesses who were watching through the door."

Captain Warren went through the black glass doors into a slick clothing store that didn't appeal to him at all. Too much black. Looked like the walking dead shopped here.

Warren found Finnerty lying in a fetal position on a checkered rug, squirming and crying and rocking himself. A bunch of twenty-something salespeople were clustered around him.

"Brian? Are you Brian Finnerty? Brian, the ambulance is coming now. Anyone else see what happened here?"

A salesgirl with white-blond hair identified herself as Angela Lanzadoro. Ms. Lanzadoro said she'd helped a couple of women tourists, sold one of them a Nicole Miller dress.

"They're mother and daughter. Susan and Serena Stanley from Ann Arbor. The older man, his name was Gozan? He friended them? He and his boyfriend."

"What makes you say they were boyfriends?"

"I've got excellent gay-dar, Officer. Anyway, I

think they made plans to have dinner with Susan and Serena tonight."

The hair on the back of Luke Warren's neck stood up. He knew full well that those douche bags were not gay.

"Do you know where the Stanleys are staying?"

"They never said."

"I need a copy of their sales receipt."

Captain Warren knew there was little he could do to put the blocks to Remari and Mazul. Even if they were caught with the stolen jacket in their possession, even if they were positively identified by Brian Finnerty, it would still be swept under the diplomatic-immunity rug.

The captain got the name of the Stanley women's hotel from the credit card company and he called their room. No one answered, so he left a message on voice mail asking them to get back to him immediately and not to go anywhere with the men they had met at Mariah Koo.

Then he called Jack Morgan.

# Chapter 33

I HAD BEEN following Tommy's car since the end of the business day. He left his office alone, drove to his house in Hancock Park by the shortest route, and not long after that, he got back into his car and headed west.

Sure, I might be wasting time and energy, but while my eyelashes grew back, and before something else blew up in my front yard, I really couldn't have too much information about what my brother was up to.

I was driving my loaner car, a black Mercedes like a hundred thousand identical cars in LA, and Tommy didn't know that I had it. I was sure that he hadn't noticed me weaving in traffic behind him, staying on his tail, but suddenly, I lost him. Tommy had made a red Ferrari disappear.

With luck, I'd be able to put a GPS tracker on his car, save me tailing him in the future.

The sun was going down as I headed east on Beverly Boulevard, passing the Wilshire Country Club on my left, looking for the Ferrari in all directions at once. That's when I got the call from Captain Warren saying that Khezir Mazul had almost killed a couple of salesclerks on Rodeo Drive and he and Gozan Remari were planning to take two women tourists out for dinner that evening.

"Drug them, you mean. No dinner."

"Jack, I don't know where to look for them. I can't even put out a BOLO, since as far as the chief is concerned, these guys are off-limits."

"I'll get back to you," I said.

I was passing through estate country, an area of expensive homes and grounds manicured to the quick. I called my hotelier friend Amelia Poole, known to her friends as Jinx. She made a few calls to her inner circle and then let me know that two men had checked into Shutters, in Santa Monica, under the name Remari.

I called Cruz and then I got back to Captain Warren, told him what I was doing. I was saying I'd check in later when Tommy's car suddenly appeared. It took a right onto Melrose, then, a short distance later, another right onto the 101 South to LA. Then the car crossed the 110.

I was three cars back, and then I was right on Tommy's tail. I thought for a second that the Ferrari had slowed so that he could check me out, but I was wrong. Tommy was taking the Broadway exit. Then he made a sharp right. And I stayed behind him.

Tommy's brake lights flashed and I saw the club up ahead.

Was that Tommy's destination?

A club?

Tommy pulled into a parking spot and I drove past him, watched him get out of his car. If he'd seen me, he'd have given me the finger. I kept him in my rearview mirror, and when he crossed the street on foot, I parked.

A minute or two later, I stuck a tracker under his bumper. Then I went toward the entrance of the homely cement block building that had once been a lightbulb factory and was now a club called the Socket.

# Chapter 34

PRIVATE INVESTIGATORS EMILIO Cruz and Rick Del Rio were sitting in loungers on the deck overlooking the canal outside Del Rio's house. It was a nice house and a nice view and a pretty sunset, but both men were wired as tight as guitar strings.

They were drinking beer and throwing bread to the ducks, and when Del Rio spoke at all, it was only to say some version of "Maybe this is the last time we'll get to do this."

And Cruz would say, "Don't be crazy, Rick. You're innocent."

Del Rio had told Cruz that he hadn't beaten Vicky Carmody, and Cruz believed his partner, but he was afraid for him. No one knew what a jury would do, and Del Rio didn't look like a choirboy.

Cruz felt awful for Rick, but after sitting with his partner for hours, there was nothing left for him to say that he hadn't already said.

Del Rio said: "This could be the last fresh air I breathe for ten years."

Cruz, half joking, half exasperated, said, "Look. I'll rent your house, Rick, okay? You'll make money, and you'll only be how old when you get out? Fifty-five?"

Del Rio looked at Cruz like he'd just said that he was having sex with Del Rio's mother.

"What did you say, you son-of-a-bitch? You think this is funny?"

Del Rio leaped from the webbed aluminum chair, grabbed Cruz by the neck, squeezed his throat with both hands, then pushed the chair over and managed to straddle Cruz while pressing his thumbs into Cruz's throat.

Del Rio was yelling, "You prick. You stupid prick. *You* want to do ten years? Huh? You couldn't do ten *days* before you'd be crying like a girl."

Cruz had a muscular neck along with the muscular rest of his body, and his arms were free. He gave Del Rio a shot to the jaw that sent Del Rio backward. It was enough to break the choke hold, but Del Rio wasn't done. He scrambled to his feet, and as Cruz got up, Del Rio hurled himself at Cruz, who stiff-armed him.

Del Rio stumbled back, recovered his footing, threw a punch that connected with Cruz's solar plexus. Cruz grunted, then lowered his head and ran at Del Rio; the force lifted Rick off his feet and sent him off the deck and into the canal.

Ducks flew up, squawking.

Del Rio sank, disappeared into the dark water, then bobbed up, sputtering.

Cruz shouted down at him, "Cooled off yet, Ricky? Are we done?"

"Shit," Del Rio said. He reached for the rope ladder.

Cruz's phone rang. He grabbed it out of his shirt pocket, flipped it open with his thumb, gave Del Rio a hand up to the deck.

The caller was Jack and he had an assignment for him: surveillance of those scumbag Sumaris, who had just checked into Shutters.

"I'm taking Del Rio with me," Cruz said.

"Fine," Jack said.

"He needs something to do. The waiting is killing him."

"I said, 'Fine.' "

Cruz stood back as Del Rio sluiced the water off

his clothes with his hands. Cruz said, "I'm sorry, asshole. Your jaw is going to be purple tomorrow."

Del Rio rubbed his jaw and said to Cruz, "So where are we going?"

# Chapter 35

THEIR CORNER SUITE at the fabulous Shutters on the Beach hotel had a wide view of the ocean and the endless sandy beach tinted by the setting sun at the horizon.

Gozan relaxed in a chaise and perused the room-service menu. He wanted a cocktail before dinner and maybe fresh oysters.

Behind him, Khezir angrily thumbed the television's remote control, speeding through the channels.

"Khezzy, your father would have loved to see the ocean. I wish he could be here with us."

"Those stupid bitches," Khezir said in Sumarin. "What a waste of our time. All day working on them and then, 'Sorry, we are not feeling well. Thank you anyway.'"

"There will be other women. This hotel is full of them."

"Don't speak to me of women."

"Okay, Khezzy."

No one understood Khezir the way Gozan did. He had been like a father to Khezzy since the day his brother-in-law, Khezzy's father, had been murdered, stabbed through the heart by his disgruntled mistress while he was asleep.

Khezir was only fifteen at the time, but he had sought the woman out and restored his family's honor, meeting blood with blood. Afterward, he inked his body with the dead woman's name.

It was the first of many tattoos.

Now Khezir threw the remote control at the flat-screen, strode to the sliding doors, and went out to the balcony. Gozan knew that Khezir was bitterly disappointed that Susan and Serena had canceled the evening's plans.

Tension was building inside Khezir, and Gozan was responsible for keeping the young man on track. Having fun was a by-product, not the objective. Much was at stake.

Gozan sighed as the sun slipped beneath the water. He was of the same blood as Khezir and he loved him.

"Khezzy," he called out. "I am ordering oysters for two and a nice bottle of champagne. Is there anything else I can get you?"

Khezir shouted back, "You'll be the first to know."

# Chapter 36

TWENTY MINUTES AFTER the fistfight at Sherman Canal, Cruz parked the fleet car in a lot adjacent to Shutters, a rangy white clapboard-sided hotel with hundreds of balconies and windows and doors looking out over the Pacific. Lights were on inside, and the place looked beautiful against the cobalt sky.

From where they were parked, Cruz and Del Rio had a clean sight line to the third floor. Del Rio affixed a small, military-grade electronic listening device to the car door, angled the receiver at the suite of rooms in the northwest corner, pinpointed and locked in the settings. They were too far away to see the Sumaris through the windows, but their voices were coming in clearly and the conversation was being amplified and recorded.

Like most stakeouts, this was going to be as exciting as Bingo night in a retirement home, but Cruz was just happy he could get Del Rio out of the house and give him something to think about that wasn't his trial.

Del Rio said to Cruz, "I'm sorry I started that fight."

"Forget it."

"One of us could have gotten killed," said Del Rio.

"That's the TV," Cruz said of the sounds coming through the receiver. "Someone is channel surfing."

Del Rio turned up the volume, and he and Cruz listened to snatches of a ball game, a real estate show, *Two and a Half Men,* an escort-service ad, and the ball game again. Then there was a cracking sound, like something had been thrown or had fallen.

Del Rio said, "Okay, they're talking to each other in Sumarin. Wait. Now in English."

One of the Sumaris said, "I am ordering oysters for two and a nice bottle of champagne. Is there anything else I can get you?"

And the other, the one with the younger, higher-pitched voice, said something from the balcony, his words blown away in the wind.

The first one put in the room-service order, asked how long it would take, and said thank you.

About fifteen minutes went by. Cruz and Del Rio listened to the TV anchors reporting the local news, and then there was the sound of a door buzzer, a door opening, the man's voice, sounding hollow because he was behind a wall, probably in the foyer.

A woman's voice chirped, "Would you like me to set this up near the window?"

Something, presumably a cart, rolled and squeaked over the carpet, and the older man said, "Let me help you with that, dear."

"I've got it, sir."

Cruz and Del Rio heard the female voice say, "Shall I open the champagne?"

There was the soft pop of a cork being ejected from the bottle, the older man calling out, "Khezzy, come and see what we have here."

The younger man said, "Maybe later."

The other man sighed deeply, said, "Ah, well. What is your name, miss?"

"I'm Luanne. When you're ready for the cart to be picked up, just call star eighty-eight and put the cart outside."

"Luanne, can you stay for a moment? I'm sorry

that my partner changed his mind. Will you have a glass of this excellent champagne?"

"Thank you very much, but I can't. It's against—"

"Oh dear, I apologize," said the one that had to be Gozan Remari. "I didn't want to put you in a difficult spot. I have been at death's door for a very long time, and now that I'm in remission, this is the first champagne I've had in five years. And I don't wish to drink alone."

"Well, that's good news," said Luanne. "I guess I could take a tiny sip."

"Good. It is good to celebrate all the important moments."

Cruz sat up straight in his seat, grabbed the car phone, and called Jack.

"Jack, it's Cruz. They've got a girl in there. We're going in."

# Chapter 37

CRUZ AND DEL RIO bolted from the fleet car, ran like hell to the parking lot on the same side of the street, then along the sidewalk fronting the hotel, which was littered with runners and ladies with strollers and bike riders. They took the front steps two at a time and arrived in the lobby of Shutters on the Beach, breathless.

Cruz flashed his badge at the desk clerk, a thin young man with a beaky nose and glasses and a look on his face like a mouse had run up his leg.

Cruz said, "A crime is being committed in a third-floor unit, northwest corner."

"What crime? How do you know that? Are you the police?"

Del Rio snarled, "Where're the stairs, dimwit?"

Cruz and Del Rio ran up two flights, pushed

open the fire door on the third floor, and sprinted to the room at the end of the hallway.

Del Rio banged on the door, banged on it again, Cruz shouting, "Open up. Do it *now*."

The door opened, and Gozan Remari, fully clothed in a white shirt, tails out over blue dress pants, said, "What is this? What is going on?"

Cruz said, "Stand aside, sir. We have to check the premises."

Remari said, "Be my guest."

Cruz and Del Rio shoved past Remari and entered the homey suite. They found the woman in the room-service outfit standing by the table at the far end of the room. She looked confused but was still in her blue uniform, her hair neat and held back in a headband. She was apparently unharmed.

She was saying, "I didn't do *anything*. What did I *do?*"

Cruz said, "We're private investigators and these men are sexual predators. Are you all right?"

"Oh my God. No. Yes. I'm fine."

Khezir came in from the other room. He was scowling, said, "What's going on here?"

Del Rio said to the young woman, "Did anyone put a hand on you?"

"No. Like I said, I'm fine."

"You should go," said Del Rio. "Get out of here, now."

The young woman scurried out of the room, and Cruz said to the Sumaris, "We know who you are. We know what you're doing."

"Oh, mind readers," Gozan said with a laugh. "And who are you again? Secret police?"

"Watch yourself," said Del Rio.

"*You* watch *your* self," Khezir said, rolling up his sleeves. "You are clowns. You need red noses and big shoes. You want to make my day?"

Cruz stepped in front of Del Rio, took a picture of the men with his phone, and said, "Your faces are going out to every hotel in LA. After today, you're going to be sleeping in your car."

Gozan was on the phone, "Suite three W. I need security. Immediately."

Del Rio and Cruz took the fire stairs down.

"I don't know. I don't think that went so well," said Del Rio.

"We got the girl out of the room."

"There'll be another one," said Del Rio.

# Chapter 38

SANDRA STOOD BESIDE the enormous bed watching the neon lights outside her windows fling spangles of color onto the white bedding. She wore her husband's dress shirt, unbuttoned all the way, showing off her large, natural breasts and her small black thong.

She said, "Harry?"

Her husband wasn't paying attention.

Actually, he wasn't breathing, but his skin was still warm, almost as if he were still alive.

Sandra gave his arm a little shake, then went to the vast marble-tiled master bath and got into the shower. She let the jet spray beat down on her for several minutes as she thought about how she'd distracted Harry all day long, keeping him too busy to think about food. When he went into

163

hypoglycemic shock, she just closed the door and let him drift away.

Not a bad death, really. Not at all.

She lathered her hair with a fragrant spa shampoo, followed up with a special rinse that made her dark mane bounce and reflect light. She toweled off with yards of Egyptian cotton, then stepped out of the stall and stood naked in front of the full-length mirror.

"Okay, Sandy. Okay, now," she said to herself. She looked really good. She twisted her body a little so she could see the elegant line of her back, her perfect ass, how long her legs looked from behind. Then she blew out her hair and returned to the bedroom.

Turning her back on Harold Wiggens III, deceased heir to the Wiggens Cough Syrup fortune, Sandra pulled on some underthings and a small, clingy white dress.

Then she sat down on the edge of the bed, put on jeweled sandals. She said to the dead man, "Harry, I'm sorry. We had a good time, didn't we? I'm as sorry as I can be."

She lifted his eyelids, one at a time, then picked up the no-name mobile phone and punched in a number she knew by heart. After two rings, Lester answered and said her name.

"Yes. It's me. It's done."

"How are you doing?"

"I'm okay. So far."

"You should call the police."

"Right after we hang up."

"I'll call you later."

"No. I'll call you."

"Sandra?"

"Don't worry, Les. I'll call you."

The newly minted widow closed the phone and mentally rehearsed what she was going to say.

*I thought Harry was sleeping. When I tried to wake him up, he was—dead. He was diabetic. I don't know what went wrong.*

Sandra picked up the landline and called 911. As she waited for the operator to answer, she put her hand over her heart, which was just going crazy. She could hardly believe it was almost over.

Without a doubt, this was the most exciting day of her life.

# Chapter 39

WAITERS ON SKATES whizzed by me as I stood in the shadows at the entrance of the Socket. Enormous cogs and gears from the original bulb factory had been burnished and highlighted to terrific effect. Iron pillars punctuated the concrete floor, and hundred-year-old light fixtures, tracks, and pulleys hung overhead.

It was still early, about seven p.m., and the smartly dressed, twenty- to thirty-something after-work crowd were filling the club, cozying up to the Line, a forty-inch-long bar topped with a steel-and-leather conveyor belt in the center of the floor.

Groups and couples, laughing and carrying on, gathered in the comfy conversation pits around the perimeter, and one young woman with a flashing tiara was having a birthday.

Tonight's music was swing, and it seemed to me that the boozy sound of the old instrumentals was putting the customers in a very nice mood.

I looked for Tommy but didn't see him on the floor, so I moved to the bar for a better view. A wannabe-actor barkeep came over with a smile and a frothy white drink, put it down in front of me.

He said, "The game starts in a minute, Tommy—actually, I think it just started."

I was an accidental clubber passing as my brother, and I had not been briefed on the game.

I sipped the drink, which looked like milk. It was, in fact, milk.

I said, "Well, I'll be a little late."

The bartender said, "Izzy asked after you, went down ten minutes ago. And there goes Billion-Dollar Bill. I hear he lightened your wallet the other night."

I swiveled on the stool, saw a guy in a pale herringbone sports coat and a good haircut heading toward the wide down-going staircase at the back of the room.

I put a twenty on the bar, said, "I guess I'll follow the money."

The bartender wished me luck, and, keeping

the herringbone jacket in view, I went down the cantilevered, concrete slab stairs to the basement. The lower level was a dance floor set up for a DJ who hadn't yet arrived, but recorded music pounded, and the crowd was getting thick, dancing in place, drinking steadily.

I tagged behind Bill, and when we came to a green door at the rear wall marked Shipping, Mr. Bill turned and clapped me on the back.

"No kidding," he shouted over the music. "Good to see you, Tom. I was hoping you'd try to get your money back."

"I don't scare off easily," I said.

I didn't know what was behind the green door and I had no plan. But, hey, I'm a pilot. I was going to have to wing it.

# Chapter 40

A CARD GAME was in progress in the sound-proofed room behind the green door. Two goons with crossed arms and bulging biceps stood just inside the entrance.

To my left, ten players sat in high leather chairs around the oblong green felt table. The players were old and young, snappily dressed and sloppily, male and female. They all looked bored, but I was sure that they were anything but. From the height and number of the stacks of chips, the stakes were very high.

The dealer wore a red-velvet vest over his starched white shirt and had a perfect black bow tie. He was sliding cards from the shoe, snapping them down in front of the players. He looked up when I came in, did a double take when he saw me.

Then he shifted his hard gaze across the table to a player with his back to the door.

That player was Tommy. A pile of chips was at his left hand and he was turning over his cards with his right. A girl with short platinum hair in a skintight black dress was draped across Tommy's shoulders like a sweater. She wore a rope of pearls turned to the back so that the long loop of them fell almost to her waist.

The dealer said to my brother, "Who's this, Mr. Morgan?" He angled his chin toward me.

Tommy turned, saw me, and jerked his chair around. His eyes narrowed and he said, "You need something, Jack?"

The platinum-haired girl was pretty, twenty-one or so. She looked up at my face and said, "Wow." I took this to mean that she thought she was seeing double.

"I'm Jack," I said to her. "Tommy's brother."

"I'm Isabella. Izzy. Tommy's girlfriend." She stuck out her hand and we shook. "Nice to meet you."

Tommy looked at his cards, folded, said to me, "Let's take this outside, huh, Jack?"

"Nice to meet you too, Izzy," I said. "Tommy didn't mention that he had a twin?"

"Nuh-uh. No. I don't know if I could tell you apart."

"Even Mom couldn't do that. You know, of course, that Tom is married. Has a lovely wife and a wonderful boy. Lives in Hancock Park under a big mortgage. And he's a degenerate gambler. Maybe you know that."

Tommy shouted, "Hey."

Izzy said, "That's not true. You're not married. Are you, Tommy?"

"Okay, wise guy. Let's cut it right here." Tommy stood up to his full six one, same height as me.

"I wouldn't get mixed up with him, Izzy," I said. "He's a liar and a cheat. And those are his good qualities."

Tommy had shaken her off, was standing with his fists clenched, and his face was clenched too. He wanted to hit me, and I wanted him to go ahead and try. He telegraphed a roundhouse punch, which I blocked; I teed up one of my own, and as my brother pulled back, I grazed his chin.

We'd been fighting for some thirty-five years and neither of us had any moves the other didn't know.

Still, Tommy was thrown off balance. He staggered back against the table, and players vacated their chairs. Drinks spilled. A woman screamed, and doormen inserted themselves between me and Tommy.

I said, "This is a warning, Junior. You come into my place and mess with me, I'm going to return the favor."

Tommy was shouting over the bouncers, "You pea brain. You ass-wipe."

"There's no problem, gentlemen," I said to the two guys with the bulging biceps and the buttons popping off their shirts. I held up the palms of my hands to say, *I'm not a problem. I'm not going to get physical.*

I backed away, still with my hands showing, then turned and left the club by the fire door, setting off the alarm for a memorable and satisfying exit.

A minute later, I was outside, crossing the street. I got into my loaner and turned on my phone. Yep, there was the GPS signal showing me the precise location of Tommy's car.

All things considered, it had been a good night's work. And it wasn't over yet.

# Chapter 41

JUSTINE SAID GOOD night to her date and waved as he drove up Wetherly and then rounded the corner at the end of her block. She stood in her driveway for another moment, watching taillights and fireflies, thinking about the evening, the temptation, and the many reasons why she should stop this while she still could.

Then she walked up the flagstone path to her darling little cottage in the flats, cute and low maintenance, protected by neighbors on all sides, perfect for a single working woman with a dog and a cat.

Her house was simple and uncluttered. She wished she could say the same for her mind.

Justine punched in the alarm code and opened the door, and her dog, Rocky, bolted out, jumping and generally making a fool of himself. She returned the joyous greeting, then led Rocky through to the rear of the house, and let him out into the backyard.

She was in her updated 1930s kitchen preparing dinner for Rocky and a purring, rubbing, lip-smacking Nefertiti when the phone rang.

Justine said to Nefertiti, "This better not be work. I am done for the day."

It was her mother, Evangeline Pogue, calling from her sailboat somewhere off Tortuga. Justine pictured Vangy in her shorts and halter top, drink in hand, sitting cross-legged on the bowsprit under the night sky, her third husband down in the galley.

Vangy said, "Justine, I've called and called." When it came to her only child, Vangy had high anxiety.

"I was out, Mom. Haven't even kicked off my shoes." She did that now, then put Rocky's and Nefertiti's food on the floor, went to the sitting room, threw herself into her favorite chair, and put her feet up on the hassock.

"Is everything all right?" Vangy asked.

Justine sighed. "Jack's car was set on fire."

"Oh Lord. Is Jack...?"

"He's fine, Mom. We were inside the house when it started. I'm trying to find out who did it."

"So, you and Jack? Thanks, Bernard. I'll be there in a minute."

Sound of Mom sipping something through a straw. "Sorry, darling. What were you saying about Jack?"

"I love him, Mom. I'm not going to lie. But it's the same stuff, different day. I've started seeing someone else."

"You are? You can do that?"

"I don't know."

"Is he married, Justine?"

"No, Mom, no. So, how are you and Bernard? What's the plan for the next couple of months? Any chance of coming out to the coast?"

"Oh gosh, sweetie. We go where the winds blow us. And right now, my dear hubby-dub is serving dessert in the aft. Will you promise to take care?"

"You bet, Mom. Don't worry about me. All is well."

That was a lie.

She loved Jack, but her heart was in play, which was uncomfortable and weird. She said good-bye to Vangy and as soon as she disconnected the line, the phone rang again.

It was Jack.

"I'm home. Do you want to come over to my place? I'd like you to," he said.

It was too much.

"Oh, not tonight, Jack. I was just dozing off. Sorry, honey."

She hung up before she weakened. She cupped her face in her hands and shook her head. She wasn't made for double-deal dating, not for long. It just was too confusing, hurt too much, made her feel too bad.

She was going to have to make a decision before she went crazy.

# Chapter 42

TULE SAT ON the floor of the large closet, way in the back, heaps of high-heeled shoes around her, her knees folded up to her chest.

She held the cell phone close to her face and made her call to Lester Olsen at his office in Vegas.

"Please answer," she said to her bare feet. "Please answer the phone."

A man's voice said, "Hello, Tule?"

She said, "Oh boy, I'm glad you answered. I'm having a panic attack."

"What's going on?" Lester had a very soothing voice.

"I'm scared," she said. "He's very big. He's very angry."

"Angry at you?"

"Sometimes at me. Sometimes he's angry at one of his kids. Sometimes he's angry at the football scores. Could be anything. He likes to be mad."

"When he's angry at you, what does he say?"

"Like now, I said, 'I had another dream about you.' Just like you and I talked about, you know? And he said, 'What are you trying to do to me, Tule? You warning me or something? Don't you know I can break your neck with one hand?' "

"Aw, jeez. What did you say to that?"

"I said, 'Oh, baby, you don't mean that.' And then I scampered away. He threw a cup at me. Missed. Hit the wall, though."

"Does he hit you, Tule?"

"No. Not really."

"Do you want to get out?"

"Maybe. No. No, this is my chance. I just needed to talk to you."

"I'm here, sweetie. I'm just glad you're okay. On a positive note, he's doing what you want him to do."

"Meaning what?" she asked. Then she whispered, "Wait. I hear him."

She listened to his footsteps on the teak floors, heard him call her. "Tuuuuule. Tuuuuuuule. Where are you, baby?"

She was breathing with her mouth open, staring at a pair of chartreuse stilettos by the light of her phone. After a minute, she said, "You still there?"

"Of course. What's happening?"

"He's gone now," she said. "Big house, you know. Lotta, lotta rooms. You were saying?"

"I was saying, his ticker is a time bomb. Keep doing what you're doing. But if you get afraid, Tule, get out. Or at least, dial it back for a couple of days."

"Yeah. Sure, Les. Thanks for listening. I'd better go. Make him some lunch. Do a little bikini dance."

He laughed, said, "That could do the trick."

She laughed too. "If only. I'd dance until he dropped dead. I'll call you soon."

"I'm always here."

"Hugs and kisses," she said. "Bye-bye."

"Bye-bye."

Tule sighed, then turned off the phone and went back to work.

# Chapter 43

JUSTINE AND PRIVATE investigator Christian Scott were in a fleet car on their way to Our Lady of the Pacific, the sixth on their list of ten schools within a five-mile radius of Jack's house. They had been canvassing schools all morning and it was now almost two in the afternoon.

Scotty wasn't surprised that they hadn't turned up any leads.

"When I was a motorcycle cop, things were black-and-white. Speeding. DUI. Collisions. This is so . . . random."

Justine said, "It's a place to start, Scotty."

"Ah. The famous square one."

"You got it. And psychologically speaking, I agree with Sci. Teenage boys like fire. It's sexy. It's exciting. They set fire to buildings, to their enemies, to toilets—you name it, a boy has set a match to it. A car-bomb spree is more sophisticated than the norm, but it fits the profile. And that's why we're going where boys are."

The private high school on Winter Canyon Road was surrounded by grassy hills and native foliage. The buildings were plain stucco over cement-block construction with attached pergolas supporting large, blooming bougainvillea.

Justine parked in the faculty-only lot, then she and Scotty crossed the busy school yard and entered the cool of the main building. They found the headmaster's office at the end of a long, sky-blue corridor.

Father Joseph Brooks was stocky, balding, smiling, and he was expecting the investigators. He shook their hands, asked them to sit down, and offered coffee.

When they were settled in, Justine told the headmaster why they were there and asked, "Can you think of a student, or maybe a group of kids, who would have the competence and the anger or brio to go on a rampage like this?"

"Oh, man," said the headmaster. He ran his hand over his head. "You think any of our kids could be such out-of-control lunatics? We have our share of cocky, rich-kid idiots, but this is over the top. In my opinion."

The headmaster's office faced south and had a sunny view over the valley. He kept bonsai trees in clay pots, and they crowded the windowsills. Justine wondered what this painstaking hobby meant to the man, reducing large plants with the potential to be huge into living miniatures, collecting them in rows.

"They might be chemistry buffs," Scotty said. "Your science teacher might be able to give us a lead."

"Mr. Peter Tong. I can tell you that Mr. Tong is a pretty traditional educator. Nothing radical or Fringe Division about him."

Justine smiled at the reference to the sci-fi TV show and asked when they could speak with Mr. Tong.

"We'd like to ask him about the chemical composition of the explosives our lab turned up in the gas tank of one of the cars. Also, we have a list of your students who've been in trouble with the law."

Father Brooks was examining the list when Justine's phone rang. Seeing it was Jack, she answered it.

"Justine," Jack said. "The cops were just here asking me where I was at six this morning. Another car went boom about two miles from my house. Look, in case it's relevant, last night I got into a fistfight with Tommy."

# Chapter 44

I HAD BEEN in court, sitting behind Del Rio, when my cell phone buzzed. I went out to the hallway to talk to Detective Tandy, who gave me the breaking news on the crispy Aston Martin in Point Dume.

He asked, "You happen to have a sleepover guest who can verify you were in bed this morning at six?"

"No. Are you actually looking at me for this, Tandy? Or do you just have a crush on me?"

"It's called thorough police work, Jack. And I'm keeping track of you to make sure you're not a target. Believe it or not, that's the truth. Do me a favor. Let me know if you plan to leave town. If I can't find you, I might worry."

"Thanks, Mitch. I'm touched."

I called Justine, and then I called Dr. Sci.

I told my chief scientist that there was a new entry in the car-explosions series and that I wanted him to go to the crime scene on Grayfox Street, check out what was left of the hundred-thousand-dollar sports car, see if he could gain some insight into the who and why.

I returned to the courtroom, stared at the back of Del Rio's head as medical professionals testified about the surgical procedures Vicky Carmody had endured after her admission to the hospital.

I was listening to the testimony, but I was thinking about this recent car destruction too. I knew where Tommy's car was this morning. I had checked my phone and read the GPS data telling me that his Ferrari had remained at the Socket until 8:45 a.m.

Since Tommy's murderous machinations last year, I've had cameras on his house, a call tracker on his phone. I could check on his whereabouts for the previous eighteen hours once I got back to the office.

Sci called and I left the courtroom again, sat on a bench in the hallway, and watched the live footage Sci streamed to my phone.

First up, a Realtor's-eye view of the fantastic homes on Grayfox Street, then the exterior of the six-million-dollar gated house in question. The gates were wide open. And inside the courtyard, lying like a small asteroid in front of the Mediterranean-style villa, were the burned remains of a once-beautiful car.

Sci's face came on my screen.

"The car is totally incinerated, Jack. Looks just like your Lambo. The fire started under the car, probably detonated by a cell phone. The gas tank is BLEVE'd, so it exploded from the inside. Safe to assume the lab will find remains of latex in the tank." Sci paused, then said, "And here they come."

As I watched, a flatbed truck from the city's forensic lab passed Sci and drove into the courtyard. The ME's van was right behind the truck. Both city vehicles came to a stop, and personnel got out, CSU techs and assistants to the ME, respectively.

I was puzzling over the presence of people from the coroner's office when the ME, Dr. Andrews himself, got out of the van and began directing his techs, who were carrying a stretcher.

"Sci, what's this mean?"

"This—this isn't good," he said.

There was a huddle outside the burned car as the two forensic divisions discussed, I assumed, procedure. I couldn't hear what they were saying, but when the ME's people backed off, CSU prepared to load the carcass of the car onto the flatbed.

I heard Sci say, "That's right. I'm talking to Jack."

Mitch Tandy's face loomed, close up in my hand.

"I'm shutting down your live feed, Jack. But I don't want to leave you hanging. There was a girl in the backseat of that Aston, sleeping off a party. That's right. This time the firebug killed a human being. That changes things, doesn't it, Jack."

# Chapter 45

MY ASSISTANT, VAL, was waiting for me on the steps outside the courthouse.

"Jack, Hal Archer has called four times in the last hour. I told him you'd call when you got out of court. But, you know. He didn't want to talk to me."

She handed me a folder of must-read documents regarding our upcoming pan-European office meeting. I thanked her, asked, "Did Archer say what he wanted?"

" 'Tell Jack to call me.' "

I walked her to her car, got into mine, checked Tommy's location—his car was parked in the lot beneath his office building.

I called Hal Archer.

Archer owned Archer's Prime, a chain of thirty

steak restaurants up and down the coast. He was an empire builder and very adept at snapping his fingers. Archer had history at Private and was part of my inheritance from my father.

He answered the call as I pulled out onto Temple and into the sluggish heart of the afternoon rush. I hardly recognized Hal's voice. Sounded like he'd been crying.

"I'm afraid for my life, Morgan. It's my wife. Tule. She's going to kill me, but I have no proof."

"Why do you think that she's going to kill you?"

"She says things. She says to me, 'Do you believe you can haunt me once you're dead, Hal?' Or, this I won't forget, 'It's such a big bed, Hal. I can get used to sleeping in such a big bed alone.'"

"Okay. She's giving you a hard time."

"I don't think you get it, Morgan. These are death threats."

"But she hasn't threatened you with a weapon?"

"She's more subtle than that, damn it."

"If you're really afraid of her, you should speak to your lawyer, right? Get a divorce?"

I turned onto West Fifth Street, heading toward my office.

"A divorce will get her two hundred million. She'll get twice as much if I die. She wants the big payoff. Before I decide to just hand her a two-hundred-million-dollar payout, I want you to come over to the house. Give her a good interrogation. What is it called? Sweat her. Scare the pants off her."

I tried not to laugh at Hal Archer being scared by the Vegas showgirl he'd married last year. Anyone stood up to Hal, he got fired. But a hundred-and-ten-pound VIP cocktail waitress had Hal Archer by the balls and then some.

"This isn't a good time, Hal. I have a meeting back in the office, and I've been away from my desk all day."

"Listen, you. You're on retainer. We have an ironclad contract. When I say come over to my house, you say, 'I'll be right there.' "

"Hal, I have prior commitments. I'm sorry. I'll call you before I leave the office."

I hung up.

I wondered if Hal's wife was really trying to kill him by pushing his buttons. Not that hard to do. Hal had had a quadruple bypass in 2012. He could be one confrontation away from a heart attack.

I called Mo-bot, our resident computer genius, and asked her to download the surveillance footage on Tommy's house and pull the cell-tower signals from Tommy's phone.

By the time I reached my office, twelve minutes later, the day had taken a very bad turn.

# Chapter 46

MY PHONE WAS buzzing as I took the stairs to my office. I looked at the screen and saw that Hal Archer wasn't taking *I'll call you later* for an answer.

I let the phone buzz, went to my desk, opened my in-box, and put the surveillance on Tommy's house on fast forward. Then I double-checked where he had been by looking at the cell-tower logs recording signals from Tommy's phone.

Tommy hadn't blown up the Aston Martin, so it stood to reason he hadn't torched my Lambo either. My paranoia hit a wall. Justine was right about Tommy—this time. But it's hard to say that I was relieved. My twin was up to something.

As long as he breathed, Tommy would be trying to get me.

In order to understand our ceaseless antagonism, you'd have to know about my father, Tom Morgan Sr.

My dad was a big man, expansive, loud, danced with my mother through the house, and spent lavishly on friends and family.

He also had a mean streak, what he called "toughening us up," and he pitted his sons against each other in competitions where the winner took all, and the loser was shamed.

I usually won. I went to Brown. My brother did two years at UCLA, then dropped out. I played college ball. My brother played the horses, ran numbers, did a little work for my father, who did undercover investigation for West Coast crime boss Ray Noccia. That much I knew. But did Dad grease cops? I thought so. He may have done more. He may have fingered some of Noccia's enemies who'd ended up in the desert or in the ocean.

In return, Noccia steered high-roller clientele to my father, probably pressured some of them. He definitely helped my father build Private up from a grimy storefront into the number-one PI firm in California.

Clients signed up who weren't gifts from the Mob. Celebrities. Corporate CEOs. The 1 percent.

The money poured in, and my father became very powerful.

My brother stayed close to my father by joining the family business, first working for Dad, then opening Private Security, a satellite company that contracted personal-security personnel to Dad's clients.

I joined the U.S. Marine Corps, shipped out to Afghanistan, and flew transport missions for three years. After the crash-and-burn of the CH-46 and the loss of all those good men, I left the Corps. Returned to LA.

By then, my father had been tried and convicted of extortion and murder and was incarcerated in a California state prison for life.

One day, two years after I got back to the States, my father summoned me to Corcoran. He said he had something to tell me, that it was a matter of life and death.

I went to see Tom Sr. in a room with a bank of telephones behind a Plexiglas wall. My father gave me a gappy smile, showed off some of his tattoos, and told me the "good news." Tommy was out. I was in. And my father made me an offer that was hard to refuse.

He said he wanted me to take over Private, that Tommy was a degenerate gambler and was running the business Dad had backed into the ground. My father wanted me to restore Private to its former glory, but to do it clean and to do it big.

He sent me the keys and a bankbook for an offshore account worth more than eleven million dollars. He had bonds and equities worth another four, and that was mine too, along with a storage locker filled with old furniture, Dad's client list, and all the dirt he'd collected on his paying customers.

He was quite a sweetheart, my dad.

I turned down his offer, and three days later, he was dead, shanked in the liver over some insignificant dispute.

His will was read. I was my father's heir and I took over what remained of Private Investigations. I built it back up, and I did it clean and big. I bought the building downtown, staffed and equipped it with the best that Dad's money could buy. I brought in a mostly first-class clientele and opened offices overseas. Private is in the black big-time.

As a result, my brother hates me more than ever. And there isn't a day when I don't think about what he's likely to do to me out of revenge. I'll bet he doesn't trust me either.

# PART THREE

# TILL DEATH DO US PART

# Chapter 47

THREE HUNDRED E-MAILS had collected in my in-box since court recessed for lunch. I responded to a third of them: the ones from clients, heads of three overseas offices, Eric Caine, Justine, and Cruz.

There was an e-mail from Hal Archer too, and I thought about how I had grown up calling him Mr. Archer, that he was loyal enough to stay with Private after my father was imprisoned, even after Tom Sr. turned the remains of his client list over to me.

I inherited Hal Archer.

He may have been my first client. But I never liked him. He was a bully. He demeaned his employees, all of them, including his contracted consultants, guys like me. Did I want to fire a client whose business was worth three million a year to Private's bottom line?

I did.

I hit my phone's Call Back button, listened as the line connected and Hal answered.

"Hal, it's Jack. I have an idea. I have a good friend, I used to work for him, as a matter of fact, and I think he would be more suited to handling your business than Private is."

"I killed her, Jack."

The air went absolutely still as I tried to process what Archer had said.

"That's not funny, Hal."

"I killed that bitch in self-defense. Maybe you'll come over to my house now, Jack. That is, if you're not too busy."

His voice was saturated with sarcasm, but the quaver was still there. Archer was afraid. And this time, he had reason to be.

"Who else knows about this?" I asked him.

"Only you."

"What about people working in the house for you?"

"They're in the main. We're in the back. Pool house."

"Don't let anyone in. I'm on the way."

"Your father would have said, 'Don't worry. I'll take care of everything, Hal.' "

"Don't go anywhere. Don't touch anything. Don't talk to anyone. I'll be there soon."

# Chapter 48

THE BEVERLY HILLS Post Office is the part of town that falls into ZIP code 90210, and it contains nearly all of the luxury gated communities in LA, including Beverly Park, where movie stars and studio heads and other moguls live and reign.

Harold J. Archer's estate cost him twenty million to build, which he did on the site of another twenty-million-dollar manse he'd bought to knock down. It fronted the best street, and from the edge of a canyon in the back, it had a drop-dead view over the city of Los Angeles.

Hal's wasn't the priciest palace in Beverly Park, but he also owned homes in Provence, St. Barts, and Bali, so I guess it added up to a whole lot of money for walls, roofs, and views.

I parked the Mercedes outside on the steep

street and sat for a moment, knowing that I was about to walk into some tremendously upscale version of hell.

I snapped out of it as a lithe young man, some kind of valet, trotted out to the curb and asked me if I was there to see Mr. Archer and was Mr. Archer expecting me?

I said that Hal had invited me to join him in the pool house. The valet checked with Archer by phone, and Archer gave the valet the okay. I followed him up the green marble pathway through a contiguous line of pyramidal teak pavilions to the entrance of what Hal called "the main."

Young-man-without-a-name opened the heavy brass and mahogany door, and I entered the foyer to the combination living room/kitchen. The entire house was tiled in golden marble, and the center of this room's floor was divided by a rill. The thin and musical stream of running water ran through the house, out the wide-open folding doors, and to the infinity pool that seemed to be running over the edge of the canyon.

To the left of the pool was another Bali-inspired pavilion. I knew that the view through the back of the structure was the broad cityscape of Los Angeles far below. But the front doors were closed.

"Can I bring anything to you?" the young man asked. He was polished and confident, but he watched my expression with the kind of intensity found in people for whom pleasing or displeasing was the difference between life and death.

I told him, "Several people who work for me will be arriving. Can you just send them back here?"

I gave him the names and thanked him. Then I circumnavigated the pool. I knocked on a wooden door that was as thick as a tree, and when there was no answer, I called Hal on his phone. After four rings, he picked up.

"Are you inside the pool house, Hal?"

"Who is this?"

"It's Jack Morgan. I believe you rang. I'm right outside, Hal. Now open the door."

# Chapter 49

HAL OPENED THE door, said, "What took you so long?"

His thick, white hair was sticking out at wild angles. His eyes were red. His belly was hanging over the sash of his maroon silk robe.

He wasn't normally a drunk, but right now, his breath was so saturated with alcohol, I could almost see the fumes.

I stepped into the pool house, said, "Stay out of my way for a couple of minutes, okay, Hal? I'm going to look at this place like a cop would look at it."

"Want something? I'm drinking scotch."

"I need to work fast, Hal. Sit down somewhere."

The so-called pool house would be most people's idea of a palace. It was built along the same general theme as the main house: the stone floors, the vaulted mahogany-and-bamboo ceiling. The wide-open, freaking fantastic view of the city way the hell down there, making it seem like the pool house was in the clouds.

There were a couple of lounge chairs facing the canyon's cliff side, a table between them, a baby watermelon cut into slices. There was also a pricey bottle of scotch, two glasses, a crystal ice bucket.

I went toward the changing room, careful not to touch any evidence, and stopped cold in the doorway.

The late Mrs. Harold Archer was lying faceup on the soft, blood-soaked carpet. She was wearing a small bikini, pale blue, pulled up over her breasts, covered with blood. She had been stabbed and slashed repeatedly.

I couldn't count the number of wounds, but they looked like they'd been delivered in a moment of high passion and fury.

Tule's left hand was flung out to her side. There was a gigantic diamond ring on her ring finger, and there was a kitchen knife six or seven inches away from her chest. The knife, her hand, her body, the white carpet, the cream-colored walls—everything was spattered, splashed, and sprayed with blood.

A man's bathing suit and a boxy printed shirt were flung over the arm of a chair. The clothes were so bloody I couldn't tell the color of the fabric.

Beyond the body, bloody footsteps led to the bathroom.

I followed the prints to the doorway and stood outside the room. I could see everything in this uncluttered space. Red footprints led to a shower stall with a lot of heads, a marble floor, and a glass wall facing the view. Bloody water was still pooled around the drain, and large handprints were on the marble, the soap, the shampoo bottle, and the glass.

Hal had cleaned up, put on his robe, and called me.

I saw the one knife that had been used to cut the melon and murder Tule Archer. And nothing else that could have been used as a weapon.

Hal was going to have a tough time proving self-defense.

# Chapter 50

I'D BEEN INSIDE the pool house for only a couple of minutes, and in another two or three, I was going to be obstructing justice. It wasn't going to take a forensic genius to figure out what had happened here, but I wanted Sci to see the scene anyway.

I left the changing room the way I found it, went back out to the larger room, where Hal had draped his large sloppy self in a lounge chair and was looking at the view. The sun was going down leaving a bloody swath of sky.

I came up behind him and said, "Hal, tell me what happened."

He spoke without turning. I had to strain to understand his slurred speech.

"She said she was thinking about my heart.

That she visualized it before she went to sleep every night. That she could see all the arteries and where they went into the valves and she could see the scars where the arteries were stitched into place."

He turned to look up at me over his shoulder.

"You see what she was doing, Zhack?

"She said she was picking at the scars every night, pulling the tissue loose. She was going to pull out the arteries with her mind. She could do it. She was a wicked girl."

He rubbed his chest with the hand that wasn't holding the tumbler of alcohol.

"She was harassing you, you're saying? She was trying to frighten you to death."

"That's it. She was trying to kill me, one night at a time. And she was going to do it, Jack. And that's why I had to put her down."

There was still time for Sci to get here, same for Cruz. But what the hell could any of us do? I'd rarely seen a crime so open-and-shut, but still, I was amazed that a big, rich, powerful man like Archer had resorted to killing an unarmed and helpless woman.

I took out my phone. I have Chief Mickey Fescoe on speed dial. I punched the number.

Hal suddenly became alert. "Who are you calling?"

"Friend of mine. Chief of police."

"*Nooooo,*" Hal shouted.

He stood up, grabbed the chair for balance, and dropped his glass. "*No, no, no.* Make this mess go away. That's what I hired you to do."

Hal flailed out to grab me, but I stepped out of his reach, said into my phone, "Mickey, I need you to send some people to sixty-five forty-seven Donovan Drive. Hal Archer's place. Go to the pool house in the back. Yep. We've got a dead body. I'll be here."

# Chapter 51

I OPENED THE pool house door for four cops I didn't know.

Hal Archer was sitting in the lounge chair again, staring out over the canyon. He had made himself a fresh scotch, and I thought there was a good chance he would pass out.

There was an equally good chance he would launch himself over the cliff, so I kept an eye on him as the detectives did a walk-through.

Detective Sergeant Joan Feeney introduced herself and her partner, Detective Phillips, told me that she and Chief Mickey Fescoe were old friends. Meaning, on this case she was reporting directly to him. As Feeney's partner went into the next room, she took out her notebook and asked me to tell her what I knew.

I told Feeney that Hal Archer was a client, that Private Investigations was contracted to do security checks on his executive staff and whatever else Archer and his family needed in the way of surveillance and security.

Feeney asked, "And what brought you here today, Mr. Morgan?"

"Mr. Archer called to tell me that his wife was trying to kill him. He wanted me to evaluate her. Tell him if I thought he was in danger. He asked me to talk to her, reason with her if I could."

"I see. You came out to reason with her."

She wrote it down.

"A half hour after he first called me, I called him back and then he told me that his wife was dead," I said.

"Okay," said Feeney. "As I understand it, the DB in the next room is the wife that was allegedly threatening to kill Mr. Archer."

"That's right."

"And did your client say that he killed her?"

"He just said that she was dead."

Lying to the police was obstruction, and I was breaking the law on behalf of my client. But I had turned Archer in; I didn't feel that I needed to put him on death row.

Feeney asked, "Did you disturb the scene in any way, Mr. Morgan?"

"Not at all. I looked. I saw. I phoned Mick."

Feeney's partner, Detective Phillips, was saying to Hal, "Did you kill your wife, Mr. Archer?"

"I don't know what you're talking about. But I do know you're blocking my view."

Phillips said, "Stand up, Mr. Archer. Put your hands behind your back."

Feeney took my phone number, closed her notebook. She looked in at the victim, called Chief Fescoe, and gave a report. Hal said to the cop, contempt oozing with every word, "I'm not standing until I feel like it. Lift a hand to me and I will sue you personally and then I'll sue all these cops."

Detective Phillips lifted him by his elbows until he was standing, and Feeney pulled Hal's right arm behind his back, did the same with the other arm, locked the cuffs around his wrists. Hal screamed, "You're going to be sorry. You wait."

Feeney read him his rights and Hal shouted over her.

*"No, you don't. Jack. Tell this rookie bitch—"*

I caught up with Hal, stayed right with him as he was pushed and hoisted through the house and along the marble walk to the curb.

213

I told him, "Cooperate, Hal. Do what the police say, but don't talk about anything that happened here."

"You fickle prick."

"Shut up, Hal. I'm calling your attorney now. You'll be neck-deep in lawyers within the hour."

Hal was looking at me like he was a pet dog that had bitten the neighbor's child and was now being dragged to the dog catcher's van. It was as if he just didn't understand what he'd done. He showed no remorse for stabbing his wife to death.

I stood on the sidewalk and watched the cops stuff a bellowing Hal Archer into the backseat of the squad car. It was true that he'd soon be surrounded by a wall of his own lawyers.

But I didn't think there was a law firm in the world that could save Hal Archer from spending the rest of his life in an eight-by-six-foot cage.

# Chapter 52

AN HOUR AFTER leaving Hal's Balinese-style estate, I cruised past scorched earth outside my house, stopped to key open my front gates, then parked my loaner inside the garage.

Security lights threw a hard glare on all the corners of my property, and once inside the house, I searched room by room, turning on lamps and overheads, hoping to find that no one had gone through the place, taken anything, touched my surveillance system, or shot a friend in my bed.

The premises were clear. Well, Colleen's sad ghost was there, as always. But there were no living souls.

I went to the kitchen, flipped on the TV, and watched the news while I put fruit, ice, and rum into the blender.

The anchorman was talking about the recent series of car bombs and so I tuned in to the report about the nineteen-year-old woman who'd been burned alive only yards from the front door of her parents' house.

Maeve Wilkinson, deceased, had a role on a popular sitcom and was regarded as a bright light with a big future. The screen behind the TV reporter flashed shots of Maeve on set and in a club, and then showed a close-up of the burned wreck of a car.

I'd already seen what remained of the car after a fire so intense that it was impossible for the ME to remove Maeve Wilkinson's body without it crumbling to ash.

The anchor turned the story over to the reporter on the scene who was one of dozens of journalists trying to get quotes from the bereaved parents.

Corinne and Lionel Wilkinson were in their forties, and they looked like people who, until yesterday, had had everything in the world to live for. Lionel went to the microphone, said that he was offering a substantial six-figure reward for information leading to the arrest and conviction of whoever had killed his daughter.

Then he broke down. His knees buckled, and a

man who looked to be a family friend caught him. His weeping wife grabbed him too. As reporters shouted questions and moved toward the Wilkinsons, their friends became roadblocks, and the victim's parents disappeared behind the gates of their home.

Seeing them in the harshest light on the worst day of their lives, knowing that they would never recover from their daughter's unthinkable, horrific, and utterly senseless death, tore at my guts.

I switched off the tube. I no longer had any doubt. The car fires weren't personal; they were crimes of opportunity. My car, the Wilkinsons' car, had both been sitting out in the open. I'd bet anything that the others had been left in similar circumstances.

I called Eric Caine and after he assured me that Rick's trial was going as well as could be expected, I went back to making daiquiris. Much later, I would realize that my phone had vibrated while I was running the Cuisinart. I wish that I had heard it and answered the call.

# Chapter 53

MY FRIEND AND former client Jinx Poole had dropped by for drinks. We lounged in chairs facing the ocean, the frosty pitcher of strawberry daiquiris on the teak table between us, a soft breeze blowing through our hair.

Jinx wore a strapless yellow dress, espadrilles, and a choker of diamonds. Hers is a swirly and girlie style, but Jinx is a hard-core businesswoman who rebuilt a low-rent hotel with a settlement from her dead husband's estate. After that, she had turned three other slummy hotels into five-star gems, each more profitable than the last.

Although when I met Jinx, she was in a bad way.

Traveling businessmen had been murdered in hotels around town and up the coast, and Jinx's hotels had gotten more than their share of dead white-collar guests.

Jinx had been frightened and angry, and she hired Private to protect her clients and her hard-won reputation. Cruz, Del Rio, and I worked the case, and Jinx and I became close. Not skintight, but good friends, anyway. There had been some electricity between us too, but we'd left it unplugged.

In the past couple of days, Jinx had helped me locate Gozan Remari and Khezir Mazul by digging into her insider's database and connecting with her hotelier network. It was Jinx who'd told me that the Sumaris had checked into Shutters, and thanks to her, I knew they were still there.

Currently, we were catching up, talking about Rick's trial, about the Sumaris, and the tragedy of Maeve Wilkinson's death. And I told her about Hal Archer but without mentioning his name.

"He's a big, ballsy entrepreneur," I said. "And given the vast number of people he has intimidated in his life, I don't understand how a twenty-two-year-old woman could have provoked him into stabbing her to death with a kitchen knife."

"Did he do a background check on her?"

"Not through us. She was a cocktail waitress. He met her in a casino. Fell for her. Prenupped her and married her in a drive-through chapel a week later. I'm having her checked out now, postmortem."

Jinx stood up, undid a hook at the back of her dress, and let the dress drop to the deck in a pale yellow cloud. She was wearing a little bikini underneath her clothes, bright pink against her porcelain skin.

I was breathing a little heavily when she resumed her position on the chaise. I poured her another drink, topped off my own, and let the sound of the ocean fill in the sudden gap in the conversation.

I remembered a time when we were having dinner together, sitting close in a booth at a nice restaurant. We were fudging the line a little between client meeting and date. Jinx had had a few tequila cocktails and said she wanted to tell me how she'd become who she was. She thought I should really know.

Her story was shocking then, and it all came back to me now.

Jinx had been working a summer job as a waitress at a country club when she met a wealthy man with a grand and engaging personality. She'd married him at age nineteen, despite her parents' protests, and learned later that they'd been right to protest.

Jinx's husband was a drinker and an all-round wife abuser. She got the last word, and twenty years later, she still blamed herself for her husband's death.

She wasn't entirely wrong to do so.

"The person you meet isn't necessarily the person you get," she said now. Her voice was soft, maybe nostalgic. Maybe regretful.

"Apparently your client didn't know the cocktail waitress very well. And she didn't know who her husband was either."

# Chapter 54

JINX SAID, "WELL, are we going for a swim or not?"

She was walking down the steps at the shallow end of the pool in her tiny, shiny bikini and I was going inside to change when I heard my name. Justine was coming through the glass doors to the deck, still wearing work clothes: dark suit and heels.

"Justine?"

"I didn't know where to park my car," she said. "I left it out front, hoping for the best."

She laughed.

I blinked at her and she kissed me, kept going out to the pool deck, still talking.

"You left your iPad in my car," she said. "I called you, Jack, but no answer, so I thought I'd run over with it."

She was taking the tablet out of her purse when her peripheral vision caught the shapely blonde in my pool.

I read the shock and then the hurt in Justine's face, and she read the reflexive guilt in mine.

"Oh," she said, looking away from me. "Hi, Jinx. It's been a long time..."

Jinx said, "How've you been?" and Justine said, "Fine, thanks," but they were speaking like actors in a British comedy of manners, no one saying what they meant.

Justine turned back to me, her eyes as hard as gun barrels. She said, "I see this isn't a good time. I'll let myself out."

I said, "No, no, join us, Justine."

She said, "See ya," shoved the tablet into my hand, then went back through the open sliding doors. I called out, "Justine. Wait," but she didn't and she was moving fast.

I shot a glance at Jinx, said, "I'll be right back." Then I went after Justine, who swept through the house and out the front door like a gust of wind through my heart.

But when she stopped at the gatepost to punch in her code, I caught up with her.

"Sweetheart, Jinx is just a friend. Nothing is going on. Come back. Have a drink."

"No, thanks, Jack. I only came by to drop off your thing, the iPad. And I've done it."

"Justine, honestly," I said, but by then she had ducked into her car. The door slammed shut, the engine started, the headlights went on, and she expertly navigated the tricky backing-up maneuver out of my driveway and onto the highway.

I found Jinx out on the deck, dressed again.

She stepped into her espadrilles, and I said what was already abundantly clear. "Justine had to leave."

"I have to go too, Jack. A little nagging headache is turning into a big nagging headache."

"Frozen daiquiris can give you brain freeze..."

She laughed. "Good one, Jack."

"Well, I'm sorry about the awkward moment. It's good to see you."

"It's okay, Jack. Another time."

I walked Jinx out to her car. We exchanged cheek kisses. I waved. She tootled her horn and got onto PCH unscathed.

I felt embarrassed, deflated, and headaches must have been going around, because I had one too. I went inside and nuked frozen Salisbury steak with peas.

Then I ate dinner alone in front of the TV.

# Chapter 55

JUSTINE TOOK A run with Rocky, even going an extra lap along the grassy median on Burton. But the three-mile jog didn't calm her down, not at all. She was mad at Jack, hurt by Jack, and freaking *furious* at herself.

At home again, Justine let Rocky into the fenced-in backyard, went to her laundry room and stripped off her clothes, threw them into the washer.

She pictured Jinx Poole: the hair, the body, the ads for her constellation of hotels with their five-diamond ratings. She could easily see Jinx and Jack together, an excruciating image that made total sense. Unlike the dumb arrangement she'd worked out with Jack so that she could be with him and still keep her options open for her own protection.

And you know what? He had every right to do the same.

She was an idiot. Correction: she was an idiot with a broken heart.

Justine went to her bathroom, stood naked in front of the mirror behind the door. She sucked her stomach in, turned to each side, then got into the shower and sat on the floor. She pulled up her knees, laid her head down on her crossed arms, and let the dual pulsating showerheads beat a three-quarter time on her body.

What was wrong with her? What was wrong with *them*?

She thought about meeting Jack five years before.

Back then, she'd been working in a mental hospital three days a week and saw private patients on the other two days in a high-rise in Santa Monica.

One day, going to work at her private practice, she got into the elevator, and Jack got in right after her. She pushed the button for her floor, shot a sideways glance at this gorgeous, confident sandy-blond-haired man. Then she watched him lose his cool when he rode with her to the tenth floor before realizing he hadn't pressed his floor number and completely missed his stop.

Both of them had laughed.

The next time she saw Jack, it was in the same elevator. He told her his name and asked her to dinner. Justine could do a quick read on anyone, a survival mechanism in her line of work. She didn't get a whiff of anything crazy off Jack Morgan.

She introduced herself, said okay to dinner, and three days later, he picked her up at home and took her to a small, very hip, quite intimate Italian restaurant.

After they ordered, Jack had fiddled with the cutlery, then told her that he'd been a captain in the Marine Corps, a pilot, and that he'd served for three years in Afghanistan. He said that the war had changed him and that he was seeing a shrink in the building where she worked, hoping to get a grip on his memories and dreams.

It was unusual conversation for a first date, but Justine went with it. It was as if Jack wanted her to know every hairy thing about him so that she could make an informed decision about whether to go forward or not.

He said to her, "Justine, when you said you'd have dinner with me, it was as if you'd cupped your hands around my heart."

She'd touched his hand. He said, "Who are you?"

She told him, and from this first date, Justine determined that Jack Morgan was open and that he wanted to grow. That was one side of him.

Months later, she said, "Jack, you're like a clam. With a rubber band around your shell." That was the other side.

He had said, "I *can't* tell you everything, Justine. I've seen too much. I've lived through too much. I have thoughts I want to keep even from myself. I keep ninety-five percent of my interior life locked up. You see the five percent that gets over the wall."

Justine had to adjust her first take on Jack as an open, emotionally expressive man, but by then, it was too late. First impressions no longer mattered.

Justine was hooked. She loved him entirely.

He loved her too. He hired her at Private, made her a partner. They bought a house and lived together. They fought about the ninety-five percent that he kept behind the wall, because walls went against everything she believed in. They went against everything she was about. Jack's lies and evasions undercut *her* integrity.

They fought, broke up, reconciled. Lather, rinse, repeat.

Justine wanted their relationship to work, but it

couldn't. Jack was who he was. As much as Justine loved him, it hurt her to be with Jack.

Maybe this time she would learn.

# Chapter 56

I WAS FEELING surly when I walked into the war room at 8:00 a.m. Twenty pairs of eyes followed me as I went to the fridge, grabbed a can of Red Bull, then took my seat at the conference table, the only piece of furniture remaining from when Private belonged to my dad.

I said, "Hello," then rested my eyes on Justine, who was sitting across from me. I couldn't read anything on her beautiful face.

I said, "I want to bring everyone up to date on Harold Archer. As some of you know, I went to his house at his request yesterday evening. I found him in his pool house with the body of his dead wife, Tule.

"Tule had been murdered; looked to me like she'd been killed in a rage. There was every manner and type of blood spray and spatter on the floor, furnishings, and walls. I saw a bloody kitchen knife, probably the murder weapon, next to the body. I couldn't count the stab wounds, but there were a lot of them. Hal had showered and left his bloody clothes across a chair."

I picked up the remote, and images of the crime scene went up on the wall-to-wall flat-screens around the room. It was all there: stark, bloody murder.

I said, "I called the police. There was nothing else I could do. Hal is in custody pending his arraignment tomorrow. He took my advice and lawyered up.

"Any questions so far?"

Cruz asked, "Did the wife have a weapon?"

"None that I could see."

"Was Hal injured?"

"Not that I could see."

Justine asked, "Did he tell you that he killed her?"

"I'm going to say no to that. Now, here's the thing. We have to do what we can to give Hal's lawyers something to work with. Mo-bot, I need you to turn up anything you can on Tule Archer— her past, her known associates, her record if she has one. Do some background on Hal too, while you're at it."

"I'll have something for you in an hour," Mo said.

I knew she would.

Mo-bot's real name is Maureen Roth. She's fifty, married with three kids, a serial slayer in the World of Warcraft, and mother hen to the younger operatives at Private. She's called Mo-bot because of her almost robotic mind. She has an eidetic memory and can multitask like an air traffic controller on speed, doesn't get frazzled or riled. I never had to think twice about Mo.

I concluded the Archer report, and Justine brought everyone up to date on the car-bomb situation, which had heated up considerably since Maeve Wilkinson's death. When she was done, Cruz leaned forward and told the group that all was quiet on the Sumar front.

"Gozan and Khezir are staying put in their hotel room, watching sports and porn," said Cruz.

The other senior investigators gave summaries of their cases, and then we were done. Notably, Del Rio's seat was empty.

"I'll be in court today," I said. "If anything blows up—cars, cases, whatever—Justine is in charge."

Mo-bot saluted Justine. There was a smattering of laughter and I asked again, "Any questions?"

There were none.

I had a wide range of questions that I kept to myself.

Why had Hal Archer gone lethal on his wife? What could I do to make peace with Justine? How would I do on the stand today when Caine called me to testify on behalf of my best friend, Rick Del Rio?

# Chapter 57

MO-BOT LOCKED HERSELF inside her corner office on the basement level, home to Private's forensic lab. She heated water in her microwave, brewed an aromatic tea of spearmint, blackberry leaves, eucalyptus, and licorice root, then began to research Tule Archer, née Tallulah Amoyo of Bakersfield, California.

Mo-bot typed the victim's name into Private's search engine, which automatically clicked through the results, organizing data by type: criminal, biographical, automotive, educational, and social. After the first sort, the intelligent software highlighted the most pertinent information and composed a comprehensive record.

The computer finished this data collection before the tea was done steeping.

Mo-bot went over Tule Archer's newly composed dossier, homed in and winnowed out, asked new questions of the search engine, and received collateral material to add to the file.

As she worked, Mo-bot took a call from Emilio Cruz, the sexiest person of either gender at Private Investigations Worldwide. She also consulted with Sci about a software suite, talking with him over the network even though he was only thirty feet away.

She relayed information from the LA lab to Sci on the chemicals used in the Wilkinson car bomb, noting that latex had been found inside what remained of the gas tank. After she finished with Sci, Mo-bot texted her husband, Trent, reminded him that he had a dentist's appointment at noon and a meeting with their contractor at two, and that their youngest son had science club at three fifteen.

Mo-bot went back to work.

The key facts about Tule were these: Born in California of Filipino agricultural workers in 1992, Tule grew up in Bakersfield, where she went to public school, got average grades, and was known as a prankster and a bit of a comic. She attended East LA College, took courses in art and theater, and then moved to Las Vegas.

Her tracks became more dramatic once she was working as a dancer and cocktail waitress.

Mo-bot watched videos of song-and-dance routines at the Black Diamond Hotel and Casino and Tule often had lead parts. Mo-bot saw both talent and ambition in this young woman.

Same time that Tule was dancing and serving drinks to VIPs, she was cited for a DUI, then arrested for having a fight with another showgirl backstage. Not long after that, according to justice court, Tule and her roommate, Barbie Summers, skipped out on their rent, leaving their dogs and furnishings behind.

Leaving dogs was telling—but what it told, Mo-bot couldn't be sure. Were they running from? Or running to?

Mo-bot got into the Clark County Recorder's Office records and found the entry for Tule's wedding to Hal Archer, and then she turned up Tule and Hal's wedding announcement in the *LA Times*; looked like they'd decided to have a second wedding, a much bigger one, back home in California.

That wedding in LA marked a dramatic turn in the life of Tallulah Amoyo, a new Real Housewife of Beverly Hills. But a few days after their first anniversary, Tule was dead, and, indisputably, Hal Archer had done it.

Mo-bot attached the LAPD's report on Tule's murder, and when the dossier was cooked, she sent a memo to Jack, copied it to Sci and Justine.

Then Mo-bot, a woman who was capable of keeping innumerable plates in the air, stopped everything to look at Tule Archer's *LA Times* wedding photo. The scene was Vibiana, a former cathedral in downtown LA, now renovated and reimagined as a thirty-five-thousand-square-foot way beautiful, over-the-top events venue.

In the picture, Tule wore a twenty-thousand-dollar wedding gown and an ecstatic smile on her face; next to her, Hal Archer looked proud and in love with his arm-candy bride.

"What happened, Tule?" Mo-bot asked the image on her screen. "What the hell went so wrong?"

# Chapter 58

LORI KIMBALL WAS in a black mood.

She pulled her SUV up to the 7-Eleven, parallel-parked it between a large motorcycle and a Chevy Volt.

What had put her in a bad state was the road repair work outside her office on South Hope Street, which had forced a detour around the block, where a red light had effectively canceled her death race home.

She couldn't blame herself. There was no need to take a point penalty, but it was depressing to lose that excellent bridge between her go-nowhere job and the terminal tedium of housewifery.

She knew that the adrenaline from the race was like rocket fuel, that it was probably keeping her brain from shorting out forty years before its time.

Damn it. She really hated being shut down.

Lori picked up her purse from the passenger seat and marched inside the convenience store, then sidled over to the cooler and selected an iced coffee, a pitiful consolation prize. She brought the plastic cup up to the line at the cash register, taking her place behind a shirtless, hairy biker and his sunburned girlfriend.

She was eavesdropping on their inane, mumbly, pothead conversation when she became aware that someone was speaking to her.

"Hey there. Ms. Kimball, right?"

She turned. It was a California Highway Patrol officer in the customary tan uniform: short-sleeved shirt with buttoned pockets and a brimmed hat. His bushy eyebrows looked familiar to her. She glanced at the gold-star badge above his pocket, saw the name Schmidt.

"Yes, I'm Lori Kimball."

Then she remembered him.

He said, "I recognized your car. You're not still speeding all to hell on the Five, are you, Ms. Kimball? Not still smoking up the freeway for the fun of it?"

"Absolutely *not*. You got through to me, Officer," Lori said, managing to throw in a merry laugh. She touched her hair, twinkled her eyes. "I don't want to lose my license. I've been very well behaved since you gave me that ticket, believe me."

"Happy to hear it."

Fuckin' power tripper.

Lori paid for her coffee, said good-bye to the highway cop, and went outside to her car. She pulled out of the lot carefully, and when she got onto the street she noticed that the officer's black-and-white Ford Crown Victoria was following behind her.

She kept well within the speed limit as she approached and then took the ramp to the 110 North. The trooper didn't follow her, but regardless, he'd definitely brought her down.

Lori got into the right lane and gradually moved into the center, other cars passing her on both sides. She was the only person on the freeway driving the speed limit, for God's sake.

The only one.

So, fuck it.

Two antique American cars were just ahead of her, one to the left, the other to the right. Lori jammed down the gas and pierced the opening between them like she was flying a silver bullet.

*Whoo-hoo.* This was better. Way better.

She motored through the Figueroa tunnels at a cool eighty-three, covering most of the death race at record speed. She was so high in the zone that she almost missed her exit. She still had time to make her move, but in overcompensating for her overshot, she jerked the wheel too hard. Her wheels screamed as she took the right onto West Doran Street, the left side of her vehicle lifting off the asphalt, then dropping back down as she made a sharp right onto San Fernando Road.

Lori was panting from sheer exhilaration. She was in the homestretch now, turning onto Grandview, passing Pelanconi Park on the right, trees on both sides lining her up with the Verdugo Mountains straight ahead. Traffic was light, no one challenging her or getting in her face, so Lori gave the engine some gas and took the car up to a very sweet seventy-two.

But it was over too soon.

Lori sighed as she slowed, then took the left onto West Mountain Street, a boring block in the boring neighborhood where she spent two-thirds of every day of her boring life. She pulled into the driveway of a small, white cinder-block-and-stucco house with blue awnings over the front windows.

Lori sat in the car for another minute, feeling her heart rate slow, thinking things over. Today had been a setback. But there was always tomorrow. Tomorrow was another day entirely.

# Chapter 59

I WAS IN court on time, clean-shaven, appropriately dressed, my face still the color of boiled shrimp from the car explosion. My brother was relaxing in the back row of the gallery, tanned and toothy, looking like a PR flack at an Oscar party. He fanned his hand in a wave.

I turned my back on Tommy and shut off my phone because there was nothing more important than being here for Rick. Didn't matter what happened anywhere else in the world.

Judge Johnson entered the courtroom with her little dog underfoot, and in a few minutes, the jury filed in and court was called to order. After Her Honor had a chat with the jury, Dexter Lewis, fittingly dressed in a gray sharkskin suit, called a witness, Sergeant Michael Degano, a detective with the LAPD.

Sergeant Degano was balding, about forty, and had the kind of five o'clock shadow that colors the jowls by noon. When he took the stand, he looked at Lewis in a way that suggested this wasn't his first testimony at a criminal trial and he wanted to get on with it.

Lewis asked, "Sergeant Degano, how did you come to be involved in this case?"

Degano said, "Our division was called and I was available to go to the victim's house. I went into the room where she was lying, and Ms. Carmody was going in and out of consciousness. The EMT didn't give her much chance of survival, so I went with her in the ambulance to the hospital.

"I sat right next to her, and when she was having what they call a lucid interval, I questioned her. I thought if she could speak, maybe she could tell me who her attacker was. That might be our best chance of bringing him to justice."

The detective swung his head a few degrees and gave Rick a short, hard look, then turned back to the ADA.

"And did you interview Ms. Carmody?"

"I did."

"And did you record this interview?"

"Yes. I got it on my phone. Later, I transferred the interview to a disk."

The computer was booted up, and the lights went down as the monitor was wheeled into the courtroom. Degano sat comfortably in the witness box and watched as the video lit up the screen with his image.

It was clear that he was recording from inside the ambulance. Degano gave his name and division, the date of the interview, and the circumstances.

The camera eye panned to a woman, whom Degano identified as Victoria Carmody. She was strapped to a stretcher and in a neck brace; she had an IV going into her arm, and she was getting oxygen through a nasal cannula. Her face and head were bruised and bloody, making it impossible to tell her age, race, or even gender.

On camera, Degano introduced himself to Carmody, said his name was Mike Degano, that he was a detective. Then he asked her if it was okay to ask her a few questions.

Ms. Carmody grunted, and Degano took that as affirmation.

"Can you hear me okay?" he asked her.

Carmody made the sound again.

Degano said, "You were found inside your bedroom. On the floor. I don't know if you know that you were badly beaten."

Carmody tried to jerk her head and made a mewling cry. It seemed to me that she knew what Degano was asking her, and the memory was fresh and very painful.

Degano said, "I'm sorry to have to ask you, Ms. Carmody, but I'm here to help you. Do you remember what happened to you?"

Carmody made a sound. It seemed to be *yes*.

"Tell me what you remember."

To Degano's credit, he used simple words, spoke softly, and had the patience to wait out an answer.

"Fight," Carmody said.

"You were in a fight?"

No answer.

"Who beat you up, Ms. Carmody? I want to find the guy who did this to you."

Carmody tried to twist on the stretcher but managed only to take in a strangled breath. Someone, presumably an EMT, said, "Wrap it up, Detective."

Degano leaned over and took Carmody's hand. "Vicky. Squeeze my fingers for *yes*. Can you do that? Good. Was your assailant a stranger?"

247

She gasped out, "No."

"Your neighbor gave me this picture of you and a man you may have had a date with tonight."

The camera image jiggled as Degano took a photo from his inside jacket pocket, showed it to Carmody, then flashed it in front of his phone. "Is this the man who hurt you?"

Carmody's one good eye opened a fraction of an inch. She said, "Rick."

Degano said, "Ms. Carmody, I want to be sure. Is this the man who hurt you? Rick Del Rio?"

Two EMTs got between the camera and the patient. We could hear Carmody say "Rick" again. Degano's voice was heard thanking Ms. Carmody, saying that he would be in touch. Then the picture went dark.

Caine had told me that I was the only person who could persuade the jury that Rick Del Rio, this tough, former U.S. Marine, was innocent of beating his ex-girlfriend nearly to death.

Now this.

What in God's name could I say to counteract Carmody's heartrending testimony?

# Chapter 60

CAINE MADE SOME notes on his tablet, then got to his feet and approached the witness.

"Sergeant Degano, you saw that Ms. Carmody had suffered grave injuries to her head. You testified that she was going in and out of consciousness. And yet you trusted the veracity of her testimony?"

"I had no choice. For all I knew, this was her last hour on earth."

"I understand. But when you showed her the picture of my client and asked if he was the one who hurt her, is it possible she didn't understand your question?"

"I don't understand yours."

"Let me rephrase it, then," said Caine. "Ms. Carmody had been physically and emotionally traumatized and had lost a lot of blood. Isn't it possible that when you asked her who hurt her and showed her the picture of Rick Del Rio, she said 'Rick' because it was his picture?"

"I asked. She answered."

"Detective, how long have you been a police officer?"

"Eighteen years."

"When you ask a person to make an identification, isn't it standard practice to show them a lineup, or a photo array?"

"There was no time to pull one together."

"So you violated procedure, and now we cannot be sure what kind of ID the victim made, can we?"

"I had the man's picture in my jacket pocket."

"Just answer the question, please, Detective. If you could have, you would have shown her an array, yes or no?"

"Yeah. In a perfect world. A world I don't happen to live in."

"Thanks, Detective. I have no further questions."

# Chapter 61

ADA LEWIS CALLED his next witness, Dr. William Triebel, a neurosurgeon of note at Cedars-Sinai. Triebel was clean-cut, fifty, his face lined from the sun. He looked confident and competent, and when he spoke, his testimony was delivered in a crisp, no-bull way.

Dr. Triebel described types of traumatic brain injury, gave a quick course in bleeding and swelling in the brain. He said that Vicky Carmody had a subdural hematoma and an intracranial hemorrhage, and he categorized her injuries as catastrophic.

"And you operated on her, Dr. Triebel?" Lewis asked.

"Yes. I did. I evacuated the subdural hematoma, managed the swelling, and all I could do about the focal hemorrhage inside the brain was wait and pray."

Lewis asked his witness, "What's her prognosis?"

"Guarded for survival," he said.

"Will she be able to walk?"

"It's too soon to tell."

"Doctor, is it fair to say that June thirteenth was the last normal day Vicky Carmody will ever have?"

Caine shot up from his seat, said, "Objection. The doctor has testified that he has no way of knowing what to expect for Ms. Carmody in the future."

"Let me rephrase that," said Lewis. "If Ms. Carmody survives, is it likely that she will fully recover from this vicious beating?"

"In a word, no."

"That's all I have for Dr. Triebel. Thank you, Doctor."

Then Lewis spoke in the general direction of the defense table. "Your witness."

Caine stood and walked toward the witness stand.

"I have a couple of questions, Dr. Triebel. Regarding the injuries to Ms. Carmody's brain that you describe as catastrophic. You've said that she suffered most of the trauma to the brain stem and the frontal lobe. Is that correct?"

"Yes."

"And do I understand correctly that these are the parts of the brain that control motor function, memory, and speech?"

Lewis spoke from his seat. "Objection, Your Honor. The doctor fully explained the extent and type of injuries to the court."

"I'll allow it anyway," said the judge. "Some of us wouldn't mind hearing this again. Please continue, Mr. Caine."

"Thank you, Your Honor. Dr. Triebel, shall I repeat the question?"

The doctor said, "That's not necessary. Yes, the brain stem and the frontal lobe control motor function, memory, and speech."

"Thank you. Now, Dr. Triebel. After help arrived many hours after the attack, Ms. Carmody was interviewed by the police, and she responded to questioning. Is it likely that her memories of the attack were affected by the trauma she sustained?"

"Maybe yes. Maybe no. Could go either way."

"Well, then, is it fair to say that any testimony she gave in this traumatized condition was questionable, even unreliable?"

The doctor folded his hands in front of him. "The brain is an amazing organ. Ms. Carmody was unconscious when she was admitted to the hospital. Without evaluating her brain function at that time, we can't know if Ms. Carmody remembered the attack accurately or not."

"Thank you, Doctor."

Lewis had put the doctor on the stand to testify about how much damage the victim had suffered at her attacker's hands. I liked the way Caine had turned the evidence around to question Carmody's ability to know what had happened to her.

I hoped at least one juror saw it as reasonable doubt.

As the witness stepped down from the box and left the courtroom, Dexter Lewis exchanged a few words with his co-counsel. Then the ADA stood, buttoned his jacket, said to the judge, "The People rest, Your Honor."

"Thank you, Mr. Lewis," said the judge. "Mr. Caine? Are you ready to present your case?"

Caine said, "Yes, Your Honor. The defense calls Mr. Jack Morgan."

# Chapter 62

I WALKED TO the box, put my hand on the Bible, and swore to God I would tell the truth. I hoped I could do that. I hoped I wouldn't have to lie.

I sat down and looked across the blond-wood floor to the defense table. Rick's expression was tight with pent-up emotion, like he was doing everything in his power not to blow.

Eric Caine, my good friend, an excellent lawyer, and Rick's defender, smiled as he came toward me.

He stopped a few feet from where I sat and said, "Mr. Morgan, you and I know each other pretty well, isn't that right?"

"Yes, we do."

"I'm employed by your firm as your in-house counsel, correct?"

"Yes."

"So I want the jury to know that you are here today as a *character* witness for Mr. Del Rio and that you have no firsthand knowledge of the crime that was perpetrated on Ms. Carmody."

"That's right."

Caine paused for a moment, then said, "Mr. Morgan, how long have you known Mr. Del Rio?"

"I've known Rick for ten years. We served in Afghanistan together."

"Will you tell the court about that?"

"How much time do we have?"

Caine smiled. He said, "As much time as you need."

I had rehearsed a few lines to get myself started, but now, as I looked at Rick's face, I forgot what I was going to say.

But the images, they were there—with sound and the stink of fear and in living color. That night, when we were shot out of the sky, I remember what affected me most deeply: the dead and dying men, and the relief in Del Rio's face after he'd brought me back to life.

But that was *my* story.

Rick had a story too, and there was a part of it that we had never talked about and that he wouldn't want me to reveal.

But I had to tell it now if I was going to help him.

I wanted to tell the jury that Rick talked to the dead.

# Chapter 63

THERE WASN'T A sound in the room, just expectant faces, every one of them turned toward me.

I began to talk about the night we were transporting troops from Gardez to the base in Kandahar. I said that I was piloting the aircraft, that Del Rio was my copilot, my wingman, and that we had fourteen war-weary Marines in the cargo bay.

"Night flights are exceptionally—hazardous. Even with NVGs, even with our heightened awareness of anomalies on the ground, there are ditches and shadows where the enemy can hide."

I said, "We never saw the ground-to-air missile that slammed through the belly of the CH-46, knocking out our rear rotor, sending us into a death spiral thousands of feet straight down. That

258

same missile set off ordnance inside the chopper and blew up the fuel tanks and started the fire that burned our helicopter from the inside out."

I looked at the faces of the jurors and told them that against terrible odds, we landed the aircraft with its struts down, and that Del Rio and I got out of the Phrog alive and uninjured. My voice cracked when I told them that when I reached the wreckage of the cargo bay, I was presented with something akin to Sophie's choice.

"You're supposed to take the man that has the best chance of survival. That's what you do—but it was dark. Men were screaming in agony, begging not to be left to be burned alive. I loved them all, but I grabbed Corporal Danny Young," I said. "I didn't know if he would make it, but he was closest to the door.

"I carried him to safety, and I had just put him down when the helicopter exploded. It's a concussive explosion. The ground *erupts*. The air *shatters*.

"I was hit in the chest by a chunk of flying metal, and my protective armor stopped it from going through. But the force stopped my heart. That's what Rick told me later. My heart stopped and I died.

"But Rick didn't let me die. He stayed with me,

pounded my chest until I was breathing. Because of him, that man sitting there, I am alive. But Danny was killed by the blast. All of our brothers in the cargo bay—dead."

I had to stop speaking. My throat closed up and my eyes watered as I remembered the unspeakable horror.

Caine's voice broke into my thoughts. He said, "What happened after First Lieutenant Del Rio brought you back to life?"

I could see it now, so clearly that I was as good as there. Could I put it into words? I tried.

"Later. The sun was coming up," I told the jury. "I was on a stretcher, with a saline drip in my arm. There were sedatives in the bag too, hard core enough to keep me down.

"But I could see through the dust and the veil of smoke that Rick was following the corpsmen into what was left of the aircraft. He came out with the body bags, helped lay them out in a line on the ground.

"We had survived and they were dead. This...there are no words...for how this feels."

Tears ran from my eyes. I just couldn't speak. Caine told me to take my time, and finally, I looked at Del Rio and said, "I'm sorry. I'm sorry."

He nodded, but he, too, was breaking down.

Dexter Lewis got to his feet and objected.

"Your Honor, I think we all understand the relationship between the witness and the defendant. There's no point in continuing this testimony when in fact it has nothing to do with this trial."

"I'll allow it, Mr. Lewis. Go on, Mr. Morgan."

I went back there again and told what I saw.

"Del Rio was squatting down maybe twenty feet away from where I was lying. He unzipped Corporal Young's bag. I could hear some of what he said. It was like, 'Danny, I hope you're still hanging around and can hear me, man.'

"He was talking and then laughing, like he and Danny were sharing a joke, and then his expression changed. I heard him say, 'Sheila.'

"Sheila was Danny's wife, pregnant with their fourth child, and I heard Rick say that when the baby was due, he would go to Lubbock, be there for Sheila. Then Rick made the sign of the cross on Danny's forehead, said, 'I'll keep you with me, Danny. See ya soon.'

"He went down the line to the next bag, unzipped it, and talked to the next Marine, and then the next, all of them as if they were living and whole.

"He said he was sorry, talked awhile, made jokes. Then he made the sign of the cross, sent them off...It was like a sacrament, a beautiful, beautiful thing."

Caine brought over the tissues and I wiped my eyes. But tissues couldn't dam the flow.

I was crying, and Rick was crying too.

I heard Caine say, "Thank you," and the judge asked Dexter Lewis if he had any questions.

And you know what? He did.

# Chapter 64

ADA DEXTER LEWIS said, "Do you need a minute, Mr. Morgan?"

"No, thanks. I'm okay." I blew my nose. Cleared my throat.

Lewis said, "Is there anything else you'd like to say about the defendant?"

"I'm sorry?"

"Does Mr. Del Rio stop traffic for ducklings? Send paychecks home to his mom?"

Caine was on his feet with an objection. "The prosecution is badgering the witness, Your Honor."

"Sustained." Judge Johnson looked at Lewis, said, "Don't do that, Mr. Lewis. Treat the witness with respect. This is a warning."

"Sorry, Your Honor."

"Ask your next question, Mr. Lewis."

"Mr. Morgan, did I understand you to say that you overheard Mr. Del Rio promise to be with Corporal Young's wife when she gave birth to her child?"

"That's right."

"Did he? Go to Lubbock, Texas, to be with Mrs. Young?"

"I . . . don't know."

"Well, I know, Mr. Morgan. And I believe you do too. Sheila Young gave birth to a daughter on March twenty-ninth of 2003. Danielle. Do you remember where Mr. Del Rio was at that time?"

"Yes."

"Speak up, Mr. Morgan."

"Yes. I know where he was."

"Please share that information with the jury."

Caine was on his feet again. "Relevance, Your Honor?"

"Overruled, Mr. Caine. Your witness opened the door. Go ahead, Mr. Morgan. Answer the question."

"Rick was at Chino."

"Why was Mr. Del Rio in prison, if you can remember?"

"He robbed a liquor store."

"Let's see. Mr. Del Rio was convicted on three

counts," Lewis said, as if he were reading notes written on his palm. "Breaking and entering. Armed robbery. Larceny. Guilty, guilty, guilty.

"I believe you spoke for Mr. Del Rio at that trial too, didn't you, Mr. Morgan? Played the hero card? Helped get him a break on his sentence?"

I didn't answer.

"Please answer, Mr. Morgan. Did you give testimony as to Mr. Del Rio's heroic acts in Afghanistan at his trial?"

"Yes."

"Thank you. So, not to rub it in, Mr. Morgan, just to state the facts: Mr. Del Rio is an ex-con, isn't he?"

"Objection," Caine shouted.

"I withdraw the question. Are you and Mr. Del Rio still close friends?"

"Yes."

"Did Mr. Del Rio ever say anything to you about wanting to get back at Victoria Carmody for dumping him?"

"No."

"Did he spy on her, Mr. Morgan? Did he use any of Private's famous space-age spyware on Ms. Carmody? Did he follow her around? Did he stalk her?"

"*Objection*," Caine said. "Once again, Mr. Lewis

is badgering the witness. I move to strike, Your Honor."

Judge Johnson shoved papers aside, asked Dexter Lewis, "Is there any basis for this line of questioning? Do you have evidence to show that Mr. Del Rio was spying on Ms. Carmody?"

"Your Honor, Private Investigations is well known for unlawful activity. It's what they do. If Mr. Del Rio was surveilling Ms. Carmody without a court order, then the jury needs to know—"

"Move on, please, Mr. Lewis."

"That's all I have for this witness."

The judge said to me, "Thank you for your service, Captain Morgan. You may stand down."

I stood up and walked across the well, meaning to put my hand on Rick's shoulder as I passed him, but Rick wasn't looking at me. He was whispering fiercely to Caine.

Caine stood and said, "I'd like to request a recess, Your Honor."

Del Rio jumped to his feet and shouted, "We don't need a recess, Judge. I want to testify and my lawyer doesn't agree. But it's my right to do it and I demand my rights."

I shouted, "Rick. *No.*"

The judge banged the gavel, and the noise in

the gallery sounded like a tornado rumbling down the interstate. There was more gavel banging, and I could hear the little dog go nuts under the bench.

Finally, a tense silence came over the room.

Judge Johnson sent the jury out, and when they were gone, she said, "Consult with your attorney, Mr. Del Rio. After that, if you want to testify, you will be heard."

# Chapter 65

DEL RIO CROSSED the room and held up his right hand, put his left on the Bible. He swore to tell the truth, and it was a safe bet he would.

But was it a *smart* bet? That, I didn't know.

I was emotionally raw, still reeling from dragging into court brave, dead men who had many times over earned the right to rest in peace. I was furious about Lewis's attack on Del Rio, and now the ADA had badgered Rick into testifying for himself against Caine's advice.

Del Rio looked like the man he was: rough-hewn, volatile. Maybe the jurors would also see my friend, a man who was so loyal, he stayed to say good-bye to the dead.

Caine approached Del Rio, said, "Mr. Del Rio,

were you in love with Vicky Carmody?"

"No. I was not."

"How did you feel about her?"

"She was a nice girl. I mean, woman. She was a nice woman. She was very sweet."

"How long were the two of you involved?"

"I don't really know to the day or anything. But most it could be was six months."

"Was Ms. Carmody in love with you?"

"Nah. She liked me, but she was ready to get married and have babies, and I'm the wrong guy for that."

"So did she break off the relationship?"

"Yeah. You don't hurt a girl like Vicky. I might have let her see enough of my rough side that she would make the decision."

"So you weren't angry with her?"

"Not at all."

"On June fourteenth, the night in question, did you go to Ms. Carmody's house?"

"Yes. I did."

"And tell the court what happened."

"I came over. I parked in her driveway. I saw the UPS guy across the street, so I waved to him."

Rick smirked. I wished he hadn't done that.

"Then what happened?"

"I think Vicky waved to him too. Then she let me in the house."

"Please go on."

"She made tea. I got a beer from her fridge. We had some uncomfortable small talk, and I gave her back her camera. Then I kissed her cheek on the way out the door. I told her to take care. She said, 'You too.'

"I drove home. I went into my house and took a six-pack into the living room and I watched a ball game. I woke up on the couch and it was about two. I went to bed. Next day, I went to work."

"Did you ever get into a fight with Vicky?"

"No. Well, I may have done a little shouting. Where I come from, shouting is like belching. It doesn't mean anything. But I never hit her. I never threatened to hit her. I never would. I've never hit a woman in my life."

I thought Rick's testimony had gone pretty well, but now Caine had to turn the witness over to the other side.

I had a very sick feeling thinking about that.

# Chapter 66

DEL RIO LOOKED confident, bordering on smug. I knew this look. It wasn't really confidence—it was his way of signaling his rage before he went crazy.

I wanted to sit him down and talk to him. I wanted to get right in his face and shout, *Don't blow this.*

But Rick didn't hear my silent scream. He just squared himself in the witness box and sat back as ADA Dexter Lewis crossed the courtroom to him.

"Mr. Del Rio, please state your full name."

"Rick Del Rio."

"Is that Rick for Richard?"

"Yes."

"That's the name you were born with?"

"I was born Ricardo Esteban Del Rio. Okay? Born in California, U.S.A."

The ADA's question was provocative, but it was smart and ethical. He was showing the jury that Rick could have aliases, that he wasn't even truthful about his name. But Rick had taken it as an ethnic slur. Twenty feet from where I was sitting, a fuse had been lit.

"Okay, Mr. Del Rio. Where'd you meet Ms. Carmody?"

"Online."

"In some kind of matchmaker chat room?"

"That's right."

"And on your first date, did you take her out to dinner?"

"You know what I did. I took her to Santa Anita. She bet on a winner. It made her happy."

"And what did you like most about her?"

"She had a nice personality. She said she thought I was interesting."

"Interesting? Is that right? So you told her that after you got out of the military, you were convicted of robbery, spent four years at Chino, and now you did a lot of sneaking around with cameras and such in your job as a private eye?"

Caine said from his seat, "Your Honor. Is there a question somewhere in that pile of garbage?"

"I'll withdraw my question, Your Honor. My

apologies. Mr. Del Rio, what did you and Ms. Carmody fight about?"

"Huh?"

"You said that you and Vicky fought. What were your fights about?"

"Nothing. Like most people. We both forgot about the fight the next day."

"You see, Mr. Del Rio, I'm asking because Ms. Carmody told Sergeant Degano in the ambulance that she had been in a fight. Now, I'd say that a fight between you and Ms. Carmody would be something like an eighteen-wheeler rolling over a Mini Cooper—"

"Objection, Your Honor. Mr. Lewis is badgering the defendant, smearing him with innuendo in a transparent attempt to bias the jury against him."

Judge Johnson admonished Lewis, said, "You surprise me, Mr. Lewis. There are remedies available to me if you continue in this vein."

Lewis dipped his head, appeared somewhat remorseful, then asked, "Mr. Del Rio, could you give us an example of a fight you had with Ms. Carmody?"

"Fights come in all sizes," Del Rio said. "For instance, there are arguments like what we're having, because I don't agree with your questions.

And I don't like your tone of voice."

Lewis mimicked Del Rio: "I don't like your tone of voice."

Del Rio was on his feet. His blood was up, and his hands were clenched into fists. "You want to fight with *me*, Lewis? Is that what you want?"

Bingo. That was *exactly* what Lewis wanted, but Del Rio didn't get a chance to lift a hand. The bailiff saw a brawl in the making, barreled into Del Rio, and forced him down into his seat in the witness box.

Caine hollered for a mistrial and the judge hollered back, "Not on your life, Mr. Caine. The defendant wanted to testify. And now he's done it."

# Chapter 67

I SWEAR TO God, I couldn't believe what was happening. The judge slammed the gavel until the courtroom came to something resembling order, but she was clearly losing control of the proceedings.

When the opposing attorneys were back behind their respective tables, when the roar in the gallery had subsided into a stunned silence, the judge put her pooch in her lap and said, "Mr. Del Rio, you are one split second from being removed from this court."

"I'm sorry, Your Honor."

"Can you control yourself? Or would you like to watch your trial on closed-circuit from a holding cell?"

"I've got myself under control, Your Honor. I

apologize to you and everyone else. But that dirtbag—"

"Stop right there!"

"Yes, ma'am."

Del Rio stared bullets at Dexter Lewis, and the jurors looked back and forth between them. Caine asked for a sidebar, and he and Lewis approached the bench.

I knew Caine was requesting a mistrial again, because there was no chance the jurors could ignore Rick's violent reaction to Lewis, even if they were instructed to do so.

There was inaudible chatter at the bench, then the attorneys stepped away, Dexter Lewis showing a twitchy smile, which told me that he was doing his best to keep a victory lap in check.

The judge asked, "Mr. Lewis, do you have any further questions for Mr. Del Rio?"

"No, Your Honor."

"Mr. Caine, would you like to reexamine Mr. Del Rio?"

"Yes, Your Honor. I would."

"Go ahead."

"Rick. Did you beat up Vicky Carmody?"

"No."

"Thank you. That's all I have. The defense rests."

The judge told Del Rio to stand down, and then she addressed the jury, telling them that she was adjourning court for the weekend, that they were prohibited from discussing the case, and that the attorneys would give their closing arguments on Monday.

The courtroom emptied and people filled in the space between Rick and me. I took an elevator to the ground floor, trusting that Caine was taking Del Rio out the back way.

I cut through the crowds in the lobby and went out the front and around to the parking lot, where a mob stampeded past me, heading to the rear of the lot, over by the ramp.

I went along with the herd and then I heard grunting and a sharp scream of pain, followed by Dexter Lewis shouting: *"You puke. You ass-wipe. You think I'm afraid of you, you fucking goon?"*

I saw through a break in the crowd. Del Rio had snapped.

Caine and assorted bystanders had pulled him off Dexter Lewis, who was holding his hands to his nose, blood running through his fingers, splashing on his white shirt and pale gray suit.

I read shock on Lewis's face, the realization that there was another kind of hardball played

277

*outside* the courtroom and that he'd just taken the brunt of it.

But Lewis wasn't going to let Del Rio get the last word.

Rick had punched out the ADA, and there would be a price to pay.

# Chapter 68

I EDGED INTO the thickest part of the crowd, got within shouting distance of Rick and the howling, bleeding, cursing Dexter Lewis. I called out to Caine and he yelled back, "Can you give me a hand, Jack?"

He and I bundled Rick into the backseat of Caine's car as cameras in a circle around us fired off shots. The raccoons reveled in the unexpected opportunity to have me and Rick in the same frame, and they peppered me with questions: "Jack, a few words, please, for Fox News?" "Morgan, d'you still believe Rick Del Rio is innocent?"

I leaned into the car, put a hand on Del Rio's shoulder, made eye contact, and said, "What the hell is wrong with you?"

"Don't worry, Jack. The jury didn't see anything."

"Might have been better if they had, Rick. This whole trial would have been scratched. That would be a good thing."

"Jack, I like this jury. They like me. I'll be fine, my friend. Just fine."

Caine didn't look fine. He looked like he thought he was about to lose Rick to the penal system. We exchanged a few pat assurances, then I swam against the tide until I reached my loaner car.

I was trying to ease the Mercedes around the mob when there was a sharp rap on my window and I turned to see my mirror image staring at me. Tommy was making the universal gesture to roll down the glass.

I did it.

He said, "Ten million, Jack. I'm slashing my offer for Private from twenty to ten. You're going to lose your clients, Jacko. They won't want to be associated with that slime bucket."

"What do you want, Junior?"

"What's rightfully mine."

"Don't move your feet," I said.

There was an opening in front of me and I stepped hard on the gas, cut out of the lot, and headed to the office. I was livid. My brother saying that Private was rightfully his was the crock-of-shit delusion that drove him.

Tommy was Dad's favorite, sure. But Dad had given Private to me and I'd built it up from an empty wreck of a company to a profitable and respected global operation—despite my father's conviction and then, some time later, his death by shiv in the showers at Corcoran.

I wondered if Tommy was even sane.

The Mercedes seemed to drive itself downtown to Figueroa. I turned into the lot under our building and took the lower-level entrance through the lab.

I passed Mo-bot's incense-perfumed cave of an office on my way to see Sci. All of Mo's computer monitors were glowing, and she was doing a funky-chicken dance with her back to the door. Acting like a little kid.

"What are we celebrating?" I said.

She screamed, startled. Then she said, "Oh, Jack. I've got something you'll want to see. This is Barbie Summers. She's Tule Archer's former roommate."

A photo filled the screen: a leggy blond showgirl wearing a feathered corset, a pair of ten-inch stilettos, and not much else.

"Show me everything," I said.

"I knew you'd say that," said Mo-bot.

# Chapter 69

MO-BOT WAS DOING her best for Hal Archer. He was obnoxious, but he was also a client who was under arrest for murdering his wife. Archer claimed he'd killed his wife in self-defense, but when the jury saw the pictures of the innumerable knife wounds on Tule's small body, Hal wouldn't stand a chance.

Mo-bot offered her chair and I sat down, clicked through the files she had set up, and scanned Barbie Summers's bio.

She'd grown up in central Florida, dropped out of college, moved to Las Vegas, and had had assorted hand-to-mouth jobs. Her arrest record was a star field of infractions: assault, prostitution, obstruction. And then there was a charge for insurance fraud that hadn't stuck.

Somehow she cleaned up her act enough to waitress at the Black Diamond Hotel and Casino. She learned to dance with a pole and moved up to the Madagascar Salon as a VIP cocktail waitress. I put her age at about twenty-three.

Mo said, "She's a piece of work. All kinds of high jinks out in Vegas. But she married well, same sort of deal Tule got."

Mo clicked on another set of documents, and I scanned them quickly as they opened in a luminous array of virtual pages that followed the movements of my eyes.

I read that a year ago, Barbie Summers had married a very prominent businessman: Bryce Cooper of Aspen. Cooper was eighty years old, a fifty-million-dollar-a-year executive in the corporate -jet manufacturing business. Another wealthy dude marrying a Vegas dolly.

Mo had annotated the document to say that Cooper paid off his four kids so that they wouldn't complain about his new bride and try to ruin his happy marriage.

Then Mo brought up the photos of Mr. Cooper. The first batch were corporate shots: Cooper shaking hands with Dick Cheney and various industrialists and movie stars. Mo showed me candid shots of Bryce Cooper competing in a statewide motorbike race, playing football with grandkids on the lawn of his enormous beam-and-glass-construction home. Then, in the past year and a half, there were a lot of pictures of Cooper on the ski slopes with a busty pink-and-platinum-haired former hoofer I recognized as Barbie Summers.

Cooper had a boyish quality—flyaway eyebrows and a wide smile. I thought I would like him.

"What do you think about all this?" I asked Mo.

"Two dolly girls, two rich old men, two marriages with the much older, very rich men within weeks of each other. I see a pattern. Don't you?"

I saw it.

If Hal Archer's story that Tule had threatened to kill him was true, her motive had to be money. If so, it wasn't a stretch to think that Tule's former roommate Barbie Summers Cooper might have the same idea.

I stood up, gave Mo a hug, and said, "You. Are. Fantastic."

"I know," she said, grinning up at me. "Here's Mr. Cooper's phone number."

I said, "There's going to be a little extra dough in your paycheck, you know."

"Yeah?"

She cupped her hands together, went into a crouch, blew on imaginary dice, and rolled them out onto an invisible craps table. "Baby needs new shoes."

"Baby can get as many shoes as she wants."

"Awww," she said. "Thanks, Jack."

I punched in Cooper's phone number, listened to the line connecting with his lodge on Red Ridge in Aspen. When Cooper answered the phone, I said my name and told him that I was the owner of a private investigation firm in LA.

"Do you have a couple of moments, Mr. Cooper? There's something I'd like to discuss with you."

# Chapter 70

BRYCE COOPER WAS understandably confused by my call.

"What's this about? Who are you?"

I repeated myself, and Cooper said, "I've got time. Nothing but time. I'm waiting for my wife to get dressed. Could be hours."

"Mr. Cooper, do you know Tule Archer?"

"Sure. I know the Archers. I went to their wedding. What about Tule?"

I did my best to tell this bad story clearly and gently.

"Hal Archer is my client, Mr. Cooper, and I'm sorry to tell you that Tule has been murdered and Hal is being held pending his arraignment."

He said, "They think Hal killed Tule? I can't believe what I'm hearing. That's crazy."

I said, "Hal said that Tule was threatening his life."

Cooper said, "He never said anything like that to me."

There was a long silence, then Cooper said, "I'm just dumbfounded. This is going to kill Barbie. She loved Tule. I guess I have to tell her."

"Of course, Mr. Cooper, but I was wondering how you and Barbie were getting along."

"What? Me and Barbie? I guess not too bad. She's a nice girl. A little wild. Aspen is kind of stuffy for a frisky kid like Barbie. But I keep up with her pretty well. Why?"

"Has she ever threatened you, sir?"

"Threatened *me*?"

He stopped right there and I let the silence go on for more time than was comfortable. The longer it stretched, and the farther it got from Cooper shouting, *Are you crazy?*, the more certain I felt that Barbie *had* threatened Cooper. That he was running over things in his mind, unsure how to answer.

"No, she's never threatened me. But I've noticed odd things. Phone calls, coming in and going out, late at night. Uh. She got a gun... Anyway, why am I telling you this? I don't even know you. And if you're looking for work, forget it. Don't call me again, Morgan."

"Mr. Cooper. Sir. Watch out for yourself. I think your wife might try to kill you."

Cooper hung up, and so did I. I didn't feel that I'd done anything more than scare him. Or maybe I'd gotten Cooper crazy enough to harm his wife in "self-defense."

Now I was worried about two people I didn't know.

# Chapter 71

SCI WAS STANDING at the tall desk in his office, transparent flex screens forming a semicircular shield in front of him. He was engrossed in the new info about the car bombs—the death of teen star Maeve Wilkinson had finally ignited the LAPD.

Sci understood the value of reciprocity. He had made friends and acquired contacts during his six years at the city's lab, and now, he and the city shared information selectively.

Ten minutes ago, Kelli Preston, head of the city lab's arson division, forwarded him reports on a firebombed Dodge Charger that might be connected to Jack's Lamborghini as well as to the Aston Martin and the other five cars.

Preston thought that the Charger was very

likely the first in the series, possibly the learning model.

The photo on Sci's center screen showed the blackened Charger chassis with its signature split-crosshair grille that had somehow survived incineration. The scene was a Ralphs supermarket parking lot, and the time of the explosion was 2:23 in the a.m.

The city's deputy arson investigator had concluded that the fire was started under the left front side of the undercarriage and that there was a chemical explosive in the gas tank, a substance that the LAPD database didn't recognize.

Preston's note to Sci said *Off the record, the LAPD closed the case on this because it was random and no one was hurt. The owner of the vehicle collected his insurance payout, and Allstate didn't raise any questions.*

Preston told Sci that the LAPD investigated the next four firebombs, but it had been a back-burner case until Maeve Wilkinson died.

Preston wrote, *Let me know if you find anything that could help us, Sci. I'll do the same for you.*

Sci sent Preston a reply, then looked again at the report from the chemical screen of the Charger's gas tank. He knew that the explosive was the same unnamed chemical he'd found in Jack's Lambo. The vehicle had been registered to Peter Tong, a science teacher at a very tony private school: Our Lady of the Pacific.

Sci fed Tong's name into his browser and got a hit on RateMyTeacher.com. This was a website students used to flame their teachers and occasionally praise them.

Peter Tong had about twenty reviews, and most of them were vile, defamatory, and anonymous.

Tong was described as a "diabolical hard-ass who liked to flunk kids just because." Another student complained that Tong was "a sadist who did unnecessary experiments on lab animals and insects. In fact, he calls us 'the insect population.' "

Sci knew that arsonists had various motivations: rage, revenge, the thrill, and, of course, the insurance money. He organized the Tong data into a single file and included it in his note to Justine.

*Justine, see attached. Also, Tong collected ten grand in insurance money. We could be looking at a killer. Be careful.*

# Chapter 72

JUST BELOW THE edge of the highway, waves charged into rocks and exploded into foam. Sunshine beat down on the asphalt, making the air shimmer. You could almost see across the ocean to Japan, the day was that clear and brilliant. Justine barely noticed.

As Scotty drove the fleet car, Justine used her phone to confirm their appointment at Our Lady of the Pacific High School. They would be questioning Mr. Peter Tong, the head of the science department, a man Father Brooks had described as ordinary with "nothing radical or Fringe Division" about him.

Justine was pretty sure that the headmaster was wrong.

Tong's car had been firebombed, and the

explosive was an unknown chemical that had been packed into a condom, stuffed into the gas tank, and set off with a time-delay incendiary charge.

Peter Tong was a chemist, a science teacher who worked in the same general location as the bombed cars. One of those cars was his.

Was he a victim? Or, as Sci suspected, a serial arsonist who had just made a fatal error?

Justine replied to the text from Mr. Tong, saying they would be arriving within the next ten minutes, then put her phone away.

Scotty said, "So, tell me about your interview with John Leonard Orr."

"Mmm. Okay. Well, it was about ten years ago. I had just started working at the Santa Monica psychiatric facility," Justine said. "I asked to see Orr, and he said okay."

"So, what was he like?"

Justine told Scotty all she knew. That John Orr had been a fire chief in Glendale, California, during a very long and devastating spate of fires that over the course of nine years had consumed sixty-five homes, acres of woodlands, and numerous retail stores and had killed four people, one of them a three-year-old boy.

Orr used a dirt-cheap and ridiculously simple

time-delay incendiary device so that by the time the fire blazed, he was long gone. Often he had gone to another fire just a few miles down the road, where he assumed his job as fire chief, an excellent cover, a brilliant alibi.

After literally *thousands* of fires, Orr's fingerprint was lifted from one of his time-delay devices, and that's how he was convicted and imprisoned for life plus twenty.

Justine said to Scotty, "When I met him, I was a kid with a PhD and a new job. He's a psychopath. I got nothing out of him except what he wanted me to believe: that he had been a terrific public servant and that he'd been framed. You know what, Scotty? Even in an orange jumpsuit and cuffs, he looked very nice, very ordinary."

"Why is it that psychos can be so beguiling?"

"Because there's a big hole in their brains where most people have a conscience. Orr doesn't give a crap about the damage to life and property he caused."

"Do serial arsonists always work alone?"

"No. Not always."

Scotty pulled the car into the teachers' lot, set the brake, and said, "Those reviews on Tong. While most of the kids who rated him hated him, he has some fans, maybe even acolytes. We don't know how many people were involved in setting those firebombs, but two at least, right, Justine? One to drive the car, one to jimmy the tank door open, stuff in the explosive, and set the device."

"Yes. Scotty, you read the review on Tong from the kid who calls himself Zero Sum?"

"Yeah," Scotty said. " 'Tong is very dark and powerful in a great and exciting way.' "

"Let's see if Mr. Tong lives up to his reviews," said Justine.

# Chapter 73

JUSTINE AND SCOTTY knocked and entered Mr. Tong's classroom, a laboratory with windows in the back wall giving a view of the upslope of the canyon.

A long desk was centered between the windows, and on both sides of the desk were floor-to-ceiling shelves lined with hundreds of jars of preserved animals and body parts.

Between the desk and where Justine and Scotty stood in the doorway were two dozen spanking-new workstations outfitted with cutting-edge microscopes and computers. Three chrome carts packed with cages of white mice were randomly parked like shopping carts in a supermarket lot.

The whole operation was impressive, and Justine thought it spoke of high tuition, generous

297

alumni support, and a faculty that wanted only the best so as to attract the best.

A man sat on a stool at the back of the lab, his head bent over a gas chromatograph/mass spectrometer, a pricey piece of forensic equipment used for trace analysis and not usually found in high-school labs.

Justine called out, "Hello, Mr. Tong?" and the man working at the GC/MS turned around.

He was Asian, of medium height and build, wearing a tight white T-shirt, black jeans, and neon-green track shoes. He wore his hair in a brush cut, and his thick glasses had red plastic frames. He had a wide and electrifying smile.

Tong bounced off his stool, stepped forward with his hand outstretched, and introduced himself to Justine and Scotty.

"I'm very glad to meet you."

"Good to meet you too," said Justine. "Thanks for offering to help."

"I will if I can."

Tong led Scotty and Justine to his desk, brought over some stools, and said, "I understand you're interested in this rash of car bombings. I was victim number one, you know. I gave the police names of people to interrogate. They refused to do it."

Scotty asked, "Why do you think they refused?"

"I told them that the arsonists were kids," Tong said, "but I had no proof."

"You had some reason to believe what you told the cops?"

"Sure. As a group, the kids here are overeducated and undercivilized. But they *are* smart. They function at college level, even in the ninth grade. They seem angelic, but they're fearless. And they don't respect authority. Not at all."

Tong polished his glasses, repositioned them on the bridge of his nose, and went on. "Add their rich parents to the mix, and you can see that the school must have kept everything quiet. Look, no one died, so no one cared—until now."

Justine averted her eyes from quart jars of assorted eyeballs. She said to Tong, "See, what worries me is that arsonists escalate."

"Dr. Smith, that worries me too. I've blown the whistle and I have rung the bell. The headmaster and the board have told me to shut the hell up or get out. If I'm blacklisted by the headmaster, I can't get another job in LA. Maybe I can't get another job anywhere."

"We're private investigators," Scotty said. "Private."

Tong nodded. He opened his desk drawer, took out a small notebook, flipped through it. Then he pulled a page out of the binding and handed it to Scotty.

It was a handwritten list of names.

"Please keep me out of this," said Tong. "One of these insects set fire to my car. Next time, they could set fire to *me*."

# Chapter 74

JUSTINE PHONED CHARLES Boyd Jr., the first name on Peter Tong's alphabetically organized suspect list. Boyd was seventeen, an A student, in the honor society, a math wonk. Tong had added a note next to the boy's name: *A vicious little centipede. A tease. A plotter. A bully. Smart, but also dumb. His parents donated three million—yes, three followed by six zeros—to the gym-renovation fund. They own strip malls.*

The Boyd residence on Malibu Road was an impeccable, many-windowed modern beach house with an unobstructed view of the Pacific. The front gates opened for Scotty and Justine's fleet car, and Scotty parked on the gravel near the entrance of the house.

Boyd had told Justine to just come in, and in

fact, after ringing the bell a number of times, Scotty realized that the door was open.

The two investigators stood in the foyer taking in the drama of waves crashing ahead of them, right outside the living-room windows. Scotty said, "I've actually never seen anything like this. I don't ever want to leave. In fact, I think I could live here and no one would even know."

Justine laughed. It *was* breathtaking. It was as if there were no walls, just white sofas and exotic animal skins on shining hardwood floors that led out to a pool, a deck, and then the beach. The anthemic sounds of Florence and the Machine singing "Never Let Me Go" pounded over expensive, unseen speakers.

"Um. Let's follow the music," Justine said.

Following the music took Justine and Scotty through many splendid rooms, all of them empty until they reached the second floor and what was likely a bedroom. The music was turned to "deafening." The walls vibrated.

Justine knocked on the door, calling, "Charles, it's Dr. Smith." But her voice was overwhelmed by the music. So Scotty beat on the door with the heels of his palms and yelled, "Charles, *open the damned door.*"

Florence and the Machine cooled their jets, and the door cracked open, releasing the heady aroma of pot.

Justine said, "Charles, I'm Dr. Smith. I called you, remember?"

The kid's face was slack, his pupils the size of Frisbees in bloodshot eyes. He wore a stained school T-shirt and red plaid boxers. His room was a rich kid's playpen, decorated by a pro and equipped with every favorite accessory of a teenage boy.

"Welcome to my abode," Charles Boyd said, making a dramatic bow.

Behind him, a teenage girl wearing only sheer black panties laughed.

# Chapter 75

THE TEENAGE GIRL sprawled across the California king. She was thin, with translucent skin and dark, messy hair. She raised herself on one elbow, looked sleepily in the direction of the open door, said, "Could you...turn up the music?"

The two kids were drinking *and* stoned, but still awake.

Justine crossed the room, opened all of the windows. Then she went to the side of the bed, picked up a cotton pullover and a pair of jeans from the floor, said to the girlfriend, "What's your name?"

"Jess. Ica."

"Jessica, put these on, please."

"But. I just took them off."

Charles Boyd lurched toward the bed and took a menacing stance between the girl and Justine.

"Leave her *alone,* " he said.

Justine gave Boyd a little shove. He lost his balance and toppled sideways onto the mattress. The teens giggled, clutched at each other, and rolled around, ignoring Justine and Scotty entirely.

Scotty said, "Are you guys insane?"

He picked up an open bottle from the floor, capped it with his thumb, shook it up, then showered the kids with beer.

The girl shouted, *"Hey. What? Are you doing?"*

Scotty plucked a blanket from the floor and tossed it at the girl, saying, "Cover up." Then he brought a chair over to the foot of the bed and sat down.

"We're not the police," said Scotty. "We're private investigators. If you help us, we're gone. If you don't help us, we'll call the cops, who will charge you with possession. Then they'll interrogate you for three days until they get everything they need to charge you with murder."

Scotty had taken a direct approach, riskier than befriending the kids and teasing it out of them, but it was a safe bet that they'd never been confronted by law enforcement before. Justine thought Scotty's method might work.

Justine said, "I'd listen to Investigator Scott,

Charles. If you play this the wrong way, your life—all of this—will be over. Understand?"

"No," Boyd said.

Scotty said, "No?"

Scotty pulled his cell phone out of his back hip pocket, started tapping in numbers. Boyd rolled onto his back. He said, "I plan on going to Northwestern next year."

"That depends on what you do in the next five minutes," said Scotty.

# Chapter 76

WHILE SCOTTY WORKED on Charles Boyd Jr., Justine stepped over to the dresser and took a good look at a metal cash box made of burnished steel, about ten by twelve and about six inches deep.

There was a combination lock showing 000. Justine raised the lid and saw a neat row of snack-size baggies filled with white powder, an opened box of Pleasure Plus condoms, and a small metal gizmo, like a mousetrap, that looked to be a remote-controlled detonator.

"Uh-oh, Charles," she said. "I don't think this looks good for you." She opened her phone, took a few shots of the makings of a car bomb, took a few more that showed the placement of the box on the dresser, kids on the bed in the background.

"I'm just *holding* that stuff," Boyd shouted. *"I'm not in charge."*

Jessica pulled the blanket up to her chin. "We're the good guys," she said angrily. "Who cares about those cars? It's a crime that they even exist. I mean, two-hundred-thousand-dollar cars that get eight miles to the gallon? You've gotta be kidding." The girl fluffed her pillow.

Justine had treated enough teens to know that their brains weren't fully formed. They lacked foresight. They didn't understand consequences. They thought things were cool that were felonious, dangerous, deadly.

In many ways, teens were still children, which was why the police couldn't interrogate underage kids without permission from their parents.

Private wasn't the police.

Scotty said, "Charles. You're losing the advantage of getting ahead of this thing. Right now, we have time to get to whoever *is* in charge. Otherwise, well, I know what my partner is thinking. The smoking gun is right here, in your possession, with your fingerprints. So what are we going to do, buddy?"

Boyd bolted off the bed, angry, blustering, chest out, hands curled into fists. Justine read his posturing as meaning that *he* was the victim here, and he wasn't going to accept this.

"Mr. Tong sent you, right?" Boyd spat. "He's a fucking douche. Zero Sum worked out the mechanics and we executed the plan, okay? We killed Mr. Tong's *car*. Are you *gone* yet?"

Justine said, kindly, "Did you kill all of them? The Bentley, the Lambo, etcetera. The Aston Martin?"

"Zero Sum did the last one solo. I was driving. But we didn't know anyone was inside that car. It was an *accident*."

"That's what you should say," Justine said approvingly. "Say that it was an accident."

Charles Boyd ignored her, but he was afraid of Scotty.

He said, "Look, don't tell my parents. I'll tell you who Zero Sum is and where he lives. He'll straighten you out. He'll tell you who the bad guys *really* are."

# Chapter 77

AS THEY LEFT the Boyd house, Justine said to Scotty, "Want to bet Charles is giving Zero Sum a heads-up right now?"

"It's okay. We're only five or six minutes away."

Justine dialed chief of police Mickey Fescoe's cell phone. A woman's voice was on the recording, Mickey's assistant saying he was away for the weekend and to leave a message.

"Mickey, it's Justine Smith. We found two of the kids involved in the serial car bombings and they have information about the Wilkinsons' car." Justine gave the name and address, then said, "You're going to need a warrant to search the house for explosives."

She forwarded the photos of Charles Boyd's bomb kit to Fescoe's mailbox.

"I hope he gets the message," she said. "Soon."

She and Scotty got into their car, pulled onto the highway, and headed for the house where Ken Capshaw, aka Zero Sum, lived with his parents in Encinal Bluffs. Capshaw was second on Tong's suspect list, and she read the note Tong had written next to the name out loud to Scotty.

"'Capshaw is a charismatic cockroach, anti-establishment and philosophically destructive. Not as bright as he thinks he is. His clueless parents travel on business. A lot.'"

Scotty grunted, stepped on the gas. They were going about seventy, but still, Justine felt the pressure of passing time. If Boyd alerted Capshaw, and if Capshaw was smart, he would immediately get behind a wall of parents and lawyers. He might leave the country.

As Scotty drove the car up the coast, Justine sent an e-mail to Dr. Sci, attaching the photos of the bomb kit. A minute later, her phone rang.

It was Sci.

"Justine. Where are you?"

"In the car with Scotty."

"Something has happened. I'm sending you a link to a video. Open it now. It's going viral as we speak."

Sirens sounded behind their fleet car, then police cars loomed in the rear window. Scotty pulled onto the shoulder and slowed as three cop cars sped past.

Justine picked up her iPad and opened the link from Sci, which took her to YouTube. She watched for a couple of seconds, then hit Pause.

She said, "Scotty. Capshaw just posted a video. Stop the car."

# Chapter 78

THE VIDEO HAD been shot in a garage, the camera angled at the BMW convertible with its top down. The kid in the driver's seat looked to be in his late teens, had a narrow, intelligent face, curly brown hair, wore denim and glasses with wire rims.

He drank from a plastic water bottle, then looked into the camera and said, "I'm Ken Capshaw and you should listen to what I have to say. You won't want to hear it, but which would you rather have, romance or the truth? This is the truth."

The kid turned away, wiped his lips with his sleeve. It looked to Justine as though he was both nervous and detached, and in her estimation, that was a bad combination.

Capshaw turned back to the camera and said, "As I speak, the world is coming to an end and it's because of us. We've ruined the planet in the last hundred and fifty years. Thank the combustion engine for that.

"We've enslaved ourselves to fossil fuel, and so we've poisoned the air and we've polluted our waters and we've taken objects like this petroleum artifact"—he waggled the bottle—"and thrown millions of them into the oceans and landfills where they will stay intact for a thousand years.

"It's all corrupt. The banks, the church, politics, corporations, the earth, the air, and the water we've ruined with our poisons and gases. And there is no sign of reversing this trend. No sign of redemption.

"You see where this is going? Do you have an exit strategy? I've warned you on my blog, and I tried to demonstrate the pernicious nature of greed by torching a few cars. But I didn't plan to kill someone.

"That was a mistake and I'm sorry. At the same time . . . at the same time, no one here gets out alive. Not even me."

Justine yelled at the image on her iPad, "*Jesus Christ. Noooo.*"

Justine and Scotty saw Capshaw take a cell phone from the top of the dashboard, type in a few numbers. There was a soft *boom,* the sound of something igniting.

Scotty bellowed at Capshaw's image, *"Get out. Get out of the car."*

Capshaw rose up in his seat. Justine saw the heavy chains around his waist, probably looped and locked around the steering-wheel column. Flames leaped around the sides of the car and then reached out to Capshaw, lighting up his clothes and hair. The boy screamed wordlessly, writhed in an agonized dance.

The bomb turned the picture a staticky white.

Justine threw her tablet down on the seat. She put her palms over her eyes. "Oh my *God.* Oh my *God.* I've never seen anything like that in my life," she said. "And now everyone in the world will see it. Every kid in the world."

Her cheeks were wet, and her hands were shaking when she called Jack.

# PART FOUR

# UNDERCOVER OPERATIONS

# Chapter 79

I WAS ON the phone with Justine when Mo-bot danced into my office. I signaled to her to sit down, told Justine that I was sorry, that she and Scotty should come back to the office.

I was shocked by Capshaw's suicide, rocked by how shit just happened. It didn't require global events or an evil twin. Just a single, unintended event—in this case, that Capshaw hadn't first looked to see if someone was passed out in the backseat of a car before he decided to fire up his protest.

It was terrible to imagine what Capshaw had been thinking when he chained himself to his steering wheel so that he couldn't change his mind at the last minute. His screen name, Zero Sum, referred to a game or an interaction where if one

319

side won, the other lost by an equivalent amount, equaling zero.

So Capshaw took his own life to balance the loss of Maeve Wilkinson's. And now, two teenagers were dead. Both deaths were regrettable.

I said to Mo-bot, "The car bomber confessed. Then he blew himself up on streaming video."

"What? No."

"It was...horrific."

I thought about my brother, that he'd had nothing to do with torching my car. But even if I was paranoid, I couldn't shake the feeling. I would still bet an arm and a leg that Tommy was planning to hurt me.

I asked Mo what brought her into the office on a weekend and she told me that she'd been doing some work for our client Hal Archer, looking into Tule's history to see if she could find anything that might help with Hal's defense.

"I uncovered this guy," she said, showing me a photo on her iPhone of a man in his early twenties with bland, unremarkable features. He could have been a corporate CEO or a serial killer or the driver of a delivery van.

Mo-bot said, "This is Lester Olsen. He graduated from MIT with a four-point-eight GPA. He has a degree in engineering, but instead of going into industry, he went to the land of no clocks and fast money."

"He counts cards in Vegas?"

Mo-bot grinned, said, "Very good, Jack," then went on. "He made a few million at poker by the time he was twenty-three, then, one dark night, the LVMPD found him unconscious in an alley with ten broken fingers and the ace of spades in his shirt breast pocket. There was some writing on the card: 'This is your last hand.'

"So, the reason I'm telling you about this guy is that after his poker career ended, he still showed up in the casinos. Lost money at craps, but he was friendly with the showgirls. And he started a new business. He became a kind of consultant. Teaching girls how to marry a billionaire."

I said, "And you're thinking Hal's a billionaire who married a Vegas showgirl who'd been trained to catch him?"

My assistant, Val Kenney, came in with my Red Bull, said, "You can learn how to marry a billionaire? I have to hear this."

I asked Val to stay and asked Mo to go on.

Mo said, "Okay, so, Lester Olsen charges ten thousand dollars for the six-week course, classroom version. But he's got a higher-end course, more exclusive, no rates mentioned. His advertising promises 'You will marry a wealthy man. Money-back guarantee.'

"So I burrowed into Tule's phone logs," Mo said. "I found that Olsen called Tule five times a week for about three months before she married Hal and he kept calling her throughout her marriage, including the day she died. And what do you know? Mr. Olsen had been calling Barbie Summers Cooper too, same time frame and frequency. He's still calling her."

Val asked, "Why is he calling these women *after* the wedding?"

"Maybe he's on retainer," I said. "Maybe he gets a percentage of the take?"

"Wouldn't you like to know?" Val said. "I mean, really, Jack. What were Tule and Olsen doing after the nuptials? What are Barbie Cooper and Olsen up to now?"

"What are you thinking, Val?"

"I should go undercover. I should sign up for Olsen's high-end course and let him coach me. See what I can find out. I'm single. I'm primed for this. If Mo-bot can give me a fake history, how is this not doable?"

Val was ambitious and she was smart. I had 100 percent confidence in her.

"Okay," I said. "You and Mo work out the details."

# Chapter 80

GOZAN REMARI HAD fallen hard for Rodeo Drive, but the Grove put Rodeo in the shade. This outdoor mall was delicious and ostentatious in the unique American way that he both loved and abhorred.

Mostly, he loved it: the wide avenue lined with excellent shops and restaurants, the electric trolley that zipped up and down between First Street and the Grove and the Farmers' Market, taking tourists through this sugarcoated Disneyland of excess.

And then, at the center of everything, there was *this*.

Gozan stood in front of the dancing fountain, watching it shoot up jets of water in time to one of Frank Sinatra's greatest hits. He couldn't keep himself from singing along: " 'The summer wind came blowing in from across the sea.' "

Someone put a hand on Gozan's shoulder, and he jerked around. Khezir was calling his name, breaking into his thoughts.

"Don't leave me by myself with them," Khezzy said, reminding Gozan that they were not alone.

The three men from Ra Galiz, standing with their hands behind their backs, were not amused by the many delights of the Grove. To them, the mall was obscene, but it was also a noisy backdrop for a meeting, a place where they would not be noticed.

They were here to issue directives and warnings to Khezir and they had given Gozan an actual headache, right at the top of his head. They didn't understand Khezzy. Talking to him as if he were slow only angered his nephew and would make him defiant.

Gozan turned his back on the incredible fountain and joined the men strolling along the street. He was thinking that there could not be a more bizarre collection of people than the five of them walking together in sports jackets among the waves of visitors in shorts and flip-flops and floaty summer dresses.

He assumed a studious expression. He walked, listened, interjected a patriotic comment every now and then, but he was also watching the women who were everywhere, shopping and smiling and showing themselves off.

He caught the eye of a lovely, plump woman who was dallying in the doorway of Nordstrom, and she returned his look, boldly. She was with a friend. Blondes, both of them. Out here, they were almost always blond.

Gozan had spent a long week with Khezzy at Shutters, keeping a low profile, as they'd had to do. But now he was hungry for the touch of a woman. He'd heard an American expression that he found hilarious: *chubby chaser*. He wanted to say it to Khezzy right now, because it made both of them laugh.

Gozan interrupted the top man of the Ra Galiz unit, said, quietly, "I think this is a good time for us to part company, Balar. Good to see you again." He shook the man's hand. "We'll be in touch. Khezzy. Come have lunch with me."

Khezir gladly fell into step with his uncle, who said, "There is a time to discuss politics and a time to be chubby chasers."

Khezzy started laughing and he kept at it until tears came into his eyes. Gozan turned back before the crowd swallowed them up, called to the men in black, "See you. Have a nice day."

Then he forgot them. He and Khezir back-tracked toward Nordstrom. Gozan hoped he could find that fleshy woman now. The way she had looked at him was promising.

# Chapter 81

VAL KENNEY WAS enjoying the first massage of her life in the spa at the Black Diamond Hotel and Casino in Las Vegas. Not only was this her first massage, her first spa, her first hotel of this magnitude and splendor, but she had never been to Las Vegas before. And what she'd seen of this town in the past four hours had been dazzling.

Too bad there was no one to tell.

Katrina's strong hands rubbed oil into Val's shoulders, and she moaned. This was sooo good, and she was so grateful to Jack for letting her run with her idea.

As of four hours ago, she was no longer Val Kenney of Private Investigations, former scholarship student at Boston and Miami Universities and part-time worker at the Miami PD, typing up files, approving expenses, and keeping the schedule logs.

Mo-bot had given her a different background, one that she was memorizing even now.

Her new name was Valerie Fernandez. Her father was a Cuban-born doctor and her mother was black, a Miami native who taught eighth grade until she died, a year ago.

Valerie Fernandez lived in Los Angeles now, a professional events planner who had created stupendous bachelorette parties for several celebrities and gala affairs for corporate clients.

As her story would go, she was twenty-five, never married, in perfect health. All true.

She would say that both her parents were dead, and that was also true.

In fact, in her real life, before her mother died, she had encouraged Val to interview with Private for a job she had wanted since Jack Morgan gave a guest lecture at her school. Val was pretty sure that if her mom could see her now—an undercover investigator, under the cover of a perfumed sheet, getting a three-hundred-dollar massage—she'd be laughing hard.

Katrina wrapped the sheet entirely around Val, tucking her in so that she was a cocoon of happiness. She rubbed Val's scalp and gently pulled her hair out to the ends. She said, "Miss Fernandez, please just lie still and rest. I'll be back in a few minutes to take you to your mud treatment, okay?"

Val said okay.

She listened to the soft music and went over her new life story in her mind. And she also thought about the $3,480 in wonderful clothes she'd charged to her expense account. Later, she would put on the sexy black jumpsuit and the crystal beads and go to the casino. She'd watch the poker players, maybe feed the slots, but all for research, and she would be in bed by midnight. And when she woke up in her amazing room tomorrow, she'd be rested and ready for her class in how to land a rich husband with Lester Olsen.

Oh, man, she could hardly wait.

Too bad there was no one she could tell.

# Chapter 82

KHEZIR MAZUL WOKE up in the darkened room and for a long moment did not know where he was. Then he remembered checking in to the Armstrong Hotel, a small, half-star place where they could be under the radar for now.

He sat up, saw the tossed bedding, the video game paused on the TV, and the fat girl in bed beside him, still trussed like the pig she was.

He reached over to the night table, grabbed the water glass that still held an inch of flat champagne, and tossed down the dregs. He looked at the clock. It was almost midnight. He fell back in the bed, covered himself with the blankets, and went to sleep.

The next thing he knew, Gozan was shaking his arm, saying, "What did you do to her, Khezzy?"

What did he *do?*

What he always did. He put something in her drink. He played with her for a while, then he passed out. Khezir said to his uncle, "What's wrong?"

Gozan had turned on the bedside lamp. He was wearing an undershirt and nothing else, and his hair was flying everywhere. The skin under his eyes sagged. He looked tired and old, and Khezir had never seen him look so afraid. Not once in his life.

Gozan bent over the girl on the bed, slapped her cheeks lightly, and cooed, "Wake up, please. Wake up."

He pinched her nostrils closed, waited. She sputtered, and then coughed, thrashed her head from side to side, said, "I'm... Don't forget...to take out...the dog."

"She's fine," said Khezir. "She's a sleepyhead. Where's my knife?"

"What do you want with your knife?"

"Cut the wrist ties, of course. Uncle, are you drunk? What is wrong with you?"

"Your knife is in my bathroom. On the floor."

"You took my knife?" Khezir asked.

"No, I did not take your knife. Would I ever take your knife? You left it in there."

"That's crazy," Khezir said.

He got out of the bed, stepped into his shorts, and walked into Gozan's bathroom, where he found the woman on the floor, blood soaking into the cream-colored bath mat and staining her yellow hair.

He stared at her. Her name was Margot or Margaret or something, the peachy woman his uncle had talked into coming back with them. Her neck was cut. He liked to do that, but lightly, sex play. Not like this, her head almost separated from her body. Yes, he had cut off heads, but not in *play*.

His knife, the one with the black stone handle and the serrated blade, was next to her.

"I didn't do this," Khezir said, looking at his uncle.

Gozan said, "Well, I didn't do it. I don't even know if I fucked her. I think I showered. My hair is wet in the back."

Khezir stared. He had bought the bottles himself at the liquor store. He had opened the bottles and poured the drinks into the glasses. He had put in the pills himself.

Had his uncle drunk from the wrong glass? Had *he*?

"The door is locked," Khezir said. "One of us

did it, but it doesn't matter. You call them. I'll shower and dress. Don't worry, Uncle."

Gozan found his mobile phone and forced himself to make the call.

"Balar," he said. "We have a problem. It was a mistake, but someone is dead."

# Chapter 83

GOZAN WENT TO the door of their shabby room at the Armstrong Hotel and looked through the peephole. He opened the door for Balar Aram and his crew, who came in, moved through the suite like smoke, looked right through Gozan.

Gozan called out, "Balar, she's in there."

Balar went into the master bathroom, saw the dead woman lying nearly decapitated on a lake of blood on the floor. Balar's eyes passed over the corpse. Then he went into the adjoining room, where the other girl was lying on the bed, her arms tied behind her back. Passed out cold.

Balar pulled the window drapes closed.

He said to Gozan in Sumarin, "This is not a holiday, stupid. This is work. And now you and your demented nephew have gone too far. Yes, Kheziralar. I mean you."

Gozan said, "I told you that this was a mistake."

Balar entered the smaller, second bath, yanked the shower curtain from the rod, spread it on the floor. He told Khezir to help him move the girl from his bed to the bathroom floor, and when she was lying on the plastic curtain, Balar took a gun from his inside jacket pocket. He screwed the suppressor onto the muzzle and shot her once in the head, twice in the chest.

*Fffut, ffut, ffut.*

Gozan felt his own blood leave him. It was as if the lights were flickering. He wasn't a crazy man. He wasn't evil. He didn't want these women to die.

Balar was saying, "Gozan, put on your shoes."

Gozan got into the small elevator with Balar, stood next to him, smelled what the man had eaten for dinner, and tried not to panic or get sick. He kept his eyes on the café menu on the panel above the buttons and asked no questions, because he knew none would be answered.

The car bumped to a stop. Gozan and Balar got out and walked toward the reception desk, where a stout middle-aged woman in a hotel uniform put down the phone and smiled.

"Good evening, gentlemen. How may I help you?"

The woman's name tag read *L. Bird*.

Balar said, "Miss Bird, my name is Colonel Balar Aram, I am from the Sumar mission to the United States." He spoke quickly and with a heavy accent.

"Oh," said the desk clerk. She looked at the ID the man presented.

Balar said, "Your guests Mr. Remari and Mr. Mazul are of the royal family of Sumar, and their lives are in imminent danger. I must take them out by the service elevator. Do you understand? No one can use the elevator until we are gone. You have the credit card imprint?"

"For Mr. Remari? Yes, absolutely."

"Consider this express checkout."

"Absolutely," the woman said again. She gave Balar the key to the service elevator and directions to the alley behind the hotel, and he gave the woman a hundred dollars.

Gozan sat with Khezir in the rear of the SUV as the Black Guard cleaned the room, removed the bodies through the back door, then returned to the reception area, where they destroyed the computer at the front desk and ripped out the surveillance camera. He could hear the muzzle fire through the glass when they shot the clerk.

Khezir said, "I hear sirens. Do you hear them?"

It was about two o'clock in the morning. Gozan wasn't sure he and Khezzy were going to see the sun come up. Since its socialist revolution in the 1950s, Sumar had been a secular state. But if Gozan had believed in a God, now would have been the time to pray.

Instead, he just said to his nephew, "Don't worry, Khezzy. Balar is taking care of us. We will be okay."

# Chapter 84

IT WAS EVENING in Aspen: birds calling out to one another, nice smell of evergreens and meadow grass in the air, no traffic on Ridge Road.

Christian Scott thought he was going to like his new assignment.

He was parked on the side of the road behind a clump of conifers, tracking Bryce and Barbie Cooper so he could warn Bryce if he saw he was about to get murdered. Jack felt he owed it to Hal Archer to get leverage that might knock some time off Archer's inevitable life sentence, so he'd sent Scotty.

With the help of Private's intelligence division, Scotty had gotten into the Coopers' enormous house, planted bugs, cloned Barbie's phone, and when their chauffeured Rolls-Royce Silver Cloud pulled onto Ridge Road heading south, Scotty knew where the couple was going.

In a little while, Robert Redford, superstar and environmentalist, would be showing his film *Watershed* at a benefit to save the Colorado River held at the summer home of publishing magnate Jean-Claude Dressler.

Scotty followed the Rolls as his laptop read out details about Dressler's forty-million-dollar home, the forty thousand square feet of glass, mahogany, and limestone in the style of Tuscany circa the eighteenth century.

Scotty was wondering how all this luxury squared with preserving the environment when he saw the compound up ahead: several gabled stone buildings with tall windows giving views across the entire Owl Creek Valley.

Scotty followed the Rolls over a bridge spanning a stream and onto the cropped lawn serving as a parking area, and the valet waved him in. Scotty got out of his car, put on his shades, rolled up the sleeves of his good-to-go-anywhere Armani jacket, and texted Mo-bot. He told her not to worry. "No one plays boring white guy like me," he said.

"As long as you don't dance," she quipped back.

Up ahead, Barbie Cooper gripped the crook of her husband's arm as she wobbled toward the house, her heels poking holes in the lawn.

Barbie filled out her small silver dress in a wonderful way, and she looked up into Bryce's face with adoration. When her wrinkly husband leaned down for a kiss, she made it *good,* pressing her supersize chest into his, putting her hand to his cheek, laying it on him for all she was worth. Which, according to the numbers they'd cranked out at Private, was half a billion dollars if he died, far less if they divorced.

That big, full-body smooch looked weird and gross and made Scotty pretty sure that Barbie Cooper wasn't looking to get divorced. Scotty felt very bad for the old man.

He started walking, caught up to the Coopers at the entrance to the Dressler manse, stuck out his hand, and said, "Bryce, I'm Chris Scofield, Scofield Systems. Oakland."

Bryce looked understandably perplexed.

"I uh, I don't quite remember..."

"That's okay. There were a lot of us there when we had lunch at Donald Ross last year. And you must be Barbie."

Barbie gave Scotty an appreciative look, patted

341

him down with her eyes. Then she said, "Scofield Systems. Is that computers, Chris?"

Still chatting with the Coopers, Scotty gave his fake name to security, and thanks to Mo-bot's superior hacking skills, Chris Scofield was on the digital guest list with a star next to his name, meaning "big donor." And as he was also engaged in conversation with Bryce and Barbie Cooper, well known in Aspen society, Scotty entered the private enclave without questions.

Now, all he had to do was stay close enough to Bryce Cooper to make sure that his cute little wife didn't kill him.

# Chapter 85

VAL KENNEY ENTERED Las Vegas's famed City Center, determined not to be awed by this glittering constellation of resorts, hotels, high-end retail shops, and million-dollar condos, all of it a monument to greed and excess.

Val had grown up poor, the child of a working single mom, and they'd lived with Grandma in Liberty City, a black 'hood in Miami. She had nothing against money. It provided necessities and comfort and also the means to help those in need, and that she loved. But Val's ambitions didn't run to amassing wealth. She wanted to raise her own bar, do good and achieve big things.

That's why she was here.

Olsen taught his how-to-catch-a-rich-husband class in his condo in Veer Towers, the residential complex composed of two buildings, each thirty-seven floors of modern luxury encased in glass and golden panels, their tops craning outward, so that neither building would interfere with the other's view of the Las Vegas cityscape.

Val took the escalator to the main floor of the North Tower, traveling up through a vast, futuristic lobby that made her feel as though she'd been living in a cave until today, when she had somehow stepped into the twenty-second century.

She told herself to get a grip.

She looked like she belonged, dressed to impress in a brilliant cherry-red-and-white print Rachel Roy dress that skimmed her curves without hiding them, the hem ending just above her knees. Her black shoes were pointy toed with three-inch heels, which would make her the tallest woman in almost any room.

As she headed toward the elevator bank, Val had an unexpected flash of fear. In a few moments, she would be entering Lester Olsen's home with a wireless microphone nestled in her cleavage, a digital recorder in her handbag. And then she was going to lie her face off.

Would she get away with *that*? Really?

Val remembered the last thing Jack had said to

her before she left LA; "I have one hundred percent confidence in you, Val. But if you become afraid for your safety at any time, get the hell out. Okay? Get the hell out and call me."

"Okay," she had said. "I'm going to be fine. And thanks for having faith in me."

No question. She had faith in *Jack*. And she would not disappoint him.

# Chapter 86

THE ELEVATOR WHISPERED Val upward, and twenty-seven floors later, the doors opened into a private foyer facing a closed mahogany door. Val tapped numbers onto a keypad beside the door, and a female voice asked her name.

"Valerie Fernandez."

A buzzer sounded and the lock clicked and Val pushed open the door, stepped into both her false identity and an astonishing room. It was elegantly furnished in white leather and steel with marble floors and modern artwork, and a great wall of windows admitted all of the light in the sky.

A very fit woman in a smart geometric-print dress, her blond hair pulled up in a ponytail, crossed the room, shook Val's hand, and said, "Hi, Valerie. I'm Norma Tiefel. I work with Mr. Olsen.

Would you please fill out this form? I'll be back in five minutes."

Val took the clipboard and went to one of the handsome steel-frame-and-white-leather sofas with an unobstructed view of the gambling capital of the world.

A silver pen with her name etched on its side rested at the top of the clipboard. Val had to smile at the pricey party favor. She used the pen to complete the form with her phony background, addresses, career history, and net worth, which she listed at $294,000, including the value of her fictitious condo in LA with its $210,000 mortgage.

She was a young woman on the way up, right?

As she answered the questions with a straight face, three other women came in, one at a time, and took seats around the room. They were all attractive, all in their twenties, and all, apparently, had ten thousand dollars to give Mr. Olsen for the secrets to marrying up. Waaaaaaay up.

Back to the questionnaire. Val checked off boxes for the traits she most looked for in a husband, writing, *I would be a great asset to a wealthy man: a social companion and intellectual peer in the form of a loving and attractive wife.*

Ms. Tiefel collected the forms and left the room.

The four women waited, made small talk, wondered if there would be an elimination round. And then, long, tense moments later, the door opened again and Ms. Tiefel came back into the room with a good-looking man in his midthirties. He was beautifully dressed in summer-weight wool, a blue jacket, gray pants. He had a clear, almost luminous complexion and remarkable long-lashed, copper-brown eyes. The one-word description that jumped into Val's mind was *winner*.

Olsen clasped his hands together and Val saw that his fingers were twisted from the breaks he'd sustained. They still looked painful, but there was no pain on his face. Ms. Tiefel said, "Ladies, I'd like you to meet a man who changed my life, Mr. Lester Olsen."

Olsen smiled, then addressed the small group.

"It's my pleasure to welcome you all to Love for Life and a day that could entirely transform your future. Please come with me. It all starts now."

# Chapter 87

VAL WATCHED LESTER Olsen swivel in a white leather chair, the panoramic view of Las Vegas fanning out behind him, a golden backdrop that suggested endless marital possibilities.

He put his hands on his knees, leaned slightly forward, and said, "You've all heard that it's just as easy to love a rich man as it is to love a poor one, and, ladies, that just isn't true. It's *easier* to love a rich man. *Much* easier.

"Love and marriage—any marriage—takes work, but being the wife of a wealthy man is work with multimillion-dollar benefits. I'm talking about priceless jewelry, classic cars, private jets, and incredible yachts. The exceptional world of the very rich includes invitations to the White House, club memberships and box seats, staffs of helpers in every home, and first-class travel to any event in the world. The wife of a multimillionaire has access to the best of everything the world has to offer.

"The very best of *everything,* " Olsen said, letting the idea have the floor. "You can have that.

"But it takes work to land your own dear Mr. Megabux, and it takes work to keep him happy. Are you ready to go to work, ladies?"

Spontaneous applause broke out, Olsen smiled broadly, and Val thought that this man was a gifted motivational speaker. At the very least.

Olsen said, "Very wealthy men are generally complex and smarter than your average white-collar guy. They can be ego-maniacal. They can be demanding and short-tempered, and, of course, they're always right."

There was appreciative laughter from the ladies. Olsen smiled and went on.

"Guess how many ultra-high-net-worth individuals there are in this country—that is, individuals worth fifty million or more. No, let me tell you. There are one million multi-multimillionaires living right here in the U.S.A.

"Now, there's a catch. Most of these men are married, and nearly all of them are in high demand.

But you can shift the odds in your favor if you know how. And that's why you're here today."

Olsen was beaming with enthusiasm. He told his little group what the course would cover, spoke of elocution, etiquette, relocation, jobs to take, events to attend, how to be a smart learner and a fascinated listener.

He said, "If you do well in this course, the odds are that *one* of you four women will marry a mega-multimillionaire. Or perhaps you'll fall in love with a regular millionaire, but you will find money and love for life. There's even a chance that *all* of you will be wearing thirty-carat diamond rings by the end of this year."

Val saw that the women sitting around her were smiling, almost purring, *Uh-huh, uh-huh*, as Lester Olsen stirred their fantasies of wealth beyond imagining.

Val wanted to make sure her mic was still in place and that her machine was still recording, but she forced herself to keep her hands still and look eager as Olsen said, "Say good-bye to Target and Payless. You have to dress well, and go where the wealthy men are." Olsen smiled at Leila, Angie, Krista, and Val. "Rent a studio in the champagne-and-caviar section of town, or simply shop there.

Be seen. Splurge on good seats at sporting events or gate-crash after the ticket takers are gone and have a drink with the guests in the hospitality tent."

Val saw an opportunity to steer the conversation where she wanted it to go.

She said, "Mr. Olsen—"

"Lester, please."

"Lester. You'd still have to be pretty lucky to meet your future husband in the produce aisle. And, actually, wouldn't a wealthy man be more inclined to date someone who was introduced to him by a friend?"

"Well, that's right, Valerie," Olsen said. "And I was just about to make this very point. When you volunteer at a sports match or a political event, you should make friends with women who travel in those circles, women who may know a lonely millionaire looking for love. Seek out the rich old ladies. Flatter them. Befriend them. They love to make matches," he said with a wink. "Even with their married men friends."

He told stories of a former pupil who got a sales job at a Mercedes dealership, and another who met her mega-millionaire at his wife's funeral.

Val took notes, and after homework had been assigned and the other women were leaving, Val said she had some questions, if Lester had a moment to spare.

"You bet," Olsen said. "In fact, Valerie, I was just thinking that you might be interested in a private service I offer to very few students. Hey. Want to talk about this over dinner?"

# Chapter 88

ALIZÉ WAS ON the fifty-sixth floor of the Palms Casino Resort, and their table was right up by the wall of steeply slanted windows. It was like being in the control tower of an airport—or, no, like being in the cockpit of an airliner, looking out onto untold miles of neon lights stretching out to the horizon.

Val had to admit to herself it was the most romantic restaurant she'd ever seen or imagined. Was it possible to get drunk on a glorious view? Delicious food? Amusing company?

Yes. Although she'd also had a good deal of wine.

Lester Olsen was looking at her with a sweet expression, and if she hadn't suspected him of professional predation and exceptional scam artistry, she might have felt attracted to him. How could she not? He had said, "Do you know how beautiful you are? How smart? What poise you have, Valerie? And yet, your vulnerability and your willingness to trust is very appealing. You are a prize. A treasure. I see a tremendous future for you."

She was getting high on his attention alone.

She thanked him, finished all but the last bite of the phyllowrapped pear and Roquefort appetizer, and allowed her wineglass to be refilled. Lester put down his wineglass and got to the heart of his pitch.

"Valerie, you were right when you said today that searching for wealthy men by yourself is hit or miss. What would you say if I told you I could make the kind of introduction that would lead you to the altar with a man who will give you the life you deserve? And this promise is guaranteed."

The guaranteed life you deserve. Exactly what Mo-bot had highlighted in the ad she'd uncovered.

"How do you guarantee love for life?" Val asked.

"Money back for the life of the customer," Olsen said, smiling. "That's the only kind of guarantee that's worth anything."

"So true," said Val. This was it. The pitch she'd been hoping for. She wondered if her pounding heart would overwhelm her microphone, smother the transmission to the recorder. She touched the mic through her clothes, tapped it with her middle finger.

"So, this isn't a free service, right, Lester?"

Lester laughed from his gut, a real warm, hearty laugh. "You're good, Val. Yes, there's money involved, but to begin with, let's go window-shopping for a man worthy of you. And that won't cost you a dime."

Val sat back as the waiter deftly placed her pan-seared breast of duck and cauliflower puree in front of her. Another waiter filled her wineglass yet again.

She smiled across the candlelit table at Lester Olsen.

"I guess it wouldn't hurt to shop," she said.

# Chapter 89

I WAS IN my office on a conference call with Jorge Suarez and Andrew Boone, operations heads of Private's Lisbon and London offices, respectively, when the GPS tracking device I'd stuck under Tommy's car alerted my phone. I checked his car's route on my screen and saw that Tommy's car had stopped in Inglewood, a very rough part of town and far from my brother's usual haunts.

When I signed off from the meeting, Tom's car was still in Inglewood and I had no plans for the evening.

Emilio Cruz was in the underground lot unlocking his car when I got there.

I said to him, "Tom's up to something, 'Milio. He's been parked on West Boulevard near

Fifty-Eighth for an hour and that's not his beat, you know? You busy? Want to take a ride?"

"Are you buying dinner too?"

I grinned at him. "Of course."

Cruz had no love for Tommy and had come to hate him even more since Tom had begun dogging Rick's trial for no good reason.

Cruz said, "I'm never too busy to watch your psycho brother, Jack. Give me the keys."

We took a fleet car, a five-year-old Chevy Impala I'd picked up at a repo sale because it can blend in anywhere. Twenty minutes later, we were parked on West Boulevard, in front of a shabby row of one-story houses and across the street from a low-budget strip mall. A spaghetti war of tangled wires hung overhead.

Tommy's red Ferrari was thirty yards up ahead, our side of the street. His ride was conspicuous by design, but in this scraping-the-bottom, have-not neighborhood, it was like waving a red freaking flag.

I didn't get it.

A clump of hooded kids were standing around the Ferrari, not jacking it, which told me that Tommy had hired them to stand guard.

Cruz got out of the car without saying why.

He's an imposing guy. Muscular, and the bulge under his jacket made it clear that he was packing.

I wasn't looking for trouble. Not this kind, and as Cruz headed toward the group of kids, I yelled, "Emilio. Come back."

He waved to me as he kept going, signaling, *Don't worry. It's okay.*

By then, the kids had seen Cruz coming toward them, and they shouted catcalls and showed a lot of junior-punk attitude. Cruz yelled out something in Spanish, and the kids stopped shouting. But they stood their ground.

The situation looked like it could break bad in an instant.

I opened the car door and was ready to join the party, but by the time my foot touched pavement, the body language had changed and the tension had died. Cruz handed something over to the biggest kid, then came back to our car.

We both got in, closed the doors, and Cruz said, "Well, that was twenty bucks well spent. Tommy's in there."

He hooked a thumb behind us, indicating the Lutheran church down the block. It was an adobe-style building with sand-colored stucco walls, a red-brick roof, and security gates on the front doors.

"Tommy's at church? That would be a first," I said.

Cruz said, "They got a Gamblers Anonymous meeting on Sunday nights."

I turned in my seat, saw that the church was emptying out, people leaving in ones and twos. I saw my brother walking with another man, and they were absorbed in intense conversation, maybe arguing.

Tommy's companion seemed familiar to me, but he was out of context and I struggled to put a name to the face. The two of them walked under a streetlight, then into the shadows, then they crossed the street and moved farther away.

Soon, I was looking at the streetlight shining on the back of the guy's balding head as he called good night to my brother and unlocked his car.

Who was he?

I couldn't quite grab the guy's name, but I knew that I had to do it, that something big was at stake. As his car door slammed and his engine caught, it came to me. I remembered him and had a good idea how he was linked to Tommy.

I had to make a move.

I had to do it right now.

# Chapter 90

RICK HAD HIS butt in his hard seat behind the defense table, and Caine was sitting beside him in a chair on the aisle. Now there was a badass cop sitting right behind Rick, keeping his eyes on the back of his head, ready to leap over the bar and throw him to the floor if he got out of his chair.

The cop was assigned because of the shots Rick took at Dexter Lewis. Lucky for him that Lewis, that prick, hadn't revoked his bail, or he would've spent his weekend in the Men's Central Jail, protecting his ass and trying not to get puked on by drunks.

Today, both sides were going to give their closing arguments, and then the jury would decide if Rick would be either (a) living in his house on the canal, working with Cruz and Jack, leading the good life, or (b) spending ten years in a cell, eating slop, being strip-searched, goaded, insulted. Having a murderous thug for a cellie—or worse.

And why was he in this jam?

Because that shit, Sutter Brown Truck, had put him at the scene of a crime he hadn't committed. He wasn't just innocent, he was as innocent as a little baby lamb. He was a retired officer of the U.S. Marine Corps, for God's sake. He'd seen action. He was *decorated*.

This whole pile of crap about Vicky was a frame.

And that made Rick want to lunge across the aisle and punch Dexter Lewis's face again. If he was found guilty, he just might do it.

There was a soft whoosh of robes as the judge came through the door behind the bench. The bailiff told everyone to rise, and they did, and then everyone sat down. In that moment, Rick turned his head, looked to see who had come to the show.

Jack was behind him, four rows back, and Cruz, his partner, was standing in the rear of the room, giving him a nod. Rick snapped his head to the front so that his friends wouldn't see him get emotional, for God's sake.

Caine put his hand on Rick's arm, said, "You okay?"

362

"Dandy."

"Something happened last night. I'm gonna take a shot."

"At what? A shot at what?"

Before the bailiff could bring in the jury, Caine was on his feet. He said to the judge, "Your Honor, I want to put a witness on the stand."

"Didn't you rest your case on Friday?" said the judge.

"Something came up over the weekend Your Honor. The defense wants to call Bradley Sutter."

Rick couldn't believe what he'd just heard. Brad Sutter, the UPS guy? That guy hated him, and now Brown was going to testify for him? That was crazy.

Lewis stood up, said, "Your Honor, we know nothing about this witness—"

"Don't be ridiculous, Mr. Lewis. Mr. Sutter was *your* witness. You know everything about him. Or you should."

"I meant, I don't know what this new testimony is about."

"Well, that's the nature of news breaking over the weekend, isn't it, Mr. Lewis? I guess we're all going to find out at the same time. Please sit down. Bailiff, please bring in the jury."

# Chapter 91

I WATCHED SUTTER come up the aisle. Last time he took the stand, I thought what a regular guy he was, how credible, what freaking bad luck for Del Rio that the UPS man with the disappearing hair and the sunburned nose was going to testify against him.

Now, Sutter looked like bad shit had happened.

Both of his eyes were blackened, his nose was swollen and bandaged, and his right arm was in a cast and a sling. He was sworn in, then he took his seat. He saw me and gave me a hard look.

I reflexively massaged the bruised knuckles of my right hand.

My brother sat in the row in front of me with his right leg crossed over his left knee. He was jiggling his foot nervously, and he wasn't smirking. Not today.

Caine approached the witness.

"Mr. Sutter, on the night of June fourteenth, did you see Mr. Del Rio at Vicky Carmody's house?"

"Yes."

"Please describe the circumstances."

"He was coming to see Vicky."

"And you knew that Ms. Carmody was expecting him, is that right?"

"Yes. Vicky had told me that Del Rio was coming over to return her camera."

"Did you mention this date to someone else?"

"Yes."

"And whom did you tell?"

"I refuse to answer on the grounds that an attempt has been made on my life and if I say who hired me, I will be erased."

"Okay, Mr. Sutter. We'll get back to that question later. Did you see Mr. Del Rio go into Ms. Carmody's house?"

"Yes, like I said the last time, I was across the street making a pickup. I saw Del Rio go in, and I saw Vicky close the door."

Caine asked, "And did you see Mr. Del Rio leave Ms. Carmody's house?"

"Yes. About fifteen or twenty minutes later."

"Then what happened?"

"After Del Rio left, I rang Vicky's doorbell and she opened the door. I told her I was just making sure she was okay, and she said she was fine. I pushed her in, went inside with her, and locked the door."

Sutter looked into space, touched his nose. Seemed lost in thought.

Caine said, "You went inside the house with Ms. Carmody. What happened after that, Mr. Sutter?"

Sutter came back to the moment.

"I beat her until I thought she was dead."

The crowd in the gallery gasped as if it had taken a collective gut punch. The gasp was loud. It echoed.

The jury, too, looked severely shocked.

Caine paused to let Sutter's testimony sink in. He did a half turn, looked at the jury, then turned back to Sutter. He said, "Why did you brutally assault Ms. Carmody?"

Sutter said, "Look, I didn't do it for fun. I did it because I was between a rock and another rock. I was in debt to some sharks who were threatening my family. There's a guy I knew from rehab who has a hate-on for Del Rio.

"We talked about Del Rio sometimes. So, anyway, I told him Del Rio was back in Vicky's life, and he made me an offer. He said it right out. He would pay off my debt if I killed Vicky and made it look like Del Rio did it."

Caine said, "And you agreed."

"I had to. I snorted a little coke to get me going. Then I beat the crap out of her. My debt went away."

"And so I'll ask you again, Mr. Sutter. Who paid you to kill Vicky Carmody?"

"Look. I'm testifying to show good faith. But, on the advice of counsel, I refuse to name the guy who hired me until my family is in witness protection and I've got a deal. In writing. And that's all I'm going to say."

# Chapter 92

I WATCHED AS Caine turned the witness over to assistant district attorney Dexter Lewis, who sneered for the jury's benefit. Then he walked over to the witness stand, kept one hand on his hip, his body language saying, *This witness is full of crap.*

Sutter cradled his bad arm. Looked to me like he was bracing himself for a grilling.

Lewis said, "That's an interesting story, Mr. Sutter. So, if I understand you, you lied when you testified last week saying you didn't see Mr. Del Rio leave Vicky's house. Is that right?"

"Yeah, obviously. I lied."

"And so now the court is supposed to believe you when you say Mr. Del Rio didn't assault Ms. Carmody, that you did it. How do we know Mr. Del Rio didn't pay you to say this?"

"Why would I confess to assaulting Vicky if I didn't do it? She could die and I could get nailed for murder. No, I'm trying to get out from under this. My life is in danger. My wife's life is in danger. My six-year-old girl is in danger too.

"All I've got going for the Sutter family is that I know who paid for a hit on Vicky. That's worth something."

Lewis shook his head, skeptical. He was flustered, expressing his disbelief not like an attorney but like a man on the street. He said to Sutter, "And so you—what? Went to the cops and turned yourself in?"

"Yeah, as a matter of fact, that's what I did."

Caine stood, said, "Your Honor, Mr. Sutter is already under arrest for the assault on Ms. Carmody. The defense moves that the charges against Mr. Del Rio be dismissed and that he be released immediately."

"Wait just a *minute*," Lewis said. "The jury has heard the case. They get to decide if Mr. Del Rio committed the crime, despite Mr. Sutter's highly suspicious, uncorroborated testimony."

It was clear that Dexter Lewis was hanging on to whatever was still within his grasp. When he'd woken up this morning, he had a conviction in the bag. Lewis did not want Del Rio to walk, guilty or not.

Judge Johnson said, "As it happens, *I've* got some questions, Mr. Sutter. I want to be convinced you were really there. What was Ms. Carmody wearing when you came into her house?"

Sutter said, "Blue-striped shirt, short sleeves, khaki pants, flat shoes. She had a chicken in the oven, and a couple of empty beer bottles were on the kitchen table. All of that can be checked with the cops. Oh, and she was watching *Dr. Phil*."

"And what did you say and do?"

"Okay. Like I said, I shoved her inside. She said, 'Brad, what are you doing? What do you want?' I punched her in the face. She staggered backward, got into the bedroom, tried to close the door. I pushed it in and I hit her again. I had no choice. It was either her or me and my family."

No one stopped him, so Sutter went on.

"She kept calling out, 'Don't do this, Brad. Stop,' and then she called, 'Rick.' Like she wanted him to save her. I picked a lamp up off the table, a blue one, about this big. And I hit her with it. She put up her arm, but I just kept beating her until she didn't move anymore."

Sutter was coughing and then crying. No one

asked him if he needed a minute. No one offered him a tissue. In a while, he stopped sobbing and said, "You believe me now, Your Honor? I did it. And I want protection from the guy who put me up to it."

The judge sighed, fixed her headband, clasped her hands in front of her. I thought she looked disgusted, like now, she'd heard everything.

She asked the jury's indulgence and then had them return to their room. The courtroom buzzed, and the judge called for order, several times.

When she had as much silence as she could reasonably expect, she said, "Mr. Lewis? Based on Mr. Sutter's testimony, you may have the wrong man on trial. What do you wish to do?"

# Chapter 93

CAINE AND CRUZ were blocking and I had my hand at Del Rio's back as we left the courtroom through a mob of people who'd been in the gallery plus the gang of raccoons who had, somehow, already gotten word that Rick was free.

Rick was in a state of shocked disbelief, like he'd been in the tunnel and heading into the light when a voice said, "Case dismissed," and he was dragged back into life.

In front of the elevator, Cruz turned, grabbed Rick into a hard hug, said, "You're okay, man. It's all over."

I thought about last night, how Cruz and I had followed Sutter from the church on West Boulevard to his house on Hickory Avenue in Torrance, then waited for him to get out of his car.

Then we'd crowded him.

Sutter saw me and yelled, "Stay away from me, Tom."

I shouted that I wasn't Tom, that I was his brother and that we needed to talk. I told Sutter that I knew what he'd done to Vicky and that I knew Tommy had paid him.

I told Sutter that I had the means to get into Tommy's financials at any time, that I'd checked Tommy's bank account and saw that he'd paid Sutter a hundred thousand dollars the day Del Rio was arrested.

In fact, I had seen the amount of the withdrawal, but not the name of the recipient. Calling Sutter out was a calculated bluff, but I was pretty damned sure that Tommy had paid Sutter to kill Carmody and hang it on Rick.

I told Sutter, "Confess what you did to Vicky Carmody and get Del Rio out of the box. Or else I'll tell Tommy that you're going to turn him in."

Sutter went pale, broke out in an instant sweat. He said, "Don't do that to me."

"Sorry," I said. "It's your choice."

Sutter made a practical decision on the spot. He agreed to tell the court what he'd done if I got my friends in high places to give him a deal.

We shook hands, and then Cruz asked Sutter if he wanted a little tune-up before we dropped him off at the precinct so that the cops would have reason to believe he needed protection.

Sutter had said, "Don't hurt my vital organs. Or my junk."

We did our best to oblige him.

I'd made my call to DA Bobby Petino, and a deal was in the works. But if Tommy was charged with conspiracy to commit murder, it would still be Sutter's word against Tommy's.

And Tommy was slick.

My brother might never spend a day in prison, but for now, all I cared about was that Rick Del Rio was free.

In the courthouse, the elevator doors opened.

My guys and I got inside and Cruz held the button while Caine and I blocked the entrance until the door closed. The ride down was exhilarating because Del Rio was finally coming back to himself, blood flowing into his face, the will to live lighting up his eyes.

He hugged me. He hugged Caine. He kissed Cruz loudly on the cheek. Then he said, "I'm buying you guys dinner anywhere you like, anyplace that will take my Visa card."

The four of us descended to the ground floor, laughing, enjoying the win for the good guys. We cut through the lobby and went out the front doors to Temple.

I said to Del Rio, "We'll take my car."

We never got to the parking lot. Dexter Lewis and the cop who'd been assigned to keep Del Rio under control were jogging down the courthouse steps. Lewis was calling Rick's name.

"Del Rio. Del *Rio*. I have something for you."

We stopped, turned. Lewis had a look in his face that could only be called *triumphant*. But what the hell could he possibly feel victorious about?

"I'm pressing charges," he said to Rick.

Lewis was enjoying this too much. He had an ugly smile, which he had probably been told his whole life was his best feature. When Rick faced the ADA, he looked like a hurricane in a bottle. Furious. Uncontainable.

"Charges? I'm *out,* asshole."

"I'm charging you with the assault and battery you committed against me. Asshole. Arrest him, Officer Brinker."

I stood by and watched as the cuffs came out. Rick looked at me wildly. "I'll be out in an hour, right, Jack?"

Caine said, "Don't make a statement, Rick. Don't say anything. We'll meet you at Central Booking."

My guts twisted. Not *this*. Not after all this.

Rick couldn't be going back to jail.

# Chapter 94

I WAS DRIVING back to the office after Cruz, Caine, and I had spent half the day at Central Booking. We were there for moral support, but we saw Del Rio for only a moment before he was taken away to be processed and then locked up pending his arraignment.

I'm a graduate of Twin Towers Correctional myself, and I can tell you that it's worse than its reputation as an overcrowded, gang-infested sewer, a brutal, dehumanizing hellhole you couldn't dream up if you wrote horror films for a living.

And I was more worried about Rick than before. Unlike in the Carmody case, Rick had actually assaulted an officer of the court in full view of about fifty witnesses.

It didn't look good for Rick. Not at all.

I was on the freeway, thinking of taking Justine out to lunch, bringing her up to date on what had just happened, when my phone rang. I glanced at it out of habit, thinking whoever it was, they could wait. But I changed my mind when I saw Luke Warren's name on the caller ID.

The captain was my connection to a couple of loathsome serial felons from a godforsaken, land-locked pile of rocks called Sumar. I had offered to help the captain for free.

I said my name, and he got right into it.

"I'm at the Armstrong Hotel, Jack, over on Brampton. There was a murder here forty-eight hours ago, but it's not my precinct, no reason for anyone to call me. Except for something a witness said to the first cop on the scene. The witness is sketchy, but I think he can ID the Sumaris."

"You said it's a homicide?"

Warren said, "Could be more than one."

# Chapter 95

THE ARMSTRONG HOTEL was a cheap joint on a run-down block at the fringes of the Cypress Park neighborhood. It didn't look out of place here with its peeling paint, blown-neon signage, cracked and empty swimming pool out front. It was hardly a hotel. More like a crash pad for locals who had no place to go.

I locked my car outside the front door, saw Captain Warren through the plate glass; he was leaning against a planter that divided the front desk from the furniture in the lobby. He straightened up when he saw me, came out, and told the uniformed cop at the door that I was working with the LAPD.

"Glad you could make it," he said, shaking my hand.

I said, "No problem. Glad you caught me."

The lobby had already been processed by CSU investigators who had left evidence of their own: yellow tape at the doorways, markers beside blood evidence, fingerprint powder on every surface. I asked Warren what had happened.

"First, I want to say, this isn't my case. I got my hands on it anyway, because if I can help, the Northeast Division will take it."

"So where are you with this, Luke?"

He ran a hand through his hair, looked past me to the front desk, as if he were trying to back up the film and see it from the beginning.

"Not far enough. It seems like two guys checked in to room four-oh-three at around ten on Saturday night," he said. "They checked out before three Sunday morning, and their room was professionally cleaned. Practically sterilized.

"We've got a dead woman behind the front desk, and the computer has been trashed, hard drive removed. Surveillance camera's gone.

"As for why, we don't know. We don't know who did it either, but we've got a lead. Hang on, Jack. I'll get our witness."

I said, "Mind if I look around?"

"Keep your hands in your pockets, okay?"

The furniture was aquamarine vinyl, looked pretty much the way it had when it was manufactured in the seventies, and that went for the planter of plastic plants as well. The front desk had taken most of the punishment. The computer that must have been there was gone, and there was a dried lake of blood on the floor, spatter on the Formica. It didn't look like the victim had put up a fight.

I was checking out the hole where the security camera had been ripped from its mount when Warren came over with a skinny, fortyish man wearing polyester pants and a wifebeater under a loud print shirt.

He said, "Jack, this is Kevin Fogarty. He's the night doorman. He's the one who found the victim—the desk manager, Lois Bird. Kevin, this is Jack Morgan. He's an investigator. Why don't you tell him what you saw?"

# Chapter 96

WE STOOD NEXT to the vending machines, the night doorman saying to Captain Warren, "I told you, I hardly know anything."

It was one in the afternoon, but Kevin Fogarty smelled of alcohol. When Warren had a chance to run his name, I was pretty sure he'd be looking at a long sheet littered with misdemeanors and outstanding warrants.

Fogarty pulled a bent half of a cigarette from the hip pocket of his shiny slacks, lit up, and when he'd framed his thoughts, he said, "I'm not going into any court to testify against anyone. Just be sure you hear me. I don't do that. That's not me. I like to keep a low profile."

"Go ahead with what you saw," I said.

Fogarty took a long draw on the cigarette,

coughed violently for too long, then: "Like I said, I saw these two guys coming in around ten on Saturday night. They was carrying brown paper bags, so they'd brought their own bar service, I guess. They were with these two women, heavyset. Bleached blondes.

"The four of them seemed like they'd been drinking for a while. They were at the elevator as I was going out on my break. All giggly, like the party was *on*, something I've seen maybe a hundred million times."

Warren said, "But something was different, right, Mr. Fogarty? You saw something that made you remember them?"

"Like I told you and the other five cops I spoke to, one of the guys was wearing a muscle shirt, no sleeves. He had some tattoos on his arms. They were like stripes going around the biceps and all the way down, and maybe words written above the stripes. He pinched one of the ladies, hard. She yelped, but that's all I saw. I remember that noise she made."

There was more smoking, coughing, and encouragement to finish the story before Fogarty continued.

"When you showed me their pictures," Fogarty

said to Warren, "I thought maybe I recognized the guy with the striped tattoos. He has a lot of hair. And a big nose."

"Did you see them again?"

"No. I came back from my break. There was nothing happening, so I told the girl at the desk to call me if she needed me. I went to an empty room right here on the main floor and I watched TV and fell asleep. When I come out here, at like three a.m., the girl, Ms. Bird. She's on the floor over there and she's dead.

"I called 911. I stayed here. I talked to the cops. And then, a little while ago, the boss calls me and fires me. Because I was sleeping on the job. I'm not even mad about that. If I'd been on the door, I would be dead too, right, Captain? I'd be dead too."

"Tell about the back door, Mr. Fogarty."

"It was open, okay? The girl had the key. So she musta given it to someone, because the rear service door was hanging open. You got enough? Because I gotta go down to the office for my check."

"Thank you," Warren said to Fogarty. "You've been a big help."

We watched the ex-doorman leave through the front door. Then Warren said to me, "I hate those guys, Jack. I hate that they're in LA, I hate what they're doing, and I hate that they're so slippery. I'll bet we don't know the half of what they've done. It's their game and they keep getting away with it."

"I want to see their room," I said.

# Chapter 97

CAPTAIN WARREN PUSHED open the door to room 403, lifted the tape so I could go in before him. He said, "This room and the one next door were likely booked as a suite. The door between them was left open."

The room was dingy blue, identical prints of a beach scene hanging on three walls and dusty gray draperies flanking windows that overlooked Cypress Avenue to the north.

A king-size bed, stripped bare, backed up against a wall and faced an armoire that held a TV and six open, empty drawers. The wall-to-wall carpet was a dark blue pattern designed to defy stains.

Hotel rooms are one of the worst possible places to collect forensic evidence, just below a strip club in Hollywood and the city dump. Hundreds of people had slept in this creepy room, all of them leaving prints, a blooming field of germs and too much DNA.

"Detectives from the Northeast got here within six minutes of Fogarty's call," said Warren. "They closed off the lobby and did a floor-to-floor canvass. When they saw four-oh-three, they locked it down. CSU was here for most of the last thirty-six hours, but as of ten this morning, they packed it in. They're coming up empty."

Just like they had in the lobby, CSU techs had left evidence of their own here; fingerprint powder was everywhere, white microfiber jumpsuits were wadded up behind the door, and discarded swab wrappers littered the place.

"CSU took the bedding?"

Warren said, "Hell no. The bed was naked when the cops got here. I'm still trying to get my mind around that. Same deal in the adjoining room."

Wiping down phones and doorknobs was Cleanup 101. But people didn't take bedding out of a room unless they were serious pros mopping up a homicide. In my one meeting with Gozan Remari and Khezir Mazul, I hadn't made them as clean freaks. I thought they were pigs.

Assuming the Sumaris had been here and had been accompanied by two women, what had happened to those women? Had the Sumaris' past pattern of sexual assault gone over the edge into murder?

Folded towels were on a rack in the bathroom, but if there had been any used towels, they were gone. Porcelain glistened under the fingerprint powder, and even the stopper had been removed from the sink.

I stood in the doorway between the two rooms and saw that 405 was a mirror image of 403. Stripped beds, fingerprint powder, no obvious trace of blood.

Professionals had made all the evidence disappear.

Warren said, "Here's the sum total of what we've got, Jack. Fogarty's five-second look at distinctive arm tattoos on a man with big hair and a big nose. He also saw the backs of two plus-size blondes. That's all, but I know it was them. Remari, that pervert. And the other one. Mazul with those tattoos."

I commiserated with the captain, and then went out to the balcony. It was sparsely furnished with a glass table and two homely lounge chairs.

The view was equally spare: a deserted service road running parallel to the distant freeway. Directly below the balcony was a foundation planting of haphazardly trimmed hedges.

The smog was eye-watering. I was about to go back inside when I caught a glimpse of something forty feet down in the shrubbery, an object that didn't belong. I called Warren and pointed until he saw the cell phone too.

He gripped the railing, exhaled hard.

"Is it too much to hope that that phone belongs to one of those pukes from Sumar?" he asked.

"Are you feeling lucky?" I said.

# Chapter 98

VAL KENNEY WAS fifteen minutes late for her 6:00 p.m. appointment with Lester Olsen, and she was worried about that. Would Olsen wait for her or not? And by the way, she was still kind of lost.

She called Mo-bot, who told her to take a sharp left on West Spring Mountain Road, go one block, then take another left into the strip-mall parking lot. Val did that but couldn't find an empty spot. She swore, apologized to Mo, then drove around the block and parked on the street.

"I'm good now, Mo."

"Good. Take a breath. Never let 'em see you sweat."

Val laughed, took a moment to touch up her lipstick. Then, gripping her handbag, she doubled back to the strip mall, walked along the row of shops until she saw the discreet, inset doorway between a pizzeria and a tanning salon, the inscription *Love for Life* etched in the glass.

Val pressed the buzzer, and a smiling Lester Olsen opened the door wide and welcomed her into his office. He looked boyish in a pink polo shirt, jeans, running shoes. She smelled peppermint on his breath.

"I'm sorry. I made a wrong turn," Val said. "It took forever to turn around."

"Forgive the mess," Lester said, ushering her through a minimal reception area into a room at the back. "This is my work space and I don't usually have people here, but we have work to do, don't we? Sit there, Val."

Lester showed her to a chair across from his desk, asked, "Can I get you anything? Coffee? Water?"

Val said, "Thanks, no. I'm good."

Lester went around to his desk chair, saying, "Are you ready, Val? This might be the turning point of your life. Pretty exciting, isn't it?"

"I cannot wait," she said.

"Me neither," Olsen said, grinning, reaching out and touching her wrist. "I've picked out five superb candidates from my prospect files, all very wealthy men who have been waiting half their lives to meet a woman like you."

He bent to his computer, clicked around, said, "They're all older than men you might ordinarily date. They're in their seventies, got a couple in their eighties. All five have more money than you could even believe."

"So you haven't told me how this works, Lester. If one of these candidates and I get married—he pays your fee?"

"Something like that," said Olsen. "Now, let's get in the right mood. Imagine that our very rich, very old dude cannot believe his luck and wants to marry you right away, because he really doesn't have much time left. He has heart problems. And he's lonely in his gigantic, double-wide, California king."

"You *are* funny, Lester."

He was not only funny but articulate and convincing. He had all the traits of a sociopathic con man.

Olsen grinned and said, "If we do this right, it's going to be fun. So, before we leave my office, we select your future husband. Then you follow my instructions on how to land him, treat him, keep him. I'll be your personal coach. Your silent partner. When he dies, you will become a very wealthy widow, and you and I will split your inheritance. How does that sound?"

"My God. I—don't know."

Olsen had laid out his plan, but where was the crime? Marrying a man for money and waiting for him to die wasn't illegal, and it didn't connect Olsen to Tule Archer's threats to her husband.

She said, "I never thought of this... I mean, it sounds intriguing, but also so... cold-blooded."

"Oh, I get you. Val, look at it this way. You're giving someone a very happy ending, someone who isn't going to need the money after he dies. But you can say no, and I hope you don't feel that I wasted your time."

Val lowered her eyes, pretended to think it over. She'd observed enough police interrogations to know when to take the lead and when to just listen.

Olsen turned his laptop around so that she could see it.

"Let's meet the contenders," he said.

# Chapter 99

VAL LEANED ACROSS the desk and peered at the file Olsen had opened on his laptop.

Olsen said, "Bachelor number one is Morris Furman."

Photo came up of an old guy of about ninety sitting in a unique handmade chair on a huge porch. He had a serious-looking drink in his claw-like hand. A TV on a cart near the railing showed what seemed to be a horse race. His hair was thin, his glasses were thick, and he had wall-to-wall liver spots on his arms.

"Attractive guy, right?"

Olsen looked up at her and winked.

"Now, listen, Val. Morris used to be head of an insurance company. A nice clean business. He has a hundred million in U.S. markets, and then he's got another bundle in real estate. He lost his wife twenty years ago, and his children are in their sixties. Has a pacemaker. His third, I think. Morris is what I call a catch and a half."

"You know him?" Val asked.

"Sure, I know him. He's my grandfather."

"He is?" Val looked up from the computer.

Olsen was laughing.

"Just joking, Val. I know him because he comes to the casinos when he's in town. Lives in Butte, Montana. He would fly you out to meet him in half a heartbeat. Which could be his last one. Or perhaps you could *cause* his last heartbeat. Just don't have sex with him until after the wedding, okay?"

Val said, "You can count on *that*."

"That's fine, Val. But, all kidding aside, you understand you don't want to marry a young tycoon who wraps you up in a prenup, then divorces you. How long do you want your husband to live?"

Val did her best to figure out how to handle this moment. Pay out the line, or set the hook? Her hands were sweating. Her skin was damp at her hairline.

"Actually, I would like some water now."

Lester got up, went to the small fridge near the

credenza, brought back a bottle of Artesian Springs. Then he sat down, and as he was navigating around his computer, Val said, "But even if the dude is old…well, there's no guarantee that he's going to die soon."

"Uh, well, think about it. The money-back guarantee depends on you. Maybe you'll have to give your antique husband a little push for that multimillion-dollar payoff, see? I can only do so much."

A little push. Tule Archer was trying to frighten Hal into a heart attack by telling him that she was killing him in her dreams. He'd responded by killing *her* in real life.

Reflexively, Val touched the microphone that was attached like a rosebud to the center of her bra and tapped it with her middle finger. And Olsen, seeing that, got to his feet fast.

He was standing right over her, boxing her in. His expression was suddenly cold and menacing.

Oh my God. What had she done?

# Chapter 100

LESTER OLSEN HAD lost his boyishness and his humor, and the man that remained was scaring her half to death.

"What just happened, Val?"

"What do you mean? What's wrong, Lester?"

"I'm a poker player, Val. One of the best. You know what a tell is? It's when someone gives himself away with an unconscious movement. Like what you just did when you touched yourself. That was a classic tell."

"I don't know what you're talking about, but you know what? I don't think this is for me—"

Val pushed her chair back, but she was up against the wall and there was nowhere to go.

"You did that at dinner the other night," Olsen said, tapping the middle of his own chest with his third finger, "and I ignored it. See how you put your water bottle between us? Another tell. I shouldn't have second-guessed myself. I bet you're wearing a wire."

He put his crippled hands at either side of the V-neck of her blouse.

"If I'm wrong, I'll apologize."

Fabric tore. Val gasped and tried to cover herself, but Olsen forced her hands aside and plucked the mic off her bra. Then, in one smooth movement, he reached around, opened a desk drawer, and pulled out a gun. He put the mic on his desk and shattered it with the butt of his gun.

Val's mind spun. She reached for a plausible explanation, then launched it. "Lester. Let me explain. I'm a reporter. I'm doing a story on how to land a wealthy man. That's all. The story is going to be good for you."

"Who are you working for?"

"*San Francisco Chronicle.*"

"Who's the publisher?"

Val sputtered nonsense, then tried to get out of the chair as Olsen swung his hand and slammed the side of the gun into her jaw. Val fell back into the seat, put her hands to her face, and stifled a cry of pain.

"Who's on the other end of the mic?"

"FBI. My people have been listening. They'll be in here any second now. I suggest you back away from me and figure out how you're going to explain what you've just done."

"Shut up, Val, and don't bother lying to me. You're an amateur and I can spot your lies before they hatch."

He lifted her purse from where it hung at the back of her chair and emptied it onto the desk with one hand. He turned off the recorder and the phone, put both in his pocket.

"Stand up," he said.

Val gripped the arms of the chair. She said, "Nothing has happened, Lester. I was taping into my *purse*. Let me go and I'll say I walked into a wall and I'll forget I ever met you."

"Stand up. Put your hands behind your back," he said. "Or I'll kill you right here and right now."

# Chapter 101

WHEN VAL STOOD up, she had to fight to keep her balance. She was feeling sick and in pain, but she was also experiencing a lot of clarity.

She understood that Olsen was protecting something more than a high-end matchmaking scheme and he was not kidding around. This was real. He could kill her and get away with it. And she understood that this was her best, last moment to regain his trust and save her life.

"I don't even understand why you're so mad," she said. "Look, you're right. I don't work for the FBI. I don't work for anyone."

Olsen spun her around and shoved her hard against the wall. She felt the gun muzzle at the back of her neck.

"Your *hands*, Val. Put your hands behind you."

He forced her right hand behind her, and she felt a zip tie go around her wrist.

"I could teach you about lying," Olsen said. "See, an innocent person doesn't go on the defensive. An innocent person goes on the attack. And here you are, pleading and defending."

"Will you let me explain?"

"Give me your other hand, Val. Or whatever your name is. I don't want to shoot you. That's the truth, by the way."

Val complied. She was shaking now, rummaging through her mind for anything she'd heard or read or seen, even in a movie, that might turn Lester around.

Lester cinched her wrists together, pulled the tie tight.

"What are you going to do with me?" she asked.

"That depends. What are you, Val? A cop?"

"I'm a freelance writer. I saw your ad online—"

"Here's what we're going to do, bitch. We're going to walk quietly out of this room and you do what I tell you to do. Okay? Say okay."

"Okay."

"I'm going to put my arm around your shoulders, and if you try to get anyone's attention, I'm going to shoot you on the spot. And then I'm going to shoot the bystander. I will then walk away."

"Whatever you say, I'll do it. Just take it easy, okay?"

"Let's go."

Olsen marched her through the office, then through the storage room. He angled her so that he could open the rear exit, then put his free arm around her shoulder and dug the gun into her side.

They were behind the strip mall, in a narrow parking lot used by the shop owners, their names stenciled on the asphalt. There was no one around, just empty cars and a couple of Dumpsters.

Olsen pushed her toward a blue Ford Taurus parked outside the back door facing the road. He changed the position of the gun, screwed it hard into her back while leaning down to open the trunk.

"Get in, Val. Or I will shoot you and stuff your body inside. You're a big girl, but maybe you've noticed, I spend time at the gym."

Val could see the traffic on the road that ran perpendicular to the alley, only fifty yards away. She pictured herself running, getting help from a motorist. If she ran, she would have a better chance than if she got into the *trunk*. No. If she ran, *he would shoot her.* As long as she was alive in the trunk, she was...alive.

"I need help to do this," she said.

He supported her as she put a leg into the trunk, then he applied pressure to her back, gave her a shove.

She fell in and curled up in the cramped space.

"Be right back," he said. "And then we'll go for a ride."

"Wait," said Val. "Look at me. I'm not lying. I'm a private investigator and our satellite is tracking me—"

Lester reached up and slammed the trunk closed.

# Chapter 102

LESTER OLSEN LEFT the goddamned girl in the trunk and went back into his office. He used Val's phone and credit card to book a flight in her name from McCarran to Honolulu, then returned her phone to her purse.

Next, he opened his briefcase on his desk, tossed in his laptop and power cords. He had a new, prepaid boost phone in his desk drawer all charged up. He put the charger into his briefcase, put the phone in his jacket pocket.

His safe was inside the supply room. He opened that, took out his passport, the wad of cash, the credit cards, put all of that in the briefcase too.

He went to the credenza, opened the doors, and took out a dust rag and a bottle of Windex. He sprayed the rag with the ammonia and wiped down the arms of the side chair, the top and edges of his desk. Then he took the rag out front and cleaned the intercom button and the door handle.

A young mom and little boy walked by, and smiles were exchanged. When they had passed, Olsen stepped back inside his doorway, locked the front door, and then double-locked it. He returned to his office, collected his case, Val's purse, and his go-bag with a shaving kit and a change of clothes. Then he left by the rear door and locked that too.

As always, the Ford Taurus was gassed up and ready, an ordinary ride with fake registration, fake plates, all matching his fake ID, all good to go. The getaway car was his ace in the hole, an ace he'd hoped he'd never have to play. But he would play it now, and he would win.

Val was thumping the lid of the trunk when he got there, but if the girl thumped and there was no one to hear it, what the fuck did it matter? His adrenal glands were pumping adrenaline overtime. He loved adrenaline. Thrived on it.

The guy who owned the tanning salon came out, Tony something. Big dumb guy. He waved to Olsen, then got into his van and started to back up. Olsen waved, then put the bags into the backseat of the Taurus.

He got into the driver's seat, adjusted the mirrors, put Miles Davis's *Kind of Blue* into the CD player, and started the engine. He called out loudly over his shoulder, "Everything okay back there, Valerie? You need anything, you let me know."

There was a muffled thump and a few words from the rear. He thought she'd said, "Please, Lester. Let me out."

"I'm over you, Val," he shouted.

He turned on the AC, then backed the car out carefully. Didn't want to bend any fenders in the damned parking lot.

A minute later, he was on West Spring Mountain Road. He waited at the stoplight, thought about how the girl might be missed today, but not at four in the afternoon. Her phone's GPS was active and if anyone was keeping tabs on her, they'd track her phone to the airport.

He used the boost phone to call Barbie.

"Barbie, it's Lester. Guess what—I'm coming out to see you. Yes. This is payday. You know what to do? Okay. Stay home, all right? I should be there by nine or so. I'll phone you later." He laughed at how excited she was. "Yes," he said. "Me too. Me too."

When the light turned green, Olsen said, "Bye"

to Barbie and disconnected the call. Then he stepped on the gas and headed toward the airport. First he had to deal with the girl.

He knew exactly what to do.

# Chapter 103

GOZAN REMARI AND Khezir Mazul were dining in Santa Monica at Mélisse, a fabulous restaurant known for its magnificent food and VIP service. Celebrities who came here were treated like gods.

Gozan wanted some god-type treatment. Actually, he needed it. He hadn't slept or eaten since the bloody horror show this morning and he felt that there was more and worse to come.

He sat stiffly in his comfortable chair under the chandelier in the richly appointed brown-and-white room, smelling herbs and roasting meat while Khezzy played the waiter for a fool.

"These Japanese cucumbers. They are like sea cucumbers that puke out their intestines, isn't that right?"

"Ah, no, sir. I don't think so. They are a type of vegetable cucumber. Sliced and pickled."

"Pickled *sea* cucumbers, am I right?"

Khezzy laughed and the waiter tried to look amused, but his eyes were fixed and his smile was tight. Khezzy loved to make people afraid. Usually, Gozan enjoyed watching Khezzy, but not now. Now, he was disturbed.

Gozan's mind went back to the woman on the bathroom floor, her throat cut like swine, Khezzy's knife lying next to her. And he thought about the subsequent killings and the dressing-down by Balar Aram that had humiliated him and made him worry that he and Khezzy would be sent back to Sumar. And if they were, how long would they be allowed to live?

"Khezzy, we should ask for recommendations, hmmm? And let this young man select for us. I am hungry."

Khezir said, "Uncle, you will eat, I promise."

Just then, Khezzy's phone buzzed. He took it out of his jacket pocket, said, "This is strange. Hello. Yes, this is Khezir." Then, angrily, "You *suck*. You can't touch us."

He slammed the phone down on the table and said, "Uncle, that pig's ass of a police captain found my number on your phone. He said he tracked my phone with the GPS...Uncle, where's your phone?"

Gozan felt his blood leave his head and run into his feet. He had lost his phone somewhere; had hoped it had fallen out of his pocket in Balar's vehicle.

The front door of the restaurant opened and two men came in, their eyes going directly to him and Khezzy. Gozan recognized the police captain from that night at the Beverly Hills Hotel with the mango and peaches women. The other one had been there too. A private cop. Now the captain showed his badge to the maître d' and angled his chin toward where Gozan and Khezzy sat.

Gozan said, "They have come for us, nephew. Do not move or they will justify shooting us. Be calm and we will be fine."

Khezzy swung his head toward the front, then whipped it around as the kitchen doors blew open. Four men in riot gear stormed into the dining room with guns drawn, yelling, "Everyone down onto the floor. Get down!"

Other cops were coming in through the fire exit like cannonballs. People screamed; dishes clattered and smashed. Diners went to the floor as the men converged on them and yelled to the Sumaris to keep their hands on the table.

Khezzy said, "You did this, Uncle. You are too stupid to live."

Gozan felt light-headed, as if his mind were leaving his body. He leaned over and vomited his martini between his shoes. When the captain told him to get to his feet, he did. He clasped his hands behind his neck, and he kept saying to Khezzy, "Do what they say, Khez. Do what they say."

# Chapter 104

LESTER OLSEN EXITED the freeway onto West Tropicana Avenue and drove past the faux-medieval Excalibur Hotel and Casino on the right. He stopped at a light and then resumed his drive, feeling pretty good, actually, glad that he was taking action and that, very soon, he was going to be enjoying the life *he* deserved.

Val was quiet in the trunk, probably thinking about how much air she had in there, how hot it was, and rehearsing what she was going to say to him when he finally stopped the car and opened the trunk.

Well, she had to be thinking how she would get away, right?

Olsen kept going on Tropicana, took a right on South Eastern Avenue, passing McCarran Airport and the busy runways on the right. Then he crossed East Sunset Road, rehearsing a few things himself, choreographing his next moves.

The entrance to Sunset Park was just past the northwestern corner of the intersection, and he made the turn, driving the blue Taurus into Sunset Park. This place was frequented by hikers and dog walkers during the day and on weekends.

But this was a weekday and the sun was down. He should have the park to himself.

Olsen took the narrow road that skirted the large pond, looking for just the right place. He found an incline under a clump of trees, pointed the nose of the car toward the lake, and put on the brakes.

There was an island in the middle of the water with some Easter Island–type heads on it, and there were some geese. That was all. He got out of the car, went into the backseat, removed his briefcase, go-bag, Val's handbag with her wallet and phone, and put it all on the ground.

Then he went around to the trunk, patted it, and said, "Val, I gotta be going. I just wanted to say nice try and good-bye."

Her voice was muffled.

"Can you give me some water, please?"

"Okay. Sure. Just a minute."

Olsen did a cursory search of the grounds, found a nice flat rock, weighed about ten pounds. He got back into the car, rolled down his window. He started up the engine, and, keeping it in neutral, he placed the rock carefully on the accelerator. Then he released the hand brake.

The car didn't budge, so Olsen got out of the car, slammed the door, and gripped the doorframe with both hands. He dug his feet in, pushed, got the car rolling, and ran with it a couple dozen yards down the slope.

When the car had a good steady momentum, Lester reached through the window, grabbed the gear shift on the right side of the steering wheel, and threw it into Drive—and the car shot straight ahead.

Winded, Olsen put his hands on his knees and watched as the car bumped over the lip of the pond and drove well into the water before the engine stalled out and the car began to float.

He watched the car settle unevenly, then sink in twelve feet of pond water until there was no trace of it at all.

The car would be found, of course, eventually. But by the time that happened, before Val's body was identified, he'd be long gone, in another country, with a new identity.

He was looking forward to that.

Olsen stood in place for a moment to reassure himself that no one was going to come running out of the bushes yelling for the police. And when he was sure he was in the clear, he walked to the edge of the pond, hurled his unregistered gun as far as he could throw it.

Then he gathered the small bags and began the three-mile walk to McCarran International.

# Chapter 105

FOUR HOURS AFTER leaving Las Vegas behind forever, Lester Olsen disembarked from the small plane at Aspen–Pitkin County Airport. He walked through the concourse, glanced at CNN on the TV screens, and saw no mention of a Ford Taurus with a body in the trunk found in Sunset Park's pond. With luck, the car wouldn't be discovered for at least another twelve hours, or maybe for days, but either way, by morning, he would be traveling as Jay Darnell in the first-class cabin of a jet heading to Tokyo.

A car was waiting for Olsen at National Car Rental, and he paid for it with Jay Darnell's Visa card. He punched Cooper's address into the GPS, then got onto Colorado 82 East toward Aspen.

When he was in the inside lane, Olsen turned

on the radio, listened to music without really hearing it. He was thinking ahead, making plans as he stayed on the highway that narrowed and crossed a bridge, still heading toward town. From the bridge, he could see across the valley and into the mountains surrounding Aspen, where he would close the biggest deal of his life.

He called Barbie and told her he would be there soon.

"I'm having drinks with Bryce right now," she said. "We're going to bed early. Right, sweetie?" she called out. "Want to go upstairs now?"

"How could he say no to that?" Olsen said. "See you soon."

Olsen took directions from the voice on the GPS; it brought him to West Main, where he continued along a residential, tree-lined corridor and from there through the commercial area of town. After passing the historic Hotel Jerome on the left, Olsen turned onto North Mill Street, which wound up the hill toward Bryce Cooper's home.

It was a beautiful drive, but Olsen was working. He had always been able to play multiple hands of poker, and he'd done the same with Love for Life. Barbie and Tule had been in play at the same time. He'd hoped to add Val to the array of games on the table, but he'd always known he might have to cash in his best hand on short notice.

He thought about his contract with Barbie, locked away in his box in Zurich. It implicated her and indemnified him against the possibility of Barbie getting weak or greedy after the fact.

Olsen tuned back in as the GPS voice said, "Turn right in one-quarter mile."

He turned off the radio, slowed the car, and switched off the headlights as he turned up the long drive to Bryce and Barbie Cooper's house. He saw the gleam of lights through the trees, then, as he rounded the turn, he saw the enormous mountain-style house that was cantilevered out over the hill, overlooking Independence Pass, Aspen Mountain, and the entire valley.

The syringe of potassium chloride was in Olsen's shaving kit, a shot he'd be able to deliver while Cooper was asleep. The drug stopped the heart without a trace. Cause of death would be written up as cardiac arrest, and it was inconceivable that anyone would contest it.

Olsen was thinking of the millions he was about to receive as he pulled the car up to the Coopers' garage. He shut down the engine and called Barbie.

"There are so many doors, Barbie. Where should I go? Give me a hint."

"Where are you?"

"Between the guesthouse and the garage."

"Stay right there. I'll come get you. I cannot believe it," she said breathlessly. "My prince has arrived."

# Chapter 106

I WAS HOME at my beach house with the air-conditioning on high, wearing a suit and tie for my nine p.m. teleconference with the COO of the Hong Kong office. We were getting into the nitty-gritty of the operations budget when I got an urgent text from Mo-bot saying, *Turn on the tube. It's about the Sumaris.*

I typed, *I was there when they went down.*

Mo-bot returned fire in caps. GO TO CNN. NOW.

I told Fred Kam that I had to call him back in five minutes, then I switched on the tube. I found the story running on CNN under the banner *Breaking News.*

I was looking at one of those picture-in-picture views. There, on the small picture, was a large, bearded man identified as Colonel Balar Aram of the kingdom of Sumar. He was behind a podium that bore the emblem of the United Nations, and he was wearing a stiff, sand-colored uniform with ribbons over the breast pocket, stars above the brim of his hat.

Surrounding the small picture of Colonel Aram was a larger picture of a violent protest on a wide, dusty street. The crawl at the bottom of the screen said, *Sumari protesters storm the American embassy in Larumin, capital of Sumar.*

The street protest was moving toward a two-story gray building with an American flag flying over the door. The protesters were highly agitated; street-wide chains of angry men with banners reading *Down with the U.S.A. Down with American pigs.* As I watched, they began throwing stones and bottles at men leaving the embassy heading toward black cars.

I tuned into the interview. Anderson Cooper was saying, "Colonel Aram, you are head of Ra Galiz. That's the special forces division of the Sumari military."

"Yes, and in particular, we are the official guard to the royal family. Both Khezir Mazul and Gozan Remari are cousins to King Naraal, may he live forever, and the royal family has sent a formal rebuke to the United States for this outrage against our country."

"As I understand it," Cooper said, "Mazul and Remari are being questioned in the murder of a desk clerk in a hotel in Los Angeles—"

"That is a lie and it is an obscenity," Aram interrupted. "Our people are principled. They would never kill anyone unless it was on the battlefield. And never a woman. Khezir Mazul is a national hero, and his uncle Gozan is a learned man, a scholar. He has no violence in him."

Aram continued, "The arrest and attempted expulsion from the U.S. is an outrage against a law-abiding nation. Prince Khezir and Prince Gozan will be released, not because of diplomatic immunity, but because the police cannot charge them. There is no evidence of any kind. This is just like when the Italian diplomat Carlo Rizzo was arrested on the word of a chambermaid."

In the background picture, cars were being rocked on the street in Larumin, protesters trying to open the car doors. It was maddening. How had Mazul and Remari become the victims of this story?

Maybe that had been the idea from the beginning.

I'd been looking at the Sumaris as criminals attacking women of Los Angeles. But maybe they'd been playing on the world stage from the beginning.

# Chapter 107

I CALLED LUKE WARREN and he answered on the first ring.

"Did you hear, Jack? About the protest at the UN special session?"

"I saw it and I think I finally get the whole Remari-Mazul crime spree. I think this was a publicity stunt," I said. "See if you agree. They did the crimes without any fear of doing the time and now the United States is being accused of setting them up. We don't have a particle of proof, so we're being painted as villains."

"The rapes? The assaults? This is *good* publicity?"

"Had you ever heard of Sumar before these guys came to LA?" I asked him.

"Not really. I wasn't much of a student," the captain said.

"Well, Luke, you've heard of Sumar now. Look what Remari and Mazul have brought home to their nation: Headline news. A beleaguered small country, a little-known hunk of rock, is victimized by the U.S.A. See? No one will remember what they were accused of and yet they're in the big time now. Sumar will be recruiting their army on this bull crap for decades."

Warren said, "Well, back here on the local scene, Mazul and Remari will be released in the morning. We have nothing on them. No confession. No evidence. No blond female complainants. No bodies. Even the drunken doorman has gone underground. We have nothing on them at all."

"I'm sorry, Luke. They played all of us. They got us good."

# PART FIVE

## A FAMILY AFFAIR

# Chapter 108

BARBIE SUMMERS COOPER was wearing short black silk pajamas when she met Lester Olsen at the veranda doors to the main house. She gasped, clasped her hands together, threw open the doors, and then, with a little shout, she jumped into his arms and wrapped her legs around his waist.

"Oh my God. Our day has come."

He kissed her on the lips, a seal-the-deal kind of kiss, and patted her behind.

"Has anyone told you lately how cute you look in black?"

"Why, nooo," she said. "But I've heard that black is the new gold."

"And in your case, a great huge pile of it."

He lowered Barbie to the ground, said soberly,

"Now, you're sure you're sure, cutie? Not having any last-minute change of heart?"

"Don't make me laugh, Lester. How about you? Any regrets? Will you please come inside, dear? Please."

Lester entered the house and found himself in a great room of magnificent proportions: high cathedral ceiling held up by impressive beams, anchored with a stone fireplace you could roast a steer in.

Barbie said, "What are we going to do, Lester? I mean, what do I do? What do you do?"

"Where's Bryce now?"

"I put the Ambien into his choc'lit. Triple his normal dose. Then I took him upstairs. He should be asleep."

Lester said, "See this?" He took a little kit out of his jacket pocket, unzipped it, showed her the hypodermic needle. "It's loaded with potassium chloride. This will stop his heart mid-beat. Guaranteed."

"Is that one of your money-back guarantees?" She grinned. "Because I have put in my time, mister. I'm ready to be cut loose. I guarantee you *that*."

"Shall we say good night to your husband?"

The staircase gripped the high fieldstone wall

and climbed to the second-floor mezzanine, which was a half-floor deep by the width of the great room. Olsen followed Barbie across the floor, feeling that he was crossing a bridge into his new life.

At the end of the corridor was a massive handmade wooden door, which Barbie pushed open with the palm of her hand.

Bryce Cooper was in the middle of an enormous bed near the windows, ensconced in soft bedding and a dozen European-size pillows. Across from him, an old cowboy movie played on a sixty-two-inch screen.

"Barbie," Lester said softly. "Sit down on the bed and just make sure he's good and asleep."

"Oh, once he closes his eyes, Lester, he is gone," she said.

"Perfect," Lester said. He held the needle up to the light of the television as Barbie gently called out, "Sweetie, I'm turning off the movie now."

A flashlight beam appeared without warning, the light coming from a dark corner between a cabinet and the wall. It shone in Olsen's eyes, blinding him and almost stopping his heart.

"Who's that?" Barbie yelped.

She switched on the lamp on the end table. A man was sitting in a rocking chair at the far side of the armoire. The man kept the flashlight on Olsen as he got to his feet.

"I'm Bryce's self-appointed bodyguard," said the tall blond-haired man. "Don't anyone move. I've got a gun."

# Chapter 109

SCOTTY PINNED BARBIE and Olsen with his flashlight beam. He had no backup and absolutely no authority to be in this house. Barbie could shoot him and be well within her rights.

Still, Pretty Boy Olsen had a syringe full of murder and would certainly send Bryce Cooper into the tunnel of death if he had two minutes alone with him.

The bedside lamp cast a romantic glow, but it left corners of the room unlit. If Scotty was going to survive this ad hoc rescue, he needed more hands—one to hold the gun, two to cuff Olsen, and another to call the cops.

Scotty saw how the situation could go wild in a hurry.

He said loudly, "Olsen, lie facedown on the

floor. Barbie, interlace your fingers behind your head and do not move, understand me?"

Olsen wasn't buying it. He said to Barbie, "Who is this guy?"

"He's in computers. I don't remember his last name. His first name's Chris."

Olsen made a move toward Barbie, casual-like, but this was no good. Scotty dropped the light, put his gun squarely on Olsen, and held it with both hands.

"I said get down, Olsen. Do it quick or I will fire and I won't miss."

Olsen dropped the needle and kit, leaned forward with his hands out in front of him as though he were going to kneel. But it was a feint. He snatched Barbie from behind, held her in front of him like a shield. She let out a surprise squeal.

"Feel like taking a shot now, cowboy?" Olsen jeered. "Put down your gun and let's talk. This is a big pie. It can be sliced three ways and everyone will be happy."

A lot happened in the next few seconds.

Scotty lowered the barrel of his gun and squeezed the trigger; the bullet struck Olsen's foot. Olsen screamed, and Barbie spun away from him. Scotty fired again and Olsen dropped to the ground, grabbed his knee, and howled even louder, "You killed me. You fucking killed me."

Scotty said, "You, Barbie. Down on the floor. Don't make me shoot you. I will do it."

Holding the gun with his right hand, Scotty pulled his iPhone out of his shirt pocket, typed in 911, but before he could press Call, there was a commotion behind him.

He turned to see Bryce Cooper shrug off the bedding, hoist himself out of bed with a gun in his hand; must've been under his pillow. Bryce stumbled toward Barbie.

"Baby," he called out. "Come to me, baby girl." He turned to Scotty and said, "I'm Bryce and you're a dead man."

Cooper's gun looked like an H&R .32 long-barrel revolver. Scotty couldn't see if the safety was off. He knew that the guy was loopy from sleeping pills but that didn't mean he couldn't pull a trigger.

Scotty fired at the man's hand, and the gun jumped into the air, landed on the carpet near Olsen. Olsen reached for the gun, then screamed as his fingers were flattened under Scotty's foot.

Scotty scooped up Cooper's gun and stuck it into the waistband of his jeans, and for the moment, the situation stabilized.

Scotty pressed the Call button on his phone, said to the 911 operator, "I need the police and a bus. Man down with two gunshot wounds. Yes, he's breathing."

He gave the dispatcher the pertinent details, then leaned against the inside of the bedroom door, kept his gun ready, and watched the show.

# Chapter 110

I WAS PULLING out of our underground lot when Justine darted out of the elevator, ran in front of my car, and slapped the hood.

"Jack. Wait."

I opened my door and got out. "Christ, I could have hit you."

"Mo-bot just got a call from a hospital in Las Vegas. Val's been in some kind of accident. I don't know what, Jack. Was she working on something for us?"

"Get in. Hurry."

Justine was pale as she worked the phone, cajoling, pleading, arguing, but all she got from the hospital was that Valerie Kenney was in the ICU.

I wove around clotted traffic, passed in no-passing lanes as if I had flashers and sirens, was close to panic as I sped toward Santa Monica Airport, all the while wondering what had happened to Val, whipping myself for letting her take on an undercover job before she was ready.

Please God, let her survive.

Mercifully, we didn't get pulled over, and when we got to Santa Monica AP, my plane was waiting for me on the tarmac, gassed up and ready to go. Justine's legs were shaking as I helped her into the copilot's seat. Justine is afraid of heights—and of flights in small planes. I thought she might be sick before we got into the air.

I climbed into my seat and reassured her over the roar of the engine.

"The Cessna 172 is an extremely stable aircraft," I said, "very forgiving, even to a beginner. Plus, I know what I'm doing, as you know."

"Let's go, okay?" she said.

She buckled up. I gave her a pair of headphones, then I concentrated on my aircraft.

The sky was dark but with decent visibility. I went through my checklist, and once we were cleared for takeoff, I made sure my compass and directional gyro were aligned to the heading of the runway, then departed with a bit of a right crosswind.

I focused on the airspeed indicator, and while keeping the airplane running straight down the runway, I waited for it to reach the critical speed of about sixty before putting a little back pressure on the control yoke. As the spinning propeller exerted a leftward force on the airplane, I pushed in a bit of the right rudder.

Then I flew the runway heading until I was given vectors to proceed on course toward Atlantic Terminal, one of the private hangars at McCarran International, an hour and fifty minutes away.

The Cessna climbed out at a fairly standard five hundred feet per minute, and once we were at five thousand feet, I leveled out the plane and got us into cruise mode.

Los Angeles was lit up below us. The cars on the roads and freeways looked like a mechanical representation of a human circulatory system. Civilization glowed. After we cleared the suburban sprawl outside of LA, the vast desert was absolutely black.

We flew in a clear, starlit sky, and finally, my lovely, profoundly loyal, and very brave friend Justine relaxed. When we were about fifteen miles from McCarran, I began pulling the power back to 2,100 rpm, which set up a nice three- to four-hundred-foot-per-minute descent to the airfield.

Ten minutes later, we were taxiing toward the hangar, the hotels on the Strip looming in the background. When we were safely at a stop, I helped a very shaky Dr. Smith to the ground.

I hugged her.

She clung to me, and then, holding hands, we trotted toward the Atlantic Terminal and the hired car waiting to take us to the hospital.

# Chapter 111

THE RIDE FROM the airport to Mountain View Hospital was swift and silent. Justine and I arrived just after one in the morning and went straight to the ICU, where a dozen hysterical parents were waiting for news of their kids, casualties of a bus plowing through the doors of a nightclub.

There was no getting to see Val.

I stalked Dr. Steven Ornstein, the attending physician, until I cornered him. He looked like he hadn't slept in a week. He told me he was sorry, but only family members could see Val.

"I'm her father," I said.

He gave me a tired smile, said, "Yes, I see the resemblance. What's your name again?"

He found my name on Val's admissions forms,

then took me into a niche in the hallway and summarized her situation.

"She nearly drowned," he said. "That's not a figure of speech. She was half dead when she was brought in. Right now, she's undergoing tests of all kinds. That means chest x-rays and CT scans as well as a neurological assessment. If her brain was deprived of oxygen for too long, she could have seizures or permanent damage."

I said, "You're saying she almost drowned in Las Vegas? In what? The Bellagio fountain?"

"She was found semiconscious on the bank of a pond, her hands bound behind her back with plastic ties. She had lacerations from the ligatures," the doctor said, indicating his wrists. "There were abrasions on her thighs, and she's got a pretty good contusion on her forehead. She could still die. It happens. But she fought like hell."

I said, "Are you saying she was dumped in this pond?"

"There's a car in there. I understand divers are going in when it gets light," the doctor said.

I wanted to curse the paint off the wall, bang my head against it. I thought of Val, terrified, bound inside a car trunk, the water coming up around her face. Christ. I wanted to kill whoever had done this to her.

I thanked the doctor, then Justine and I took up a vigil in the waiting room outside the ICU.

During the following hours, we put down several quarts of coffee. At around four, I went to shake down the snack machine, and when I returned with Bugles and Doritos, Justine was laughing.

She said into her phone, "Three against one? Are you some kind of ninja? I'll tell him. Yes, I'll call Caine. Get some sleep."

Justine hung up, still smiling.

"You okay, princess?"

She said, "You bet," and filled me in.

"Lester Olsen and Barbie Cooper were about to kill Bryce Cooper with an injection of potassium chloride. That would have been fatal in a couple of seconds, but Scotty was waiting for them. He shot Olsen twice. Not fatally."

"Damn. That's a damned shame," I said. "How did Scotty miss?"

"Jack." She laughed some more. "Anyway, Olsen is hospitalized under guard. Barbie is in lockup. Scotty was released after the APD questioned him. He said—" Justine cracked up again. She was a little manic, but still, she was enjoying herself.

"Scotty said to me, 'I don't know if Bryce Cooper is going to press charges against me for breaking and entering or if he's going to throw me a parade.'"

I laughed with her, then shared my salty snacks as we talked about Olsen, that psycho with the twenty-four-karat-gold balls. Scotty hadn't known about Val's encounters with Olsen, but we were sure that before Olsen flew to Aspen, he had tried to kill her.

He'd almost done it.

How had Val survived?

I desperately wanted to know.

# Chapter 112

BY EIGHT IN the morning, Val had a room of her own, and Justine and I had seats on either side of her bed. Val looked like she'd done time inside a cement mixer.

The left side of her face was bruised and she had a line of stitches and sutures over her left eyebrow. Both of her wrists were bandaged, and leads went from her body to an array of beeping machines around her.

She looked small and very frail.

It broke my fucking heart.

I touched her arm above the bandages, and Val opened her eyes and looked at me. Recognition spread across her face and she lit up with such happiness, my feelings of remorse and guilt almost dropped me to the floor.

I said, "Val. How are you? How do you feel?"

"I feel like the world's biggest jerk, since you ask." Tears filled her eyes and spilled down her cheeks. I was so relieved that she knew me, that she was lucid, speaking in complete sentences, for God's sake. It was as if sunshine had flooded the hospital room. I squeezed her arm and said, "I'm so glad you're back."

"I really blew it," she said, squinting her bloodshot eyes. "I'm so sorry."

Justine said, "Val, you were heroic. That's the truth."

Val turned and saw Justine gripping the bed rail, looking like she was going to bawl. Val reached out with both arms and Justine hugged her. I found a box of tissues, handed them around, took some for myself.

There was some crying, and then Val collected herself and got very serious. "We have to find Lester Olsen," she said. "He tried to kill me."

Justine quickly sketched in the story of Scotty's night in Aspen, then said, "Olsen and Barbie are guests of the Aspen PD, and Scotty is in a first-class hotel without a scratch on him."

"That's the best news I've ever heard," Val said.

I said, "If you're up to it, Val, what the hell happened?"

"Oh God." Val sighed. "Yesterday, I think it was yesterday, I went to Lester's office to pick out my so-called future husband."

Val told us about the error that gave her away, about Olsen's stuffing her into his trunk at gunpoint, about the car going into the water, and about the moment when she realized she was going down.

"I couldn't get my hands free of the zip ties."

Her voice broke. She looked at her bandaged wrists.

"I kicked through the divider, and then I kind of rolled into the backseat.

"The driver's-side window was down," Val said. "Water was flooding in like a dam had broken, and it was pinning me inside the car. But there was a bubble of air at the ceiling, and when the car was underwater, I took a deep breath and swam for the window. I'm a Miami girl, remember. I can *swim*."

Val eked out a brave smile, then I asked her to go on.

"I remember cracking my head on the door-frame, Jack. I lost some air when I did that, but I pushed off from the car and got onto my back and just kicked until I surfaced. And that's the last thing I remember until I woke up here."

"You're amazing, Val. No other word for it," I told her. "I'm sorry this happened. You took a mic and a recorder to a gunfight, and that's my fault. I should have sent someone to back you up."

"It wasn't *supposed* to be a gunfight, Jack. Or any kind of fight. I was just trying to get the guy to incriminate himself. And now I don't even have the recorder."

I said, "You have your life. And we have you. You're going to be a great investigator, Val. In fact, you should take my job. You'll do fine."

"It's a deal. You heard him, Justine."

Val had a great smile and a very decent handshake.

I hugged her. "I'm very proud of you," I said. "You've got a gigantic future at Private."

# Chapter 113

JUSTINE AND I had just arrived at the Atlantic Terminal for our flight back to LA when I got a phone call from a man I'd hoped I would never hear from again. I was wrung out from my night at Mountain View Hospital, but it was either speak with the head of the Noccia crime family or wonder what Ray Noccia wanted until he showed up at my door.

I chose the find-out-now option.

I stabbed the Answer button on my phone and said my name, then listened as Ray Noccia said, "It's been a long time, Jack. A couple of years, right?"

"What can I do for you, Ray?"

Rain was starting to come down. Justine and I ducked into the closest hangar as the downpour began in earnest.

Noccia said, "I've got some business to discuss with you."

"You know that's not going to happen, Ray. I'm not interested in your business. I thought we'd been over this."

"Don't be dramatic, Jack. I want a conversation. That's all."

I told him I was working, that I'd call him after I checked my schedule.

"And, listen, Ray, I'll pick the time and the place."

I hung up, and, standing under a dripping overhang, I said to Justine, "Want to grab something to eat when we get to LA?"

She looked drained, but then, we were about to get into a plane again.

"What does Ray Noccia want with you?" she asked me.

I shrugged.

"Like always with the Noccia family. It will be what I least expect, when I least expect it."

# Chapter 114

IT WAS SUNNY in LA when I dropped Justine off at her house and then called DA Bobby Petino from my car. I left him a message saying that I had to speak with him urgently.

Then I drove home, took a shower, and was dressing for work when Bobby returned my call.

I said, "Bob"—and he cut me off.

"Jack, you're on my call list. I heard about Lester Olsen and what he did to your assistant and the rest of it, but the Love for Life racket is a job for the Vegas DA, not me."

"I was calling you about something else," I said. I put Petino on speakerphone, sat on the edge of my bed, and pulled on my shoes.

"As I said," Petino went on, "you're on my call list. I need a minute and I've only got a second."

The man is an attack dog, all the way. I know Justine likes him and might even be dating him. I don't understand how she can stand him.

"Go ahead," I said. "Talk to me."

"It's about Hal Archer."

"Uh-huh."

"Your client, right?"

"Yep. He's mine."

"Well, FYI, even though he may have been a Love for Life target, it doesn't matter. Even if Archer was set up, manipulated, whatever, there's no case for self-defense. Archer outweighed his little wife by a hundred pounds and she was unarmed."

I went to my closet, picked out a tie, looped it around my neck.

Petino said, "I've got enough evidence to indict him a hundred times over. So I'm going forward."

"I never doubted you were going to prosecute, Bobby," I said. "Meanwhile, I need a favor. And I need it right away."

"I'm listening, Jack. What do you need?"

# Chapter 115

TWIN TOWERS CORRECTIONAL Facility is a deceptively modern-looking prison system on ten acres. The main entrance at 450 Bauchet opens into a clean, well-lit, and tiled lobby called the Inmate Reception Center, as if the IRC were a hospitality suite at a convention center rather than central booking for the two thousand inmates who are bused in daily and warehoused in this cesspool until their arraignments and trials.

Bobby Petino had left my name at the front desk. I picked up an escort, Officer Eugene Calhoun, who kept his own counsel, escorted me to an elevator, and took me up to the sixth floor, where I glimpsed the tier of overstuffed pods jam-packed with desperate, unwashed humanity. The sickening sight of this hellhole brought back memories of a wretched time I wanted to forget.

Calhoun and I passed through a series of steel-barred gates, arriving at last at a cubicle divided by a wall of glass that is generally used by prisoners and their attorneys.

The room was furnished with a shelf in front of the glass, a telephone, an aluminum chair, and a caged light overhead. I took my seat, drummed my fingers until I heard footfalls in the hallway.

Calhoun unlocked the door, showed Hal Archer into his side of the bisected room, and locked the door. He came back to me and said, "You've got ten minutes."

"Stick around, Officer," I said. "We won't be that long."

Archer had been incarcerated in this medieval snake pit for a week and had lost a few pounds. His skin sagged, and his knuckles were abraded. He was doing pretty well, considering.

He sat down heavily, gave me a scathing look; he picked up the receiver on his side of the Plexiglas wall and I picked up mine.

"It's about fucking time you got here, Morgan. I'd be on a yacht right now if your father were still alive."

Hal Archer was a heinous prick as well as a conscienceless murderer.

"My father's dead and I think you've been on your last yacht. This is a courtesy call, Hal. I came to say that there's nothing I can do for you. Good luck in the joint."

I hung up the phone, took the elevator downstairs to the IRC. I made a couple of calls from the lobby to check that Petino had made good on his promise, and then I walked out the doors of the prison and around to the back of the jail.

I didn't have to wait long.

Rick came through the doors of the prison wearing jeans and an ugly green shirt. A guard opened the gate for him and he came through, his face lighting up when he saw me. He extended his hand. We shook, embraced, broke apart still smiling. He smelled bad but he looked good.

"Hungry?" I asked him.

"How come I'm out?"

"Dexter Lewis had more important things to do than try you for punching him in the nose."

"So you leaned on Bobby Petino."

I grinned.

"Good," Rick said. "Once I've had a shower and a shave, order will be restored to the universe."

"I'll run you by your house."

"You were saying something about lunch, Jack? Where are we going?"

"Feel like having lobster with a mobster?"

"If the lobster doesn't mind, it's okay with me," said Rick. "Where'd you park the car?"

# Chapter 116

RICK AND I sat at a table on the open deck at the back of the Lobster, a charming old eatery on Ocean Avenue at the head of the Santa Monica Pier.

From where we sat, I could see the Pacific Wheel, the Carousel Building, and the red awnings over a paved walkway that zigzags down toward the pier and water.

Rick was leaning over a bowl of clam chowder, shoveling it in. He hadn't had a meal worthy of a human being in two days, and I didn't see why he should wait for Ray Noccia.

I sat back in my seat, tried to enjoy the pretty scene, but the truth was, I was worried.

Last year, despite my wanting nothing to do with organized crime, Ray's oldest son, Carmine, coerced me into recovering millions in stolen pharmaceuticals belonging to the Noccia family.

We did the job perfectly. The Noccias got screwed without knowing it. Private was kept out of sight and I was sure that we'd left no trace of what we'd done.

Now I was having doubts.

About half a year ago, Carmine Noccia had teamed up with Tommy to blackmail me. Carmine suspected I'd double-crossed the Noccia family with the pharmaceutical case—but I got him off my back easily enough. Ray Noccia was a different story. He had the power that Carmine didn't.

If Ray Noccia had found me out, he might be looking at me to pick up the ten-million-dollar tab. Actually, people had been killed for much less.

Rick finished his soup, mopped up the remains with his bread. He burped and was going for the last of his wine when a gray-complexioned, gray-haired man in a gray sports jacket came up the stairs with a couple of goons at his heels. They stood in the entrance as a smiling Ray Noccia approached our table.

"Good to see you, Jack," Noccia said to me. "Don't get up. You too, Rick. Sit."

Noccia reached for the back of a chair and at

the same time turned his head toward the stairs. Looking past his protection, he said, "Oh, here he comes now. I asked Tommy to join us for lunch."

My brother, Tommy?

My unease turned to dread when I saw my twin coming into the restaurant. Ray Noccia had more notches in his gun belt than Clint Eastwood in a spaghetti western. Tommy lived to take me down and he had history with Ray Noccia through our father. An alliance between these two could not be good for me.

"Hey, Jack," Tommy said, closing in on our table. "I'm really glad to see you, bro."

Tom sat down. Noccia sat down. The waiter came over with menus, and the don ordered Pellegrino for the table.

After the waiter walked away, Noccia said to me, "I really didn't have to be here, Jack. I just wanted to see your face when Tommy said his piece. Tommy?"

Tommy accepted the handoff with a gracious nod, looked as pleased as if he'd won the trifecta at Santa Anita.

"Let me give you the short version," he said.

"Take all the time you want," I said.

"Thanks, Jack. It's like this," Tommy said. "And

I'm going to use the legal term for it, okay? You 'improperly influenced' Dad so that he would leave Private to you. He had long promised Private to *me*. You *duped* him and that's a fact. Now, Jack, I offered to buy you out, and my offer was pretty generous. You blew me off and left me no choice. So I'm taking you to court—"

"Let's go, Rick," I said. I stood up, opened my wallet, dropped a few bills on the table. "Lunch is on me," I said.

"You can run, but you can't run far," Tommy said. "I've got witnesses who will swear Dad was leaving Private to me until you visited him at Corcoran. He changed his will just before he died. So I'm going to sue you, Jack. And I'm going to win."

Del Rio and I went out to the car. I said, "He's full of crap. No jury is going to take the word of Ray Noccia."

My best bud, Del Rio, agreed.

But I didn't convince myself. Ray Noccia could buy off any number of jailhouse rats for pocket change. If he got twenty mugs to say that my father was leaving Private to Tommy before I talked to him, that much testimony could add up to a preponderance of evidence.

It might persuade a jury, and if Dad's last will was overturned, the prior will would be enforced.

Tommy could try, and I knew he would use every angle and maybe come up with a few new ones. But I wasn't going to let my brother steal Private from me. I couldn't let that happen.

No fucking way.

# EPILOGUE

# AT CROSS PURPOSES

# Chapter 117

IT WAS CASUAL Friday, Lori's favorite day of the week, because the office closed at one.

Lori made sure that the boss was good and gone. Then she grabbed her handbag, jogged down the stairs to the underground garage, and got into her platinum-colored Infiniti, her silver bullet, her wonder car.

She strapped in, checked her mirrors, and felt for the timer on the cord around her neck. Then she turned the ignition, and, as the gates rolled up, she gunned the engine and zoomed up the parking-garage ramp. As soon as the front tires hit the street, she pressed the timer's start button. She drove a speedy half mile through light traffic, then peeled out onto the ramp taking her to the 110.

Lori had a good feeling about the upcoming twelve minutes. Like, maybe she could knock a few seconds off her best time, like she'd been trying to do for a couple of weeks. She was in a wide-open lane now, moving at seventy-three, the roadway rolling out in front of her like a satin ribbon. She spun the steering wheel with her wrist and took the Infiniti into the inside lane, accelerated, and got up to seventy-six, now eighty, easy-breezy.

As Lori sped toward her own personal finish line, a goddamned paneled van up ahead wandered across the center lanes in some kind of trance. She had her rules: no horns allowed, no *brakes,* so Lori stepped on the gas and kept to the inside lane, flying so close to the van, she brushed its side panels.

She glanced into her mirror, saw with supreme satisfaction that the van was already a dot behind her—and that she'd gained four seconds on her previous best time for this point in the race. OMG.

Lori was flying through the Figueroa tunnels, and now traffic was merging onto I-5 North. She was passing the Glendale exit on her right at a cool eighty-five, heading toward Griffith Park and her exit onto the 134, when it hit her.

Today. Right now, she was going to break her all-time record by more than twenty seconds.

The exit was coming up and Lori was doing beautifully, all open road and smooth sailing, until a big orange-and-white box-store tractor-trailer began edging her out of her lane, mindlessly sending her away from her turnoff to her right and toward the median strip to her left, giving her no room to maneuver and no time to fade back.

*This was just wrong.*

Lori had no choice. She gunned the engine, shot into the sliver of lane between the sixteen-wheeler and the median strip. Her left rear tire bumped up against the low concrete wall, climbed it, and spun the Infiniti into a right-handed yaw toward the semi.

Instinctively, Lori wrenched the wheel hard left against the turn, felt the car buck, jump the center strip entirely, and clear it, sending her into oncoming traffic at ninety miles an hour. Her elation was gone, replaced by anger, fear, and then horror as the blue Bentley barreled toward her, looming large. She saw the fear on the face of the driver. He turned his wheel and hit the brakes as the distance between them closed.

Rubber burned, and despite Lori standing on

the brakes, using every muscle she had to stop her car, there was nowhere to go, no way out.

"Jesus Christ," she screamed a split second before the cars collided, before the fireball bloomed, before she died.

"*Noooooo.*"

# Chapter 118

KHEZIR COULD HARDLY believe how quickly their lives had changed. Three days ago, he and Gozan were on the verge of deportation to be followed by either summary execution at Sumar International or exile to the wilderness in rags.

Now, thousands of Sumaris were protesting in the streets across their nation, and Khezir and Gozan had become celebrities. There had been an avalanche of press and TV interviews, countless calls and letters of support from their countrymen.

And now this: the cherry on top.

Khezir and Gozan sat together inside the Bentley in the parking lot of Warner Brothers Studios, just grinning at each other, saying in unison, "Can you believe this?"

They laughed as one, then Khezir adjusted the

visor, started up the wonderful car, and drove past the guard's booth to the exit onto Forest Lawn.

As Khezir waited for an opening in the four lanes of traffic, he dialed up the air-conditioning. And he thought about the luncheon meeting Gozan and he had just had in the executive dining room with five serious young people who wanted to know more about them.

Those highly intelligent kids had an idea for a three-part miniseries and had "spitballed" ideas with them over cold potato soup and Kobe beef sandwiches. Khezir was still high on the intelligence and fierce energy of these young movie people. He admired their creativity and their structured ideas.

Gozan said, "You can go," and Khezir pulled out of the Warner Brothers lot onto Forest Lawn Drive.

The car picked up speed, giving Khezir a lovely feeling of riding on clouds. He was going to buy a car exactly like this one. The latest model. Then he would find a willing young girl, his type, and take a road trip with her, sharing big beds in hotel rooms across America.

Gozan said, "This is the life, right, Khezzy? This is the American life." Gozan started singing a song from that prewar period of America that he liked so much.

" 'Blue skies, la-la-la-la. Nothing but blue skies, from now onnnnn.' "

Khezir laughed. "This is our theme song, Uncle."

Gozan beamed.

"Khezzy, I think they liked us. I know they said they love us, but even if they are only warm on us, I think they will make this TV show."

"I love *them,* " Khezir said. "*Raiders of the Lost Ark* meets David and Goliath. I don't know exactly what they mean, but I like the way they said it."

He banged the steering wheel with his fist for emphasis and sped up Forest Lawn, passing the cemetery, heading toward the Ventura Freeway. He hit the ramp for 134 East, and the lovely car zoomed past Griffith Park on their right.

Tonight they would be back in the Beverly Hills Hotel. They had a bungalow in the garden, an even better one than last time. This one had an enclosed private pool.

Khezir took the exit to I-5 South, the Golden State Freeway. Khezir leaned down to adjust the air-conditioning controls, and when he looked up, he saw something unimaginable.

A silver vehicle had jumped the barrier between

the two lanes and was hurtling toward them. The car was out of control.

"*Uncle,*" he screamed. He jammed on the brakes, twisted the wheel as the silver vehicle filled his windshield.

There was an unfathomable clash of metal and plastics exploding together, and Khezir was thrown violently against the seat. Glass fired on him like an ice storm, and horns blew like the wind roaring through the rocky clefts of Sumar.

# Chapter **119**

JUSTINE WAS RUNNING with Rocky, her five-year-old rescue who was part dachshund, part beagle, part comedian, and all-around best pooch in the world.

Rocky was giving her the happy-dog grin, letting her know that he had been waiting forever for this run, and that he wasn't going to forget a minute of it, and that he really loved the guy who was running with them.

The best-looking guy in the world was also enjoying their run on the wide grassy divider between the lanes of traffic on Burton Way. All three of them had been running for a half hour at a nice even pace, although it was becoming harder for Justine to keep up because she was laughing so much.

"Pick it up, Justine," he said. "Try this. It's good for your calves."

And then he did sideways leaps over Rocky as the dog ran on the leash ahead of them, unaware or uncaring that he'd become exercise equipment.

"Now you try it."

"No, sir, no way," Justine shouted. "Look," she called out. "I think we should go out for dinner."

"You're crazy," he said. "I've already marinated the fish. You saw me, Justine. I made my special marinade."

"We can freeze the marinade," she said.

"Really? Not where I come from. Listen to me. You'll chop a few vegetables, throw them in a bowl, make a salad. After that, all you have to do is open the wine and pour me a glass. Sound okay? Still with me?"

"Yes, I'm with you."

She was. She was so with him, it was ridiculous.

They passed Il Cielo, a place she loved that wouldn't require her to make a salad or wash dishes. Instead, she could put on this really lovely dress she'd just bought, black, gauzy, deeeep neckline, short very flirty skirt.

There would be air-conditioning in the restaurant, no sweat, and after dinner, they could go back to her house and sip wine out by the pool and listen to music. For a little while.

"I'm gonna grill the fish that I've been marinating, thank you, and it's going to be the very best snapper you've ever tasted. And then, Justine, I'm going to clean the grill. How long has it been since that grill got a good shine?"

"I don't know. Never?"

"That's what I thought. So, after dinner, after I clean the grill, I'm going to show you a couple of moves you've never seen before."

Justine laughed loud and long. He was making a good case for staying home, that's for sure.

"Here's a preview of one of them," he said.

He stopped running and she pulled up short, put her hands on his chest. He looked right into her eyes. Then he got a grip on her waist and brought her close.

Justine's insides fired up and heat flashed through her body, making her want to get naked, right then and right there, with the cars honking at them—she was that damp and hot and hungry for him.

She looped her arms around his neck and pressed up against him, and he kissed her, softly at first, then got into it really good as the dog ran around their legs, corralling them, tying them together with his leash.

"Good one," she said when they broke from the kiss.

"I've got a few more of those I've been saving up for you," he said with a grin. He kept his eyes on her, looked as messed up as she was, his mouth still soft from their kiss.

He said, "But you're going to have to wait. Until after I clean the grill."

# Chapter 120

THIS WAS ONE of those times when the news was too big to text or e-mail or even say on the phone. I wanted to tell Justine, and I wanted to see her face when I told her.

I drove to Wetherly, a neat little street in the flats, and parked outside Justine's three-bedroom 1930s house that was just as solid and sweet as a house could be.

A lot of cars were parked along her block. School was out and it was a pretty summer night. Kids rode by on bikes, sprinklers slapped at the lawns; TVs turned the windows blue and added a cool glow to a nice domestic scene.

Justine's car was in her driveway and I was glad that she was home. I took the walk to her front door. Rapped on it. Rang the doorbell. Called her name.

There was no answer, so I went around back to her yard that is fenced in for Rocky and curtained with shrubbery. There's a patio back there and also a pool.

As I approached the backyard, I saw Justine picking up some glasses and a wine bottle from a table by the pool. Her hair was wet, and she was wearing a white terrycloth robe. Cool jazz came over the speakers, which explained why Justine hadn't heard me at the door.

Before I got to the chain-link fence, I called out so I wouldn't startle her.

"Justine, it's me."

But she jumped anyway and grabbed her robe at her throat. Then she saw me through the leaves and said, "Jack, what's wrong?"

"I've got news," I said. "Why don't you go around front and let me in?"

"What's the news? What happened?"

"Nothing much. Maybe just proof that God exists. Or that there's justice in the world." I laughed, opened my arms expansively. I couldn't wait to tell her.

"This had better be good," she said. She put down the glassware and came closer to the fence.

"The Sumaris," I said. "A car going about ninety

the wrong way on I-5 slammed into them. Khezir and Gozan are dead."

"Oh my *God*," Justine said. "So much for diplomatic immunity."

"You want to say, 'Jack, come in'?"

She shook her head no.

I tried to read her expression and that's when I put the wineglasses and the music together. I looked past her and saw someone hauling himself out of the water at the far side of the pool.

He called out to her, "Justine? Is everything okay?"

Cruz hooked a towel around his waist. His long hair dripped water down his chest as he came across the yard toward us. "Jack?"

I grabbed the fence, rattled it hard, and shouted, "What the *hell* is this, Emilio? What the *hell*?"

# ACKNOWLEDGMENTS

OUR GRATITUDE TO these top professionals who were so generous with their time and expertise during the writing of this book: Captain Rich Conklin of the Stamford, Connecticut, Police Department; Attorney Philip R. Hoffman of New York City; Dr. Humphrey Germaniuk, medical examiner and coroner of Trumbull County, Ohio; C. Peter Colomello, pilot, of Tillson, New York; and Chuck Hanni, IAAI-CFI, of Youngstown, Ohio.

As always, we are grateful to our excellent researchers, Ingrid Taylar and Lynn Colomello, and to Mary Jordan, who keeps it all together.

Turn the page for a sneak preview of

# TRUTH OR DIE

Coming June 2015

"WHERE EXACTLY DID it happen?" I asked.

"West End Avenue at Seventy-Third. The taxi was stopped at a red light," said Lamont. "The assailant smashed the driver's side window, pistol-whipped the driver until he was knocked out cold, and grabbed his money bag. He then robbed Ms. Parker at gunpoint."

"Claire," I said.

"Excuse me?"

"Please call her Claire."

I knew it was a weird thing for me to say, but weirder still was hearing Lamont refer to Claire as Ms. Parker, not that I blamed him. Victims are always Mr., Mrs., or Ms. for a detective. He was supposed to call her that. I just wasn't ready to hear it.

"I apologize," I said. "It's just that—"

"Don't worry about it," he said with a raised palm. He understood. He got it.

"So what happened next?" I asked. "What went wrong?"

"We're not sure, exactly. Best we can tell, she fully cooperated, didn't put up a fight."

That made sense. Claire might have been your prototypical "tough" New Yorker, but she was also no fool. She didn't own anything she'd risk her life to keep. *Does anyone?*

No, she definitely knew the drill. Never be a statistic. If your taxi gets jacked, you do exactly as told.

"And you said the driver was knocked out, right? He didn't hear anything?" I asked.

"Not even the gunshots," said Lamont. "In fact, he didn't actually regain consciousness until after the first two officers arrived at the scene."

"Who called it in?"

"An older couple walking nearby."

"What did they see?"

"The shooter running back to his car, which was behind the taxi. They were thirty or forty yards away; they didn't get a good look."

"Any other witnesses?"

"You'd think, but no. Then again, residential block . . . after midnight," he said. "We'll obviously follow up in the area tomorrow. Talk to the driver, too. He was taken to St. Luke's before we arrived."

I leaned back in my chair, a metal hinge somewhere below the seat creaking its age. I must have had a dozen more questions for Lamont, each one trying to get me that much closer to being in the taxi with Claire, to knowing what had really happened.

To knowing whether or not it truly was . . . *fuckin' random.*

But I wasn't fooling anyone. Not Lamont, and especially not myself. All I was doing was procrastinating, trying hopelessly to avoid asking the one question whose answer I was truly dreading.

I couldn't avoid it any longer.

"FOR THE RECORD, you were never in here," said Lamont, pausing at a closed door toward the back corner of the precinct house.

I stared at him blankly as if I were some chronic sufferer of short-term memory loss. *"In where?"* I asked.

He smirked. Then he opened the door.

The windowless room I followed him into was only slightly bigger than claustrophobic. After closing the door behind us, Lamont introduced me to his partner, Detective Mike McGeary, who was at the helm of what looked like one of those video arcade games where you sit in a captain's chair shooting at alien spaceships on a large screen. He was even holding what looked like a joystick.

McGeary, square-jawed and bald, gave Lamont a sideways glance that all but screamed, *What the hell is he doing in here?*

"Mr. Mann was a close acquaintance of the victim," said Lamont. He added a slight emphasis on my last name, as if to jog his partner's memory.

McGeary studied me in the dim light of the room until he put my face and name together. Perhaps he was remembering the cover of the *New York Post* a couple of years back. *An Honest Mann,* read the headline.

"Yeah, fine," McGeary said finally.

It wasn't exactly a ringing endorsement, but it was enough to consider the issue of my being there resolved. I could stay. I could see the recording.

*I could watch, frame by frame, the murder of the woman I loved.*

Lamont hadn't had to tell me there was a surveillance camera in the taxi. I'd known right away, given how he'd described the shooting over the phone, some of the details he had. There were little things no eyewitnesses could ever provide. Had there been any eyewitnesses, that is.

Lamont removed his glasses, wearily pinching the bridge of his nose. No one ever truly gets used to the graveyard shift. "Any matches so far?" he asked his partner.

McGeary shook his head.

I glanced at the large monitor, which had shifted into screen saver mode, an NYPD logo floating about. Lamont, I could tell, was waiting for me to ask him about the space-age console, the reason I wasn't supposed to be in the room. The machine obviously did a little more than just digital playback.

But I didn't ask. I already knew.

I'm sure the thing had an official name, something ultra-high-tech sounding, but back when I was in the DA's office I'd only ever heard it referred to by its nickname, CrackerJack. What it did was combine every known recognition software program into one giant cross-referencing "decoder" that was linked to practically every criminal database in the country, as well as those from twenty-three other countries, or basically all of our official allies in the "war on terror."

In short, given any image at any angle of any suspected terrorist, CrackerJack could source a litany of identifying characteristics, be it an exposed mole or tattoo; the exact measurements between the suspect's eyes, ears, nose, and mouth; or even a piece of jewelry. Clothing, too. Apparently, for all the precautions terrorists take in their planning, it rarely occurs to them that wearing the same polyester shirt in London, Cairo, and Islamabad might be a bad idea.

Of course, it didn't take long for law enforcement in major cities—where CrackerJacks were heavily deployed by the Department of Homeland Security—to realize that these machines didn't have to identify just terrorists. Anyone with a criminal record was fair game.

So here was McGeary going through the recording sent over by the New York Taxi & Limousine Commission to see if any image of the shooter triggered a match. And here was me, having asked if I could watch it, too.

"Mike, cue it up from the beginning, will you?" said Lamont.

McGeary punched a button and then another until the screen lit up with the first frame, the taxi having pulled over to pick Claire up. The image was grainy, black-and-white, like on an old tube television with a set of rabbit ears. But what little I could see was still way too much.

It was exactly as Lamont had described it. The shooter smashes the driver's side window, beating the driver senseless with the butt of his gun. He's wearing a dark turtleneck and a ski mask with holes for the eyes, nose, and mouth. His gloves are tight, like those Isotoners that O. J. Simpson pretended didn't fit.

So far, Claire is barely visible. Not once can I see her face. Then I do.

It's right after the shooter snatches the driver's money bag. He swings his gun, aiming it at Claire in the backseat. She jolts. There's no Plexiglas divider. There's nothing but air.

Presumably, he says something to her, but the back of his head is toward the camera. Claire offers up her purse. He takes it and she says something. I was never any good at reading lips.

He should be leaving. Running away. Instead, he swings out and around, opening the rear door. He's out of frame for no more than three seconds. Then all I see is his outstretched arm. And the fear in her eyes.

He fires two shots at point-blank range. *Did he panic?* Not enough to flee right away. Quickly, he rifles through her pockets, and then tears off her earrings, followed by her watch, the Rolex Milgauss I gave her for her thirtieth birthday. He dumps everything in her purse and takes off.

"Wait a minute," I said suddenly. "Go back a little bit."

LAMONT AND MCGEARY both turned to me, their eyes asking if I was crazy. *You want to watch her being murdered a second time?*

No, I didn't. Not a chance.

Watching it the first time made me so nauseous I thought I'd throw up right there on the floor. I wanted that recording erased, deleted, destroyed for all eternity not two seconds after it was used to catch the goddamn son of a bitch who'd done this.

Then I wanted a long, dark alley in the dead of night where he and I could have a little time alone together. Yeah. *That's* what I wanted.

But I thought I saw something.

Up until that moment, I hadn't known what I was looking for in the recording, if anything. If

Claire had been standing next to me, she, with her love of landmark Supreme Court cases, would've described it as the definition of pornography according to Justice Potter Stewart in *Jacobellis v. Ohio.*

*I know it when I see it.*

She'd always admired the simplicity of that. Not everything that's true has to be proven, she used to say.

"Where to?" asked McGeary, his hand hovering over a knob that could rewind frame by frame, if need be.

"Just after he beats the driver," I said.

He nodded. "Say when."

I watched the sped-up images, everything happening in reverse. If only I could reverse it all for real. I was waiting for the part when the gun was turned on Claire. A few moments before that, actually.

"Stop," I said. "Right there."

McGeary hit Play again and I leaned in, my eyes glued to the screen. Meanwhile, I could feel Lamont's eyes glued to my profile, as if he could somehow better see what I was looking for by watching me.

"What is it?" he eventually asked.

I stepped back, shaking my head as if disappointed. "Nothing," I said. "It wasn't anything."

*Because that's exactly what Claire would've wanted me to say. A little white lie for the greater good, she would've called it.*

She was always a quick thinker, right up until the end.

NO WAY IN hell did I feel like taking a taxi home.

In fact, I didn't feel like going home at all. In my mind, I'd already put my apartment on the market, packed up all my belongings, and moved to another neighborhood, maybe even out of Manhattan altogether. Claire *was* the city to me. Bright. Vibrant.

Alive.

And now she wasn't.

I passed a bar, looking through the window at the smattering of "patrons," to put it politely, who were still drinking at three in the morning. I could see an empty stool and it was calling my name. More like shouting it, really.

*Don't,* I told myself. *When you sober up, she'll still be gone.*

I kept walking in the direction of my apartment, but with every step it became clear where I truly wanted to go. It was wherever Claire had been going.

Who was she meeting?

Suddenly, I was channeling Oliver Stone, somehow trying to link her murder to the story she'd been chasing. But that was crazy. I saw her murder in black and white. It was a robbery. She was in the wrong place at the wrong time, and as much as that was a cliché, so, too, was her death. She'd be the first to admit it.

"Imagine that," I could hear her saying. "A victim of violent crime in New York City. *How original.*"

Still, I'd become fixated on wanting to know where she'd been heading when she left my apartment. A two-hundred-dollar-an-hour shrink would probably call that sublimated grief, while the four-hundred-dollar-an-hour shrink would probably counter with sublimated anger. I was sticking with overwhelming curiosity.

I put myself in her shoes, mentally tracing her

steps through the lobby of my building and out to the sidewalk. As soon as I pictured her raising her arm for a taxi, it occurred to me. *The driver.* He at least knew the address. For sure, Claire gave it to him when he picked her up.

Almost on cue, a taxi slowed down next to me at the curb, the driver wondering if I needed a ride. That was a common occurrence late at night when supply far outweighed demand.

As I shook him off I began thinking of what else Claire's driver might remember when Lamont interviewed him. Tough to say after the beating he took. Maybe the shooter had said something that would key his identity, or at least thin out the suspects. Did he speak with any kind of accent?

Or maybe the driver had seen something that wasn't visible to that surveillance camera. Eye color? An odd-shaped mole? A chipped tooth?

Unfortunately, the list of possibilities didn't go on and on. The ski mask, turtleneck, and gloves made sure of that. Clearly, the bastard knew that practically every taxi in the city was its own little recording studio. So much for cameras being a deterrent.

As the old expression goes, show me a ten-foot wall and I'll show you an eleven-foot ladder.

The twenty blocks separating me from my apartment were a daze. I was on autopilot, one foot in front of the other. Only at the sound of the keys as I dropped them on my kitchen counter did I snap out of it, realizing I was actually home.

Fully dressed, I fell into my bed, shoes and all. I didn't even bother turning off the lights. But my eyes were closed for only a few seconds before they popped open. *Damn.* All it took was one breath, one exchange of the air around me, and I was lying there feeling more alone than I ever had in my entire life.

*The sheets still smelled of her.*

I sat up, looking over at the other side of the bed . . . the pillow. I could still make out the impression of Claire's head. That was the word, wasn't it? *Impression.* Hers was everywhere, most of all on me.

I was about to make a beeline to my guest room, which, if anything, would smell of dust or staleness or whatever other odor is given off by a room that's rarely, if ever, used. I didn't care. So long as it wasn't her.

Suddenly, though, I froze. Something had caught my eye. It was the yellow legal pad on the end of the bed, the one Claire had used when she took the phone call. She'd ripped off the top sheet she'd written on.

But the one beneath it . . .

## Also by James Patterson

### ALEX CROSS NOVELS

Along Came a Spider • Kiss the Girls • Jack and Jill •
Cat and Mouse • Pop Goes the Weasel • Roses are Red •
Violets are Blue • Four Blind Mice • The Big Bad Wolf •
London Bridges • Mary, Mary • Cross • Double Cross •
Cross Country • Alex Cross's Trial (*with Richard
DiLallo*) • I, Alex Cross • Cross Fire • Kill Alex Cross •
Merry Christmas, Alex Cross • Alex Cross, Run •
Cross My Heart • Hope to Die

### THE WOMEN'S MURDER CLUB SERIES

1st to Die • 2nd Chance (*with Andrew Gross*) •
3rd Degree (*with Andrew Gross*) • 4th of July (*with Maxine
Paetro*) • The 5th Horseman (*with Maxine Paetro*) •
The 6th Target (*with Maxine Paetro*) • 7th Heaven (*with
Maxine Paetro*) • 8th Confession (*with Maxine Paetro*) •
9th Judgement (*with Maxine Paetro*) • 10th Anniversary
(*with Maxine Paetro*) • 11th Hour (*with Maxine Paetro*) •
12th of Never (*with Maxine Paetro*) • Unlucky 13 (*with
Maxine Paetro*) • 14th Deadly Sin (*with Maxine Paetro*)

### DETECTIVE MICHAEL BENNETT SERIES

Step on a Crack (*with Michael Ledwidge*) •
Run for Your Life (*with Michael Ledwidge*) •
Worst Case (*with Michael Ledwidge*) • Tick Tock
(*with Michael Ledwidge*) • I, Michael Bennett (*with Michael
Ledwidge*) • Gone (*with Michael Ledwidge*) • Burn (*with
Michael Ledwidge*) • Alert (*with Michael Ledwidge, to be
published September 2015*)

## NYPD RED SERIES

NYPD Red (*with Marshall Karp*) •
NYPD Red 2 (*with Marshall Karp*) •
NYPD Red 3 (*with Marshall Karp*)

## STAND-ALONE THRILLERS

Sail (*with Howard Roughan*) • Swimsuit (*with Maxine Paetro*) • Don't Blink (*with Howard Roughan*) • Postcard Killers (*with Liza Marklund*) • Toys (*with Neil McMahon*) • Now You See Her (*with Michael Ledwidge*) • Kill Me If You Can (*with Marshall Karp*) • Guilty Wives (*with David Ellis*) • Zoo (*with Michael Ledwidge*) • Second Honeymoon (*with Howard Roughan*) • Mistress (*with David Ellis*) • Invisible (*with David Ellis*) • The Thomas Berryman Number (*to be published May 2015*)• Truth or Die (*with Howard Roughan, to be published June 2015*) • Murder House (*with David Ellis, to be published July 2015*)

## NON-FICTION

Torn Apart (*with Hal and Cory Friedman*) •
The Murder of King Tut (*with Martin Dugard*)

## ROMANCE

Sundays at Tiffany's (*with Gabrielle Charbonnet*) •
The Christmas Wedding (*with Richard DiLallo*) •
First Love (*with Emily Raymond*)

## OTHER TITLES

Miracle at Augusta (*with Peter de Jonge*)

**FAMILY OF PAGE-TURNERS**

## MIDDLE SCHOOL BOOKS

Middle School: The Worst Years of My Life (*with Chris Tebbetts*) • Middle School: Get Me Out of Here! (*with Chris Tebbetts*) • Middle School: My Brother Is a Big, Fat Liar (*with Lisa Papademetriou*) • Middle School: How I Survived Bullies, Broccoli, and Snake Hill (*with Chris Tebbetts*) • Middle School: Ultimate Showdown (*with Julia Bergen*) • Middle School: Save Rafe! (*with Chris Tebbetts*)

## I FUNNY SERIES

I Funny (*with Chris Grabenstein*) •
I Even Funnier (*with Chris Grabenstein*) •
I Totally Funniest (*with Chris Grabenstein*)

## TREASURE HUNTERS

Treasure Hunters (*with Chris Grabenstein*) •
Treasure Hunters: Danger Down the Nile (*with Chris Grabenstein*)

## HOUSE OF ROBOTS

House of Robots (*with Chris Grabenstein*)

## KENNY WRIGHT

Kenny Wright: Superhero (*with Chris Tebbetts, to be published May 2015*)

## HOMEROOM DIARIES

Homeroom Diaries (*with Lisa Papademetriou*)

## MAXIMUM RIDE SERIES

The Angel Experiment • School's Out Forever •
Saving the World and Other Extreme Sports •
The Final Warning • Max • Fang • Angel •
Nevermore • Forever (*to be published May 2015*)

## CONFESSIONS SERIES

Confessions of a Murder Suspect (*with
Maxine Paetro*) • Confessions: The Private School
Murders (*with Maxine Paetro*) • Confessions: The Paris
Mysteries (*with Maxine Paetro*)

## WITCH & WIZARD SERIES

Witch & Wizard (*with Gabrielle Charbonnet*) •
The Gift (*with Ned Rust*) • The Fire (*with Jill
Dembowski*) • The Kiss (*with Jill Dembowski*) •
The Lost (*with Emily Raymond*)

## DANIEL X SERIES

The Dangerous Days of Daniel X (*with Michael
Ledwidge*) • Watch the Skies (*with Ned Rust*) •
Demons and Druids (*with Adam Sadler*) •
Game Over (*with Ned Rust*) •
Armageddon (*with Chris Grabenstein*)

## GRAPHIC NOVELS

Daniel X: Alien Hunter (*with Leopoldo Gout*) •
Maximum Ride: Manga Vols. 1–8 (*with NaRae Lee*)

For more information about James Patterson's novels, visit
www.jamespatterson.co.uk

Or become a fan on Facebook